Dear Mom,

At dinner tonight Cal told all of us we should be sure to write letters home. I was going to write you, anyway. Things are kinda boring here. I've played lots of soccer, and I'm studying real hard, but I miss being at home. Last night after dinner we had a talent show. Billy, who is from New Mexico, put on a black cape and a kind of Spanish hat and played the guitar. It was so bad it was funny. I drew a picture of it for you. I miss you a whole lot. Please come visit me soon.

Love,

Jason

Please address questions and book requests to: Harlequin Reader Service
U.S.: 3010 Walden Ave., P.O. Box 1325, Buffalo, NY 14269
CAN.: P.O. Box 609, Fort Erie, Ont. L2A 5X3

NEVADA

JANICE KAISER

Chances

Harlequin Books

TORONTO • NEW YORK • LONDON
AMSTERDAM • PARIS • SYDNEY • HAMBURG
STOCKHOLM • ATHENS • TOKYO • MILAN
MADRID • WARSAW • BUDAPEST • AUCKLAND

HARLEQUIN BOOKS
225 Duncan Mill Road, Don Mills,
Ontario, Canada M3B 3K9

ISBN 0-373-47178-5

CHANCES

Copyright © 1987 by Belles-Lettres, Inc.

This edition published by arrangement with Harlequin Books S.A.

® and TM are trademarks of the publisher. Trademarks indicated with ® are registered in the United States Patent and Trademark Office, the Canadian Trade Marks Office and in other countries.

Printed in U.S.A.

Dear Reader,

In 1984, when I gave up practicing law to write, I'd never have guessed that twelve years later I would have published fifty books! *Chances* was my sixth novel, and as I look back on it, I realize that many of the themes I wrote about then continue to interest me.

Like many of my heroines, Blaine Kidwell was a good woman in a not-so-good situation. She is a widow, trying to make a living as a professional poker player, and her son is in trouble with the law because he got into a fight with another boy while trying to defend his mother. Life isn't easy for Blaine or her son.

Meeting Cal Rutledge, the man who runs a ranch for troubled boys, changes both their lives. For Jason it's a chance to stay out of reform school, and turn his life around. For Blaine it is a chance to find true love…if Cal can accept her for the woman she is, and not try to change her.

Jessica Kaiser

For Ruth Small Kaiser, whose love, devotion
and sacrifice have made so many things possible.

CHAPTER ONE

SHE STOOD PASSIVELY at the window, her bony fingers toying with the pearls at her ample bosom, her eyes following the progress of the soccer ball across the parched grass. Agnes Kidwell watched it skid along the ground till it came to the man's extended foot, where he trapped the ball between his toe and the turf. Then, with several boys running headlong toward him, he stepped back and kicked the ball in a high arc to the far end of the field.

The old woman continued to eye Caleb Rutledge as he playfully grabbed one of the boys and tousled his hair. Then he seemed to say something to the group of youngsters before turning and walking toward the ranch house where she waited. As he approached she glanced at the luminous Nevada sky and the silhouetted buildings of the Rutledge Ranch and School for Boys. She stepped back into the shadows when he drew near, so she could take her measure of him, discreetly.

Rutledge was tall and athletically built, having both his father's rugged western demeanor and his mother's eastern refinement. He was a man of the land like Agnes Kidwell's own husband and son— both of whom were dead—but there was that other side of him, the refined side, that she neither liked nor trusted.

Still, this man had become the key to the future of the Kidwell family and she would have to deal with him. Caleb Rutledge with his rumpled blond hair and sweat suit, Caleb Rutledge who owned hundreds of thousands of acres of ranch and farmland all over the West, this man who controlled a fortune but preferred to work and play with his boys, *he* was the key.

When he disappeared around the corner of the house the old woman went to the chair she had been shown to by Rutledge's secretary and sat down to wait. A moment later he opened the door to his office and stood there, a broad grin on his face.

"Well, Mrs. Kidwell, I didn't expect you. To what do I owe this visit?"

"Hello, Mr. Rutledge. I'm sorry to drop in on you unannounced.

It was important enough I decided to fly down from Washington and see you. I was hoping we might have a little talk.''

"Certainly. But—" he looked down at himself "—I'm not exactly dressed for either socializing or business. Will you give me a few minutes to clean up and change?''

"It's not necessary. I know what it's like to be around men who work hard. Please, come in. What I have to say won't take long, and you may wish to get back to your game.''

Rutledge went to his desk and sat on the corner of it, wiping his brow with the sleeve of his sweat suit. He looked at the woman, sensing something weighty was on her mind.

"My grandson, Jason, wasn't out there with you, was he?''

"No, he hasn't been at the school long enough to have developed a taste for soccer. But it's something I interest most of the boys in before they leave.''

They looked at each other awkwardly for a moment.

"How's Jason doing?'' she finally asked.

"Well, I think. The usual adjustment problems, but nothing major. The counselors have no complaints and I haven't detected anything to be concerned about. I believe he misses his mother, but that's not uncommon.''

The woman's expression grew pained. "Yes, that's partly what I came to speak to you about.''

"Oh?''

"Let me be direct, Mr. Rutledge. I'd like for you to have a talk with my daughter-in-law and discourage her from trying to see Jason. I've learned she plans on moving to Nevada to be near him, and I want you to talk her out of it.''

"Why is that?''

"Blaine's responsible for the boy's problem. She's an unfit mother, and I am convinced it's in his interest to be completely free of her influence, at least for a while.''

Rutledge studied the sober face before him, etched with deep lines. After a moment's reflection he walked around the desk to the window. Pausing there briefly, he watched the boys running back and forth across the playfield.

During the past half dozen years since he'd built the school on his family's ranch, his life and the old place hadn't been the same. He'd returned to Nevada after his parents' deaths, but living alone and running the family empire had not been enough. Something inside him had demanded a purpose to living—a *real* purpose.

He'd started with a little project to bring troubled boys to the ranch for exposure to nature and companionship in a wholesome environment. That program turned eventually into a home for boys, and then into a school for junior-high-and high-school-age delinquents. The Rutledge Ranch became recognized by the state as an alternative to correctional institutions, and boys from around the country were sent there.

Rutledge had watched it grow until now he had nearly two hundred boys, a staff of twenty-five and a work load that kept him from devoting the necessary attention to his business interests. But size had its price. He'd found it difficult to continue to run the school as a personal charity, and had had to look to individuals active in the church, such as Agnes Kidwell, for their contributions.

He hated the money-raising aspect of running the school, especially when it meant he had to deal with people like the Kidwell woman. Before facing her again he looked at his boys.

With the sun dropping toward the snow-tinged mountains to the west they would soon be abandoning the soccer field to clean up and study awhile before supper. It was early May and the air was cool. Rutledge wished he was still outside with the boys.

He turned to the sour-faced woman. "Mrs. Kidwell, my hands are full with the boys and the school. And of course there are my personal business interests. I hardly have the time, or the right, to meddle in family affairs when the child is not directly involved."

The woman gave him a disapproving look. "But this *does* affect Jason. Directly or indirectly, how does it matter? Besides, why would it be meddling if *I* request it? I *am* his grandmother."

"Yes, I'm aware that you're his grandmother, Mrs. Kidwell, and that he's here because of you. But you are asking me to get involved in the politics of your family when technically my mandate is from the juvenile courts."

"Mandates and technicalities mean nothing to me," she snapped, waving her hand with annoyance. "*I* brought Jason here and *I* arranged for a very generous donation to your school's endowment." The level look she gave him said she had taken off her gloves and was prepared to be as forceful as necessary to have her way. "I would think that my small request would have had a more sympathetic reception."

Rutledge let his piercing blue eyes settle on her. Her anger had chased his geniality away, and he was beginning to feel as he did when a business negotiation became acrimonious. For two cents he would have told her to go to hell, but his training forbade such heavy-handed behavior, and he didn't let himself do that sort of thing...not with a woman like Agnes Kidwell.

Rutledge knew her money might entitle her to certain prerogatives, but he wouldn't let her push him farther than he thought justified. Still, what mattered was the boy's welfare and, if there was a germ of truth in what this woman was saying, his duty was to check it out.

He sensed she would have her way in the end, and he didn't like it. When he finally replied, his voice was as genial as he could make it. "What makes you think the boy's mother would listen to me?"

Agnes Kidwell's face grew smug. "I know Blaine, Mr. Rutledge. She is a determined woman, strong in her own way—though no match for me and the resources at my disposal—but she *can* be reasonable."

"But why me? Why won't she listen to you?"

"Because she hates me every bit as much as I hate her." The hard words were followed by a little smile. "It's best to be honest about it. Neither Blaine nor I have made a secret of our contempt for each other since my son's death. She's the mother of my grandson, so I'm stuck with her. I control the boy's inheritance and his future, so she's stuck with me."

"What makes you think my asking her to stay out of Nevada will do any good?"

"Once she meets you, Mr. Rutledge, she'll realize that Jason is in good hands. Her only reason for opposing his coming here was her hatred for me. Everything I want for the boy she immediately opposes. I'm sure you'll have no trouble convincing her to stay away from him. If she moves to Las Vegas as she's threatened, she'll interfere continually. I know it."

Rutledge sank into the high-backed chair behind his desk and studied the old woman's sour face. "She *is* his mother."

Agnes Kidwell shrieked derisively. "Mother! She's a gambler! Earning a living playing cards? Carousing with men in casinos? She might as well be a whore!"

Rutledge sat upright. The woman's shrewish manner was starting to annoy him. "She hardly sounds like the ideal mother, but there's been no allegation that—"

"Allegation? It's obvious what that woman is! All of Prosser knows, and half of eastern Washington for that matter. If she had been a fit mother Jason would never have gotten into that fight and hurt that boy. She's unfit, I tell you. If it weren't for me, he'd be in a home for juvenile criminals now.

"No, Mr. Rutledge, don't talk to me of 'allegations.' I want that woman back home where she can't see the boy all the time. All Jason needs is to be free of her, to grow a little on his own. I want her back in Washington and I expect you to convince her.''

"Mrs. Kidwell, she's a free woman. She can live where she wishes and she can visit the boy during visiting hours. I can't prevent that.''

"Maybe you can't prevent Blaine from seeing him, but I'm sure you could convince her it's in Jason's interest that she stay away from him.''

"Why are you so sure?''

"Because you'll tell her that *I'm* not behind this and that it's *your* idea.''

Caleb Rutledge knew it would take all his willpower to keep from lashing back at this bitter old woman. She didn't own *him* and he yearned to make that plain to her. Instead he searched inside himself for patience, though in the end it was his business instincts that came to the rescue.

Agnes Kidwell's financial support over the coming years was reason enough to grant the favor. This was a case where discretion clearly was the wise course. "All right, Mrs. Kidwell. I'll have a talk with her. But I'll use my own judgment in the matter and I won't promise you anything.''

The woman straightened her shoulders and the slight smile on her face betrayed a hint of triumph. "That's all I can ask, Mr. Rutledge,'' she said softly. "And as luck would have it, you'll be spared a trip up to Washington to see her. I'm told she's in Las Vegas for a couple days for one of those disgusting poker tournaments she plays in. Perhaps you can go and see her there in her *natural* environment.''

The sarcasm seemed doubly final when Agnes Kidwell rose. Rutledge realized the interview was over. Gratefully, he stood as well and stepped around the desk. The woman looked him up and down as he reached for her outstretched hand.

"You're a fine figure of a man,'' she said in a rather proprietary tone, as her eyes settled on his handsome face. "Not unlike my son, Frank.''

Rutledge saw a flicker of nostalgia on her face. She smiled at him as she continued. "I'm glad you decided to come back to the West. You look like a man of the land—like your father, bless his soul.'' She turned toward the door. "I met him once, you know. It was years ago. My late husband, Edward, and he were both young ranchers, just starting their lives.''

Rutledge opened the door to his office.

"When I'd heard you'd settled down back East, I decided it was your mother's influence. But seeing you like this, I realize you *are* your father's son, after all."

They left the building and walked toward the black limousine parked in the driveway. Stopping at the door that the driver held open, Agnes Kidwell turned to her host. "I take it you'll call me after you've had a talk with Blaine?"

"Yes, of course."

A moment later she was gone, and Rutledge started back toward his office. Fleeting thoughts of his parents went through his mind, replaced by thoughts of his boys. Finally his mind turned to this unknown woman, the poker player named Blaine Kidwell.

He dreaded the task the old woman had given him. Being a boy's keeper in the face of a hostile parent was never a pleasant circumstance. But, wanting to get it over with, Rutledge decided to make the long drive into Las Vegas that evening. He would call a few of the casinos and track down the poker tournament first. Reaching for the phone, he dialed information.

THE CHAPARRAL WAS just another glittery gambling factory to Caleb Rutledge. He didn't like casinos, didn't believe in them, but had to admit to a begrudging fascination. As soon as he walked in the door he felt electricity in the air—the energy of the vast congregation of gamblers.

He had changed enough over the years that instinctive thoughts of sin didn't leap into his brain, as they once had. Still, the realization that it was the place where he'd find the mother of one of his boys "working" didn't sit well.

As Rutledge walked through the throng his ears were assaulted with the sound of coins cascading into metal trays in slot machines and laughter signaling a turn of fortune at one of the gaming tables. Beneath it all was the steady hum of the machines, the clicking of the wheel of fortune, the tumbling clatter of wooden balls over roulette wheels.

Surveying the scene, Rutledge looked over a sea of blackjack tables in one direction and a field of craps tables in the other. Ringing the entire pavilion were one-armed bandits being fed a steady diet of coins by a motley army of tourists and local addicts.

In a distant corner of the casino he spotted a dense crowd of people and a banner against the wall reading Western Poker Championships. He made his way through the packed hall, hoping he would quickly find Blaine Kidwell and that he wouldn't have to wait long to speak with her.

As he drew near the card room, Rutledge saw the bright lights of a television crew through the mob of spectators. He was surprised, not having realized the event was sufficiently important to attract the local media.

From the outer fringe of the crowd, he was able to see a table on a low platform perhaps thirty feet behind a railing. Craning his neck to peer around a cowboy hat in front of him, Rutledge was struck by a totally unexpected sight.

The woman at the table, opposite the crowd, was lovely. Her face, framed by glossy black hair, was pale porcelain, masked in concentration. As Rutledge watched, her gray eyes turned first to the man on one side of her, then to the other, before settling on the cards lying facedown before her. She seemed in almost a meditative state. Her mouth was expressionless and betrayed no hint of her thoughts.

Rutledge beheld her with fascination, his eyes moving over her narrow shoulders, which were neither rigid nor relaxed, and her slender fingers, which toyed unconsciously with a stack of chips. There was a fragility about her, despite her control—a hint of vulnerability beneath the facade. He wondered if she could be Blaine Kidwell.

The woman looked totally unpretentious in a plain white silk blouse. She wore no jewelry and only light makeup on her eyes. There was just a hint of color on her lips and cheeks, giving her a fresh and innocent appearance that he hadn't expected. She seemed much too young to be the mother of Jason Kidwell, a boy of fourteen, yet he saw a resemblance between them. Could he be mistaken, though?

Rutledge turned to the man next to him. "Who's the woman?"

"Blaine Kidwell, Queen of Hearts," the other replied, without taking his eyes off the drama at the poker table.

"Queen of Hearts?"

"Yeah, that's what they call her."

"Why?"

The man looked at Rutledge as though he was some kind of visitor from outer space. "I don't know about you, pardner, but I think she's a damn good-lookin' woman. Besides, she's a helluva poker player." He gestured with stubby fingers, pointing toward the table. "That ain't penny-ante poker, mister. There must be thirty or forty thousand on that table."

Rutledge looked again at the woman. She had just pushed a pile of chips into the pot.

"She's callin' Pickins," the man next to Rutledge said. "This ought to make or break him."

The slender man sitting on one side of Blaine Kidwell announced a flush, jack high. He smiled nervously and looked at the woman. She said something inaudible to the audience, but showed her cards, indicating a winning hand. Pickins rose, nodded in Blaine's direction and left the table. The dealer turned to the spectators and said that the winning hand was a full house, threes and sevens.

There was a murmur in the crowd and Rutledge's neighbor turned to him and winked. "Now it's down to just the two of them, the Queen of Hearts and Bedrock Butler. He's the best there is," the man explained. "That girl's done good to get down to the last pair with a player like Butler."

The dealer was shuffling and Blaine Kidwell had just finished re-stacking her chips. She remained serene, not looking at her opponent, who sat behind his own formidable winnings, staring at her.

"What's happening now?" Rutledge asked the genial man at his side.

"Bedrock dropped out of that last hand that finished Pickins. Him and the girl got about the same amount on the table. It's between the two of them for the prize money—twenty thousand to the winner and seventy-five hundred for second place, plus what they've won playin'."

"You mean they get more than just the prize money?"

"Shucks, the players have to put up twenty-five hundred just to enter, then they need bettin' money. These two have already won most of all the losers' grubstakes—I'd guess fifty or a hundred thousand, anyway. If they play to the death, one of these two could end up with it all."

The men turned their attention to the game. Butler had just taken the pot when Blaine declined to meet his bet. He smiled and said something to the woman.

Rutledge let his eyes settle on her pretty face again. Her demeanor was strangely at odds with her beauty. She seemed out of place to him, like a delicate rose growing in rocky desert soil.

There was some current in her that intrigued him, something curious beneath her facade of self-control. He surmised it was an inner conflict. The years he had spent helping troubled boys enabled him to see things most observers missed.

"She's going to lose," Rutledge whispered to his companion.

"Wouldn't surprise me," the other replied. "She's good for a woman, but she has a way to go to get in Bedrock's league."

The next hand had been dealt, and obvious emotion filled Blaine's face. The subtle signs Rutledge had first noticed spilled out now for everyone to see. After a moment of hesitation, the Queen of Hearts calmly laid her cards on the table and stood up. Butler looked surprised. She said something to him in a low tone, then turned to speak to an official, none of her words audible to the audience.

The tournament official stepped to the edge of the platform and announced that the game and championship had been conceded to Butler.

"Well, I'll be damned," the man next to Rutledge said with surprise. "Bedrock must have psyched her."

They watched as Blaine Kidwell placed her winnings in a chip tray and Butler stood up, a big grin on his face. Rutledge's eyes were on the woman, who had regained her calm. When she had finished with her chips she extended her hand to her opponent. Butler put a burly arm around her narrow shoulders and whispered something in her ear. The smile she gave was controlled.

"You can be sure he's psyching her for the next time they meet," Rutledge's neighbor said with a laugh.

Blaine Kidwell turned away as the television people came forward. Butler was now in the winner's circle, but Rutledge couldn't take his eyes off the woman, who had stepped to the cashier at the rear of the card room. He found himself admiring the trim lines of her slender figure, revealed by the plain black slacks she wore.

She was a beautiful woman. Rutledge was shocked, he hadn't expected it. As he watched her he couldn't help wondering if the whole thing was a joke of some sort. Might this be Agnes Kidwell's idea of temptation—sending him off to meet with this lovely creature?

He had to smile at the absurdity of his thoughts. Would he ever stop seeing the world as divided between good and evil? Perhaps it was the old woman's contemptible hatred that had set him off.

But what of this beauty, Blaine Kidwell? He contemplated her and felt a growing desire to discover the woman behind the porcelain mask. He sensed an enigma in her, an enigma that sparked his own brooding masculinity.

BLAINE KIDWELL WATCHED as the cashier carefully stacked her chips into piles on the counter between them. A supervisor stood behind the cashier watching the process, mentally calculating the player's winnings along with her.

Blaine never took her eyes off the chips as the cashier quickly worked, finally announcing the total at $36,865. Under the scrutiny of the supervisor, the cashier prepared a receipt for Blaine's signature, then counted out her winnings in cash, placing it in a neat pile.

"Would you like it bundled, Ms Kidwell?" the cashier asked.

"Yes, please." She watched as the money was placed in several piles and secured with heavy rubber bands. When the job was done, Blaine signed the receipt and pushed it across the counter to the cashier. "Could I have my purse?"

The supervisor opened a drawer and removed a heavy black leather shoulder bag and handed it to her. She opened it and glanced inside, ignoring all the contents except for the thirty-eight-caliber pistol on top. "Thank you," she said, and wedged the bundles of cash down beside the gun.

As she turned around Blaine saw Lloyd Harris, the casino manager, talking to one of the tournament officials. Upon seeing that she had finished with the cashier he walked over to her.

"Are you okay, Blaine?"

"Yes, I'm fine."

"The TV people want to talk to you."

She frowned. "Do I have to?"

Harris shrugged. "I can't make you talk to them, but you seem to be the story and it's awfully good publicity."

"For you or for me?" she smiled.

The man grinned back at her.

Blaine Kidwell knew she owed a lot to Lloyd Harris. He had been instrumental in getting her into her first major tournament two years earlier, and she wanted to reciprocate whenever she could. Still, she didn't feel like an interview just now. Considering her a curiosity as the only woman in big-time poker, the media had begun paying a fair amount of attention to her during the past year or so.

The questions were always the same. How did you get into poker? What's it like being the only woman in a male fraternity? How much of your success is attributable to luck and how much to skill? What does your family think? How much money have you won?

The publicity was the worst part of Blaine's success as a poker professional—she relished her privacy. But the publicity also made her valuable to the establishment. Her cooperation assured her a degree of protection and privilege in a cold and lonely world.

"Would they settle for an interview tomorrow, instead? I really don't feel like talking to anyone."

"I can ask. What happened anyway, Blaine?"

"I was more than thirty thousand to the good. I just didn't feel like playing anymore."

Harris nodded his silver-maned head. "You know what they'll say, though."

"Let them say what they like. I'm the only one besides Butler who left with thirty thousand."

Harris glanced over at the poker champion, who was being interviewed under the bright lights. "He's already crowing, Blaine."

"Doesn't bother me, Mr. Harris. There'll be another time. Besides, that'll give you something to beat your drum about—a rematch at the National Championships."

"Yeah, Blaine, it's good for me, but what'll it do for your confidence?"

She gave him an even look. "Right now all I care about is my headache."

Their eyes met and the casino manager conceded with a smile. "When and where can they have their interview?"

"How about tomorrow morning, before I check out?"

"Okay, you can use our conference room. Shall I tell them ten?"

"Make it eleven."

Lloyd Harris patted her arm. "Okay. Want a security guard to walk you out?"

"At least to my building. I'm in one of the garden suites, out by the pool."

"Sure you'll be all right?" Harris asked, gesturing toward the purse Blaine had tucked under her arm.

"I've got old Betsy," she replied confidently, as the manager turned away with a smile. He signaled to a guard.

SOME OF THE SPECTATORS had begun drifting away, including the man who had befriended Caleb Rutledge, but he himself had not moved. He was intrigued by the woman he'd come to see. The dark-haired beauty was an unexpected surprise. Pleasantly so.

But Rutledge's mind turned back to the purpose of his trip into Las Vegas. This attractive poker player was the unfit mother Agnes Kidwell had complained about. And he had been given the task of discouraging her from seeing her son. The notion didn't sit well, but Rutledge did feel an obligation to get a reading of the situation, if only to better know how to deal with the boy.

His eyes moved over the shapely figure of the woman as she stood at the cashier's counter, talking to the casino official. Rutledge found her very attractive, even arousing. He smiled at the irony. He had come seeking her for the purpose of making an unpleasant request, only to be taken by her physical appeal.

Maybe he had been neglecting his social life too long. Maybe that was what was wrong. It had to be a sign when a card player—a lady

of the casinos—intrigued him. Given her record and profession, she
had to be rather common, notwithstanding her beauty. Rutledge decided he had better concentrate on what he'd come there to do.

While he was preoccupied with his thoughts, the woman had
walked with a security guard to an exit at the side of the card parlor,
moving quickly down an aisle through the surrounding slot machines.
Gathering himself, Rutledge went off after them, knowing that if they
were to talk he'd have to catch her before she got lost in the crowded
casino.

It was now after the dinner hour and the building was packed,
making it difficult for him to do much more than keep pace with the
woman. She seemed as intent on avoiding their meeting as he was
on effecting it.

Hurrying in pursuit, Rutledge saw Blaine Kidwell and the guard
turn up a side corridor leading out of the casino. By the time he
reached the spot where they had turned, they had disappeared. He
looked up the carpeted passageway at the bobbing sea of people, but
she was nowhere in sight.

Rutledge ran up the corridor, slipping through gaps in the flow of
the crowd. Near the end of the passageway was a lobby area with a
restaurant and some shops. Could they have entered one of them? It
seemed unlikely.

Rutledge had almost decided he had lost them when he caught a
glimpse of the dark-haired beauty and her uniformed companion
walking outside, along a pathway toward the pool. He ran after them,
but they were already nearing one of the buildings.

They stopped at the entry and the guard tipped his hat at her, then
walked away. Rutledge almost called out, but decided instead to
hurry and catch her in the building where she would be alone. Inside
he opened the door to the ground floor rooms, but the hallway was
empty. He ran up the stairs to the second floor, breathlessly pulling
open the door.

She was three-quarters of the way down the corridor. Her back
was to him and she was standing in front of a door, fishing her room
key from her purse. As he approached she took a quick look over
her shoulder at him, a touch of dismay on her face.

When he was thirty or forty feet away he called out, "Mrs. Kidwell!"

Blaine spun around suddenly, sending the bag on her shoulder
thumping into the door. Her eyes were filled with terror, her white
teeth bared. The sheer hostility on her face stopped Rutledge dead in
his tracks.

It was only then, in the tense instant in which his eyes drifted from her face to her hands, that he realized she was pointing a gun square at his belly.

CHAPTER TWO

BLAINE KIDWELL EASED the pressure of her finger on the trigger as the man's hands slowly rose to the height of his shoulders. She knew she was in control but her heart continued to rage nonetheless, like a trip-hammer gone berserk.

Through the blur of fear his face drifted into focus. There was fright in his eyes, and the way he was staring apprehensively at the gun told her he expected to be shot at any second. But Blaine knew he was safe, she could never shoot anyone, unless perhaps she was about to die herself.

She felt her gun hand begin to tremble and she redoubled her anger to make sure he understood she meant business. His eyes met hers. She saw him swallow and the vaguest hint of a smile touched his mouth.

"Don't shoot," he said softly. "I just want to talk to you."

Blaine glared, convinced that it was duplicity. "Talk? What about?"

"Your son, Mrs. Kidwell. Jason."

"Jason? What about him? What have you done?" The gun began shaking so violently that Blaine had to support it with both hands.

"Nothing," the man hastened to reassure her. "I've done nothing. He's all right."

"Who are you?" she snapped, fear and suspicion seizing her.

"My name is Caleb Rutledge. I run the ranch where Jason's staying."

"Rutledge? Father Rutledge?"

He looked a little exasperated. "The boys call me that. I haven't been a priest for seven years."

Blaine suddenly comprehended the absurdity of what was happening. She had a gun pointed at the man who was responsible for her son—Father Rutledge, the operator of the Rutledge Ranch and School for Boys. She looked questioningly into his eyes, then her arms dropped to her sides, the pistol hanging from her right hand like a rock on a string.

He, too, lowered his hands and took a deep breath, his relief obvious. "I'm sorry I frightened you, Mrs. Kidwell."

Blaine felt a swirl of turmoil inside. Their confrontation, the gun, what he must think, all struck her. She looked at the ruggedly handsome face of the man who was now guardian of her son.

There was no accusation in his eyes. They were clear, gentle. His entire face was full of compassion. The green turtleneck sweater, camel-colored pants and calfskin jacket he wore belied his role, but in spite of it all she knew he was Father Rutledge, the man Jason had written her about in such glowing terms. His countenance authenticated the fact. But why had he come to see her?

"What's happened to Jason? Why are you here?"

"Nothing has happened. I've just come to talk with you about him. We haven't met before and obviously have a mutual interest in his welfare." He cleared his throat. "I heard you were in town and I thought I ought to take advantage of the opportunity to—"

"How did you know I was in Las Vegas?" she cut in. Blaine was beginning to sense the hand of Agnes Kidwell, and she searched the man's face for corroboration. He looked uncomfortable.

"Agnes Kidwell, your mother-in-law, mentioned that—"

"I might have known! Her again!" Blaine's face grew sober. "Okay, Father Rutledge, why did she send you?"

"It's Cal Rutledge. Cal."

"Sorry. It's just that—"

"Yes, I understand." He drew a deep breath. "Look, can we go someplace to talk?" His eyes fleetingly drifted down her body.

Blaine looked at him, seeing a man instead of the image of a priest she had carried in her mind. The sandy blond hair, clear blue eyes and chiseled face were not the look of a priest, and yet there was a sensitivity underneath the facade. The man who moments earlier had been a robber was now a former clergyman, but something more, too.

Finally Blaine lowered her eyes when she felt his clinging too tenaciously to hers. "I don't feel like going anyplace," she replied. "I'm wrung out."

"Is this your room?"

"Yes."

"Can we go inside and talk?" He glanced at the gun still hanging from Blaine's hand. "I think we're a bit of a spectacle here in the hallway."

Blaine knew there was a small fortune in her purse and she only had the man's word that he was Caleb Rutledge, but she was too weary to doubt him. She had the thirty-eight, but she felt vulnerable anyway, defeated by the situation. Cal Rutledge was her son's keeper. What choice did she have? "Perhaps for a few minutes, Mr. Rutledge, but—"

"My name's Cal. I'm not 'Father,' and I'm not 'mister,' either, Blaine."

"Okay, Cal. I'd like to hear what you have to say about Jason. But I'm awfully tired and not feeling very well...."

"I realize this is not the best time, but I didn't know another way to get a hold of you. The hotel wouldn't even confirm you were staying here."

She nodded. "Yes, I'm in a rather delicate business, as you can see. I try to be careful." Blaine took the room key from her purse and started to open the door. When there was a six-inch crack in the doorway she froze.

"What's the matter?"

She closed the door as quietly as she could, then turned to him with wide eyes. "The lights are out. I left them on," she whispered. "Someone is in there."

Caleb Rutledge took the key from Blaine and she stepped behind him. "Maybe they've gone, or it could have been the maid," he said, as he inserted the key and slowly opened the door a crack. Reaching in, he flipped on the light switch and eased the door open wide.

The room, or as much of it as they could see, appeared empty. A curtain was billowing in the breeze of an open sliding glass door to the balcony.

"Did you leave that open?"

"No."

"I think whoever it was has left, but let me go in and check." Cal took the pistol from Blaine's hand and searched the bath, closet and under the bed before calling to her that it was safe.

As she approached him, he handed her the gun. "You'd better put this thing away before somebody gets hurt."

"Oh, it's not loaded."

"Not loaded!" he exclaimed. "You let me walk in here with an empty gun?"

Blaine couldn't help smiling. "It stopped *you*, didn't it?"

Cal eyed her. "I advise you not to let the word get out."

"Oh, I have bullets. They're in my makeup bag. But I almost always forget to put them in the gun."

Now Cal laughed. "Messing with you is a little like playing Russian roulette."

"I suppose it is," she said vacantly.

"Why do you carry that thing anyway?"

Blaine shrugged. "I walked into a dark motel room once, got punched in the face and lost six thousand dollars."

"I think you're in the wrong business."

She looked at him for a long time. "Is that why you're here—to tell me that?" She watched him study her, apparently considering his response carefully. Blaine knew she had struck a nerve.

"Your profession is not my main concern," he said at last. "What matters is what's best for Jason."

His words were not unexpected—it was a familiar refrain—but Blaine felt resentment nonetheless. She was always being judged, criticized, told what to do with her own son, how to live her life. And now Agnes had sent this ex-priest to have his go at her.

Cal Rutledge looked a little surprised at the emotion that must have been playing on her face. "Am I wrong?"

"No, of course not. Everybody wants what's best for Jason." Blaine felt her blood rising. "How many times do you suppose I've heard that?" The tears started welling in her eyes. "I've been told to give him up, that he'd be better off if I was dead."

She sank to the bed, trying to maintain control. Finally she looked up at him through tear-brimmed eyes. "All I've done is love him," she implored. "He's a good boy. It was an accident. They've treated him like a criminal and he's just a boy. He didn't mean to hurt that kid, not like that anyway." Sorrow swept over Blaine and she lowered her head, fighting her tears.

Cal sat next to her on the bed. "Look, I'm here to discuss Jason's welfare with you, to work out what's best for him."

Blaine listened, though she didn't look at him. His words were reassuring, but the circumstance gave them an air of unreality. Cal Rutledge represented another enemy, another obstacle between her and her son—she was sure of it. The fact that Agnes was behind it was all the proof she needed.

"Don't be upset," he said in a soothing voice. "I'm concerned for both you and the boy."

Blaine looked at him warily, seeing several men, several contradictions. He was Agnes's agent—her surrogate—but he was also a man of the church, whether he practiced as one or not, and he was just a human being, someone whose job happened to be caring for her child.

She scooted a few inches away from him, feeling uncomfortable at his proximity, even if what he intended was pastoral warmth. She didn't trust him, but she didn't exactly mistrust him, either. "What is it you want from me, Cal?"

"Your help and cooperation."

"What do you mean?"

Rutledge took out his handkerchief and handed it to her. Blaine dabbed her moist eyes. She was aware of his gentleness, but he was a man and she had learned to be distrustful of all men.

"What do you mean, my cooperation?" she asked again.

"I'd like to know what your plans are."

She straightened her shoulders, knowing it was Agnes's question. "I plan to move to Las Vegas and see Jason as often as possible."

"I see."

She studied him as he studied her. She knew he'd have to come out with it, so she waited. She didn't know his hand yet, but she could tell he wasn't playing it straight. "Is there a problem with me living in Las Vegas?"

"Not necessarily."

Annoyance flickered through her. "Please say what you're thinking."

"What I'm thinking isn't the issue."

"Will you answer me one thing? Did Agnes put you up to coming here?"

"She asked me to talk to you, yes."

Blaine couldn't help a tiny smile of triumph. "What's the message? As though I need to ask."

Cal looked irritated. "Agnes Kidwell doesn't tell me what to say or think. No one does."

"What do *you* think then?" she asked caustically. Anger passed across his face and Blaine felt pleasure at having smoked him out.

"I haven't decided."

She laughed. "Isn't it obvious? You think I'm a model mother, don't you? Just the sort of person you'd have raise a boy like Jason. I mean, what could be better? You've just seen it all—guns, cards, cash...the whore Agnes probably told you you'd find." Her irony turned bitter. Tears welled again. "Go ahead! Tell me what you think. Give me your pious, saintly speech about morality, good and evil!"

"You chose this life," he replied angrily, and rose to his feet.

Blaine watched him pace in front of her. "Yes, I chose it. I play poker because I'm good at it! See that purse?" she said, pointing a trembling hand. "There's thirty-six thousand dollars in there. I slaved for two years as a bank clerk in Prosser, Washington and barely made half that much!"

"Money's not everything. You can become a slave to *it* just as easily."

Blaine felt fire surge through her veins. She rose to her feet and faced him, hands on her hips. "Let me tell you about slavery, Mr. Rutledge. For twelve years I've been a slave to that woman. She's done everything in her power to keep me tied down and docile, dependent on her for the money I couldn't earn. She's kept me hostage with Jason's inheritance, knowing I wouldn't move away and deny him that opportunity. Well, several years ago I had enough. I decided to make money on my own, to earn enough so Jason and I could have everything we need without *her*."

"So you play poker."

"Yes, Mr. Rutledge, I play poker. I play professionals. I don't fleece tourists. I don't cheat. What I do is no different than what hundreds of thousands of men in three-piece suits do speculating in the stock market every day. They try to win at the other guy's expense, and so do I. The only difference is they bet on whether a stock's going up or down. I bet on whether my hand's better than the other guy's."

"Funny how gambling is such a noble endeavor in your mouth."

Blaine seethed. "I'm *not* a gambler! I'm a professional poker player. I play odds and I play people, my opponents. I'm successful because I'm good at what I do. I understand numbers and I can read people. I've also got guts, Mr. Rutledge. Luck has nothing to do with my work. Gambling is for fools. I've never shot craps or played roulette or blackjack in my life."

"And all that makes you a model mother?"

She opened her mouth to respond, but the utter futility of it struck her. He was as self-righteous as the rest of them. It was not the first time she'd encountered the attitude, so she wasn't surprised. Still, it hurt. It always did.

Glaring at him through her pain Blaine saw remorse on his face instead of the smugness she expected. Perhaps he had gone further than he intended, but it didn't matter now, it was too late. All at once the damned-up emotion spilled out and Blaine sank onto the bed again and began to cry.

She felt his hand on her arm. "I'm sorry," he said softly. "I shouldn't have said that. It was out of place, insensitive. I shouldn't have said it."

Blaine looked at him through her tears. There was contrition on his face, but she knew it didn't matter. "Whether you should have said it or not," she sobbed, "it's what you think."

"You don't know what I think, Blaine. I was provoking you, yes. Maybe it was cruel, maybe I shouldn't have done it, but I learned at lot."

"What?"

"I learned that the situation is a lot more complicated than I thought when I came here tonight." Cal handed Blaine his handkerchief again.

"What are you going to do, Mr. Rutledge?" she asked, wiping her eyes.

"Call me Cal," he commanded.

"Cal, Mr. Rutledge, what does it matter? You've got my son."

"Okay. Let me be blunt then. I came here to determine what kind of an influence you were on the boy. You weren't what I expected, Blaine, and you certainly aren't the loathsome creature Agnes made you out to be." He looked squarely into her eyes. "I don't know what to make of you, frankly. I don't really know you, but I find myself sympathetic. I...I've seen nothing that says you're bad for Jason."

"So, my work is okay with you now?" she asked skeptically.

"No. To be honest, I don't approve. It's your affair, not mine, I realize, but as far as the boy is concerned I do have an interest, a responsibility."

"My self-appointed judge. Isn't that what you're saying?"

"Judge, no."

"Oh, come on, Cal. You're here to judge and to influence me, it's obvious. Agnes would prefer I never saw Jason again, and you're here to try to keep me from him." She wiped her eyes.

"Isn't it possible a little time apart might be good for both of you?"

"You see!" she exclaimed. "You are trying to keep me from my son! Why don't you just come out with it? Why can't you be honest?"

"Now just a minute, Blaine. I'm only raising considerations. Agnes wants that, I'll admit. But I haven't drawn any conclusions yet."

"You've already said you don't approve of what I do."

"That's true, but it doesn't necessarily reflect on your qualifications as a mother."

"How do you presume to judge that any more than you can presume to judge my work?"

"I don't presume anything."

"Ha!"

He touched her arm. Blaine pulled it away.

"I'm not your enemy," he insisted.

"You won't try to stop me from seeing Jason, then?"

"No, of course not. I couldn't prevent you from seeing him if I wanted to. You have a right to come to the ranch on the two Sundays a month we have visiting hours. Any more than that would be up to me."

She searched his eyes. "Do you want me to see him?"

He hesitated. "I'd like to say yes, but I don't know."

Blaine felt disappointment, but she wasn't surprised.

"When was the last time you saw your son?"

"A month ago, in Washington, before they sent him down here."

"Did you see him often up there, after the hearing?"

The tears were forming and she fought them back. "No, only three times—three times in two months," she replied, her voice cracking.

She saw that her unhappiness was upsetting him. Unexpectedly he took her hand, squeezing it sympathetically. His frustration was apparent.

When an errant tear ran down Blaine's cheek, Cal reached over and brushed it aside with the back of his fingers. The warmth of his touch made her aware of his masculinity.

"Please, don't pity me," she whispered.

She stole a glance at him and saw the emotion on his face. There was affection in his eyes. Was she confusing his sentiment with priestly compassion? Or was her own vague attraction to the man clouding her perception?

"I don't feel pity for you, Blaine. I just feel uncomfortable in the position I'm in—between you and Jason."

"I just want to see my son." She watched him and waited. Blaine knew that Cal Rutledge had the bet. It was all up to him.

Finally Cal broke his silence. "Would you like to see him tonight?"

"Tonight?" A smile broke across her face. She hadn't expected this.

"You can ride back with me to the ranch. It'll be on the late side by the time we get there...it's more than a three-hour drive. But I'm sure Jason wouldn't mind getting out of bed to see his mother."

"Are you serious?"

He smiled. "After what I've put you through, it's the least I could do."

Blaine took both of Cal's hands and squeezed them gratefully. She beamed.

"You can stay the night—we've got plenty of space—or I can

bring you back, if you prefer." He looked at his watch. "It would be pretty late by the time we made the round trip, I'm afraid."

"It doesn't matter, as long as I get to see Jason."

He glanced around the room. "Frankly, the idea of you staying here doesn't sit well with me. Apparently someone was rather interested in what you've got in that purse."

Blaine sighed. "Yes, I wasn't looking forward to tonight."

"How long will it take you to pack?"

"I just have to throw a few things in my bag."

"While you do, I'll call hotel security. They ought to know about this," he said, pointing to the open slider.

Several minutes later Cal was standing at the door when Blaine approached him with her suitcase in hand. She put it down and looked up at him. "I want you to know how much I appreciate this, Cal."

Before she knew it, she had leaned into his arms. He held her tightly. His strength made her feel small and vulnerable and terribly aware of how good it felt to be held. Cal brushed her cheek affectionately with his fingers.

When the emotion of the moment had passed, Blaine became aware of who the man was who was holding her in his arms. She grew embarrassed at the intimacy she had initiated and gently pulled herself free—not because what he did wasn't pleasurable, but rather, because it was.

CHAPTER THREE

"MORE FRIES?" she asked.

"Yeah. Please." Cal took the steering wheel with the fingertips of his milk-shake hand and reached into the sack she held. He took his eyes off the road just long enough to give her a little smile. "Thanks."

Blaine looked at the handsome profile of the man in the dark: his straight nose, the fullness of his lower lip and his rather stubborn chin. There was a sexuality about him that moved her. Instinctively she resented him a bit for it—men were not supposed to affect her that way. "Were you really a priest?"

He smiled slightly, but didn't look at her. "An Episcopal priest, yes. But that was a long time ago. Why?"

"I don't know. In a way you don't seem like a priest, or even a preacher. But in a way you do."

"I'm not. That's all part of my past."

He popped another French fry into his mouth and Blaine turned to look out the window at the night. The moon was just rising in the east and she could see the vague profiles of the desert landscape passing by in the moonlight. She wondered about Caleb Rutledge.

"How did you get into poker?" he asked unexpectedly.

She gave a little laugh and he looked at her in surprise.

"What's so funny?"

"I don't know. I guess it was that 'what's-a-nice-girl-like-you-doing-in-a-place-like-this?' sound in your voice."

Cal shot her a glance. "In my voice, or in your head?"

She studied him. "Maybe you do seem like a priest, after all."

"What are you trying to say, Blaine? That I'm being judgmental?"

"Maybe."

"Well, I'm not. It was a serious question. I wasn't judging you one way or the other." He sucked on the straw of his milk shake, but, by the sound, it was empty.

Blaine reached over and took the cup, putting it in the paper sack at her feet. "Want any more fries? There're only a few left."

"No, you take them."

"I don't want them."

Cal's attention was focused on a truck approaching them on the narrow desert highway. With his eyes intent on the road he groped with his hand, first touching her wrist, then sliding his fingers over her palm until he found the sack of fries. Blaine shivered at his touch, surprised at each manifestation of her physical awareness of him.

After watching him trying unsuccessfully to get into the sack, she finally took the remaining fries out herself, then reached over to put them in his mouth. As the truck passed he turned and smiled at her. It wasn't the look of a priest.

She thought she detected amusement hidden in the shadows on his face. There was more going on in his mind than he would likely admit. Or was it in *her* mind?"

Stealing glances at him she realized that his attractiveness had become a source of irritation to her, mainly because she wasn't accustomed to it. Blaine had managed to keep men at a distance for years, but Cal Rutledge had accomplished something no man had in a long time: he had aroused her, just by his presence.

"So why did you leave the priesthood? Because of worldly concerns?"

Cal grinned. "If that was an oblique reference to women, the answer is no. Actually, it was more the opposite—loss of a woman."

"What happened?"

His voice grew somber. "I was engaged to be married—there's no celibacy in the Episcopal church, you know. My fiancée developed cancer and died within a period of four months."

"I'm sorry."

"I had a church in Massachusetts," he continued, apparently wanting to get the story out, "and after Laura's death I decided to leave the ministry. It was not so much a case of shaken faith as doubts about what I wanted to do with my life. I felt the need to help people a little more immediately and tangibly than in a spiritual sense alone, so I came back out to the family ranch and opened the school for boys." He turned to her with a grin. "Now my only vice is hard work."

"Too much of anything can be bad for you, you know."

"Yes, Mother."

She turned. Their eyes met. Jason hadn't been mentioned since they left Las Vegas, and Cal's remark unintentionally brought their earlier confrontation to mind.

"I didn't mean to be flip, Blaine."

"It's okay. I know."

There was a difficult silence. "Look, I'd like to talk about you and Jason," Cal said, "if you don't mind."

"No, I don't mind. I'm sure that was Agnes's intent."

"No, Blaine, this has nothing to do with Agnes. I want to know about you and the boy.... I want to know what went wrong."

"Nothing went wrong. He got into a fight at school, like boys will. The injury to the other child was accidental, but no one seems to be willing to accept that."

"I've read the file. There seemed to be a consensus that Jason went further than was reasonable under the circumstances."

"I won't try to justify what he did. But he was very, very upset about what the boy had done."

"You mean the things he'd said about you?"

Blaine bowed her head.

"You're blaming yourself, and that's not right, either," Cal said.

"I can't blame my son," she snapped.

"This is not a time for blame. It's a time for healing. Let's talk about what matters. Let's talk about you and Jason."

Blaine felt a wave of fear come over her. This moonlight drive across the desert was an innocent enough setting, but she knew she was really on trial. What this man thought, what he decided about her, could profoundly affect both her life and her son's.

"Look, Cal, if we're going to talk about Jason and me, we may as well talk about my career, too. I know my poker-playing is the crux of the issue. It's been Agnes's ax to grind since she found out about it, and it doesn't take a genius to figure out you have your doubts, too."

Cal reached over and took Blaine's hand, holding it firmly. "Okay, we'll talk about whatever you wish. But I want you to know that I'm not going to let my own feelings affect my judgment of you as a parent."

"But you can't separate them, either. Not completely. I am who I am. I'm a poker player *and* I'm Jason's mother."

"Blaine, I don't want you to think I'm equating gambling with sin."

"Cal, I know you mean well, but you really don't understand. I'm *not* a gambler. I play poker. It's a contest of skill and guts." He had not released her hand and Blaine felt the emotion flowing back and forth between them. They were two human beings joined only by their humanity and their mutual concern for a boy. She had never felt so close and yet so far from a man at the same time.

"Let me put it this way," Cal said in a soft, affectionate tone, "I care about you as much as I do about Jason."

There was an intimacy in the man's words that Blaine hadn't expected. She was sure he felt a desire that went beyond human compassion, but *his* desire didn't distress her nearly as much as her own. This man—she knew instinctively—offered no real promise, only temptation.

Right now she needed him because of her son, but she had to be careful. She had to guard against her own weakness. Everything she had done, and everything she would do, he'd judge her by. Agnes Kidwell was looking over his shoulder. Blaine knew she couldn't forget that.

"Please tell me about yourself, Blaine," he said, releasing her hand.

It was a challenge of sorts, but she also saw it as an opportunity. If he was fair-minded, the truth might not hurt. She could only hope. "My life story? Is that what you want?"

"I want to know who you are."

"I'm your basic kid from the wrong side of the tracks," she began matter-of-factly. "Not that there was anything horrible about my family. We were just unfortunate, and we were poor. My mother died when I was in the fifth grade. My father was a good man, but he was weak. He gambled.

"When I was in my first year of high school Dad lost so much money that the little farm we had went to the bank. He tried to gamble us out of hock, but ended up losing everything. It wasn't much, but it was ours. We finally moved into town in a place the banker let us rent for next to nothing—to assuage his guilt, I guess, not that it was his fault." Blaine fell silent as images of her youth came to her from the darkness of the desert night.

"Was that in Washington?"

"Yes. Prosser's a little place between the Tri-Cities and Yakima. It's not a bad town but, like any small place, being from a poor family doesn't make you queen of society. In high school the boys were all interested in me for the wrong reasons.

"By the time I was a senior I managed to climb out of the hole I was in. I was going with Frank Kidwell, the son of the richest family in the county. He was a few years older and was already running his family's farming operation. Frank had spent a year at Washington State and dropped out.

"We got married secretly at Christmas in Oregon. I got pregnant a few months before graduation. I thought I was in love, but I suppose I was really taken in by the status and respectability he represented.

"Some people in town, especially Agnes, said I tricked Frank so he'd marry me, but it wasn't true. I thought he was my one true love and I wanted a new life with him. I was seventeen and...well, you know how that is."

"Was it a good marriage?"

Blaine laughed bitterly. "No, the only good that came from it was Jason. Frank was twenty-one and no more ready for marriage than I was. He spent most of his time carousing with his friends. He drank a lot. Finally killed himself one night a year after Jason was born when he got drunk and ran himself off the highway in his pickup."

"Did he treat you badly?"

Blaine sighed. "Nothing terrible, no. He used to boss me around a lot, but most men do when they're young and insecure. Worst thing he did was make me go with him every Sunday to my dad's house. I'd have to stand there while he gave Daddy a hundred-dollar bill. My father was too sick to work and all he had was his gambling. Frank was his keeper. He just wanted to rub my nose in the fact that I owed him everything. It made me feel cheap, and I hated him for it."

"So after your husband died Jason was all both you and Agnes had."

"Yes. She'd been widowed for years. Frank was her only relation until Jason was born. I meant nothing to her. We never got along. She helped me financially after the accident, but it wasn't altruism. She wanted to keep me in Prosser and used Jason's inheritance to tie me down. Everything I got was contingent.

"Of course, we did benefit. I didn't have to go to work until Jason was in school. When I did take a job, Agnes arranged something for me at the bank to make sure I didn't have to leave town. But I did manage to get my degree in psychology in Ellensburg at Central Washington College of Education. Agnes must have called three times a week. She was sure that I was going to meet somebody and get married."

"So how did you get to be a poker champion?"

"I learned to play from my father. He was actually pretty good, but he played emotionally when he got desperate. He gambled and had a tendency to let the cards play him. I used to drive Daddy to the state-licensed card room in Kennewick when I was in high school. Eventually, they let me watch."

"Then you've played since high school?"

"No, I never played until after Daddy was gone. It was while I was in Ellensburg, at college. I got into a game at a fraternity party, almost by chance. I took home a hundred and fifty dollars."

"And you got hooked?"

"No, Cal, I don't gamble. It's not an emotional thing. I don't do it for thrills. I didn't play again until several years later when I went into the card room in Kennewick on an impulse. Agnes had given me a hundred dollars for Christmas, and I was headed into the Columbia Shopping Center when I decided to get a little revenge. I wanted to get back some of the money my father had lost over the years. I was making some kind of statement, I guess."

"You won?"

"Nearly seven hundred that first night."

"But you weren't hooked?"

"No, I knew why I was winning."

"Didn't you ever lose?"

"Oh sure, but it was because of mistakes. I learned from that, too, though. I made sure I never bet more than I had and I never used anything but my winnings to play with."

"What made you start to play regularly?"

"After the first big win in Kennewick the regulars nagged and baited me. They wanted a chance to win it back, and I wanted to teach them a lesson for my father's sake."

"How'd you get into the big time? Just get too good for the local boys?"

"Partly. There was an old pro who took me under his wing. Said he knew talent when he saw it, and I kind of became the son he never had. He was a real estate broker from Pasco, but he loved poker. He taught me how to spot cons. Things like partners and other tricks we never saw much in the small towns because we were leery of strangers. I always picked my games carefully and never went over my head, unless I was in it to buy a lesson."

Blaine turned to Cal and their eyes met. She looked up the lonely stretch of highway at the lights of an oncoming car on the next ridge. Neither said anything for a while. "What are you thinking, Cal?"

"That you're a fascinating woman."

"You never met a professional poker player before?"

"Not like you, no."

Blaine chuckled.

"What?"

"I was thinking you're about as noncommittal as a poker player," she teased.

Cal smiled. "What were you expecting?"

"I don't know. Something. Approval, disapproval, something."

"You're obviously a very capable woman."

"What about *mother*?" she asked, feeling frustration.

He hesitated. "I don't know about that."

They fell silent again. She thought about the man, about Jason, about the predicament she was in. The prudent thing to do was to lie back and wait, but Blaine couldn't control her frustration. She had to know what he intended. "If I seem to be on edge, Cal, it's because I'm uncomfortable when a man gets leverage on me."

"What do you mean?"

"I don't like being under a microscope, and I don't like being beholden to anyone." *And I don't like feeling attracted to you,* she wanted to add, but didn't. She knew Cal represented temptation, and she'd have to resist it. Weakness had destroyed her father and, as a result, she had taught herself to be strong. She was determined not to succumb, no matter what.

"You're not beholden to me in any way," he said insistently.

"You determine how often I see my son."

"His welfare is the only consideration."

"As judged by you."

"You're afraid I'll be unfair?"

"I don't know. I'm not sure what I think."

"Don't worry," he said.

"I know you don't approve of what I do. That's hardly reassuring. Otherwise, I have no idea what you think of me."

"Do you care?"

"Of course I do."

"Because of Jason?"

Blaine sensed the advantage had slipped to Cal. "Yes," she said softly, but she knew in her heart that it was only a half-truth. She cared for herself, as well.

For the next fifteen or twenty minutes neither of them spoke. Cal turned on the radio, but after fiddling with the knob he turned it off.

Blaine felt a tension in the air, almost as if there had been a lover's quarrel and each of them regretted the spat, but couldn't bring himself to apologize. She knew the notion was silly because they weren't lovers and they hadn't really quarreled. But why was the air thick with regret? Was she imagining it?

She looked at his handsome face as though she might find the answers to her questions there, but it was unfathomable. Cal Rutledge was having an effect on her that she wasn't used to. He moved her, and that didn't sit well.

It was twelve years since Blaine had been with a man that she cared for. Since her husband was killed she had learned that men tended to prey on women in her situation. There had been a couple of brief relationships, but they hadn't ended well.

While in college she had been hotly pursued. An attractive young widow with a small child seemed to fit everyone's fantasy. Blaine had fended off the more obvious opportunists, but there had been one young man, the son of a prominent lawyer from Tacoma, who managed to breach her defenses.

She soon realized that he was only interested in the adventure and had no intention of becoming serious, of taking on the responsibility of an instant family. She had bitterly broken off the relationship, suspicious of college boys thereafter.

For a time, when she worked at the bank, Blaine had dated the manager of a car dealership in Richland, but he was divorced and more interested in a sexual companion than a meaningful relationship. She concluded it was a mistake to look for a husband and a father for her son, so she concentrated on living her life and being a good mother to Jason. Being strong and independent was the best policy.

Now that she was the Queen of Hearts, Blaine Kidwell could have her pick of men. The irony was that she wanted none of them. She knew they courted her for the wrong reasons, and there was no changing the world.

The only thing she had control over was her own feelings. No man could control her life or affect her emotions—no man until she met Cal Rutledge.

Strangely enough, the knowledge that he had such power was more troubling than compelling. She'd get over the physical attraction for him easily enough—she always had in the past. It was his control of Jason that concerned her more. He sat in judgment, like King Solomon.

And yet it intrigued her that the first man to move her in years should be an ex-priest. How ironic—the Queen of Hearts and a man of the cloth. The little poker player from the wrong side of the tracks and Father Rutledge, the rich rancher and shepherd of wayward boys.

Blaine decided that Cal was a man of contradictions. She tried to imagine him as a priest and, in spite of his masculine aura, there *was* something about him that was spiritual and caring.

She remembered what he had said about leaving the priesthood—

it had been the death of his fiancée that had prompted it. Blaine wondered about the woman. What kind of person would have moved him to marriage? But for the tragedy, who would have been Mrs. Caleb Rutledge?

After the long silence Cal's voice intruded unexpectedly into Blaine's thoughts. "Do you mind if I ask you something?"

"What?"

"Tonight at the tournament you surprised everyone and quit. Why?"

"Because I was ahead and I didn't feel right. I didn't have the control I needed to play well, and I felt the mental leverage was against me."

"I saw the last few hands," Cal explained, "and asked the man standing next to me what happened. He said your opponent psyched you out."

"More like I psyched myself out. I'd prefer to think I was smart enough to know that I'd lost the mental edge. You see, if I continued to play under those circumstances, it would have been gambling. Any time you play out of pride, fear, greed or desperation, you're dead."

"But it's a game, a contest."

"A serious one, if you earn your living at it."

He smiled in the darkness. "There's more to what you do than meets the eye."

"The only reasons for me to stay in that game tonight were either fear or greed—fear of losing or greed for the prize money. Either of those things will kill a poker player if he's not on top of his game. I wasn't."

"What happens if you play that fellow again?"

"Hopefully, he'll be overconfident. I have the advantage of knowing why I quit, he can only guess. Butler's not stupid. He's one of the best in the world, so I need every advantage I can get. In July there's the National Championship tournament. I might find out then."

"What if he suspects you dropped out tonight on purpose—as a psychological gambit, I mean?"

"He might. And that's why I'm not going to be overconfident the next time I play him."

Cal laughed. "I have to admit you've given me a respect for playing poker."

Blaine couldn't help smiling to herself. Cal's admission was a small victory, but she'd take each one she could get.

After another five minutes they left the highway and headed on a secondary road toward the foothills to the west. Cal told her they were almost at the ranch, and Blaine felt her heart swell with excitement at the thought of seeing Jason again.

She forgot all about Cal Rutledge and the things he had done to her mind and body the past hours. Her maternal love transcended everything, and her child, his problems and unhappiness, again occupied her mind as they had for months. By the time they pulled into the compound she was so jittery she could hardly sit still.

RUTLEDGE PUSHED the wadded-up newspaper under the fireplace grate then stood, looking along the mantel for the matches. Glancing behind him, he saw Blaine and Jason on the couch talking quietly, their dark heads touching as they huddled. Her arm was around the boy's neck. Both of them had tear-streaked faces.

Rutledge had driven Jason to his house from the dormitory so that the boy wouldn't have to get dressed and disturb the others more than necessary. Sitting with his mother now in his pajamas and bathrobe, he looked more as if he was spending a quiet evening with his parents than stolen minutes with a mother from whom he was separated.

Rutledge saw Jason wipe his cheek with his sleeve when their eyes met, and he knew he was intruding on their privacy, embarrassing the boy. If it hadn't been important for him to evaluate the character of their relationship, he would have left them in private.

Instead he turned to his task, lighting the fire he had spent the past few minutes preparing. When he had managed a good strong blaze, he turned to mother and son. "This fire should take the chill off, but I personally need something warm inside. Can I interest you two in some hot chocolate?"

Jason nodded. "Yes, please."

Blaine also assented. "That would be nice, Cal."

From the kitchen Rutledge was able to see them, though he couldn't hear the softly spoken words they exchanged. At one point Blaine kissed Jason on the cheek. He hugged her back fiercely and they clung together for a long time.

It was apparent that they were close, that this meeting was special to them. He was glad he had arranged it, smiling at the film of moisture that had come over his eyes and the lump in his throat.

"It may not be world class," he said a few minutes later as he entered the room with a tray and three mugs of chocolate, "but it sure tastes good on a cold night."

Blaine smiled at him through eyes brimming with tears, and the lump swelled up in Rutledge's throat again. The little nod he gave her said, "You're welcome."

He looked at the boy, who had his mother's pale gray eyes and refined features. "Jason, I hope you've been telling your mom what a great school we've got here." Rutledge dropped into an easy chair.

The boy hung his head shyly. "Well...not exactly."

Rutledge chuckled. "What's the matter? Don't you like the math?"

"Oh, it's okay. But I've had most of it before."

"Well, maybe I'd better have a word with your math teacher."

Jason's face immediately filled with a look of regret.

"Don't worry, I won't tell him what you said. I'll just ask him to review your test scores."

The boy looked relieved and Rutledge shot Blaine a glance. "It takes us a while to find the bright ones and get them up to where they belong."

She squeezed the boy's shoulders. "Jason's a hard worker."

"Oh, Mom," he mumbled, obviously embarrassed by her maternal pride and loyalty.

"Well, that's important," Rutledge said. Then he added, "If you're half as dedicated and determined as your mom, you'll go a long way." He winked at Blaine, who had a glow of happiness on her face that he hadn't seen before.

Letting his eyes linger on her as she playfully cuffed her son, Rutledge felt a special rapport with the woman. The love he had seen in her belied her facade, exposing the softer aspects of her femininity that she kept hidden.

As he watched mother and son interacting, Rutledge felt a yearning—a desire for the elemental woman, the female with her offspring. Looking at her, he hated himself for having judged her. But he knew he also hated the life she led.

BLAINE LAY BACK with her head resting on the couch, her eyes staring dreamily into the fire. Between the final session of the tournament that afternoon, the encounter with Cal Rutledge and her emotional meeting with Jason, she felt completely spent, wrung out.

As soon as Cal left to take Jason back to the dormitory, Blaine had collapsed with fatigue, too tired, too full of emotion to think about her situation. Yet she knew he would be back shortly. She would have to decide what to do.

The thought of the long drive into Las Vegas was too much to bear, she would have to stay at the ranch. But she wasn't sure what arrangements he had in mind. They hadn't had a chance to talk about it, but she was sure from what he had said that there were suitable accommodations.

Although she was alone in a strange house, Blaine felt curiously secure, even comfortable. Cal had been wonderful with Jason. He seemed completely understanding and accepting, which made seeing her son a warm and happy experience. Perhaps he saw their closeness. Maybe he would become an ally in her cause.

Still, she sensed the disparity in their lives was much greater than any spiritual connection between them. In a way he and his family were not unlike the Kidwells when she had first encountered them as a girl.

And, despite her fame as the Queen of Hearts, it seemed she was still on the outside looking in. With Frank Kidwell it had been the promise of respectability. With Caleb Rutledge it was the fate of her son and what that required: Cal's approval of her.

He had given her hope, but she knew their worlds were far apart, that the chasm between them could never be breached. Their only tie was a mutual concern for Jason, and a vague attraction Blaine sensed he felt as much as she.

How ironic—two unlikely people set apart by who they were and the circumstances in which fate had placed them. Blaine smiled into the fire, loving and hating her bittersweet life.

When the front door slammed she realized that Cal had returned. He swept into the room, bringing with him some of the cool desert air. Blaine shivered slightly as she looked up at his robust face.

"You've got a helluva boy, Blaine. He's a good kid," Cal said, as he removed his jacket and tossed it on a chair. He looked at her in a kindly way. "You've had a rough day. I bet you could use a drink. I know I could."

His blue eyes seemed good-natured and friendly. There was nothing pernicious about the man, but something inside her told Blaine there were dangers to be avoided. Yet, to refuse to join him for a drink seemed somehow ungrateful, a repudiation of his kindness and generosity. "Maybe one drink, but I'm awfully tired," she finally said.

He stepped to a cupboard in the corner of the room. "What would you like? A cocktail? Cognac? A liqueur? I think there's wine and beer in the refrigerator."

"What are you having?"

"I think I'll have a brandy."

"That sounds good."

He took two brandy snifters from the shelf and poured out the cognac.

"Where are your guest quarters?"

"Well, there are several choices. I think the best bet would be for you to stay in the guest room here in the house. This was my family home, so there's plenty of room and privacy for you."

"Okay. Whatever is easiest."

Cal walked to the couch with a brandy snifter in each hand and dropped down beside her. His sudden nearness disrupted her composure and, when he put the brandy in her hand, his fingers brushed hers. Instinctively she recoiled.

As her eyes searched his warily, Cal touched her glass with his own. "To the Queen of Hearts," he murmured in a half whisper, one corner of his mouth curving provocatively.

And Blaine realized the man had taken off his priestly mantle. He was addressing the woman in her, not the mother of one of his boys.

CHAPTER FOUR

BLAINE WAS GLAD for the crackling fire. She was glad for the stinging warmth of the brandy—it helped distract her, but not completely. Though Cal Rutledge was sitting quietly beside her, he assaulted her senses by his very presence. She didn't trust him; she didn't trust the feelings inside her; she didn't trust anything.

Although she looked at the fire instead of him, Blaine could feel his awareness of her. It radiated from him, making her feel more uneasy still. She knew instinctively it was wrong for them to feel that way because it invalidated the very thing they both cared most about: Jason's welfare.

Nevertheless the attraction was strong, involving another side of her, a part deep in her feminine soul. At this moment her desire seemed every bit as strong as her ability to resist it, and Blaine knew it was weakness—the kind that could defeat her.

She and Cal were from two different worlds, ruled by two different gods. Desire was not reason enough to cross the no-man's-land that separated them.

Common sense told Blaine that if Caleb Rutledge wanted her, he wanted her physically. If so, he was as much a victim of his own delusions as she was of hers. Even if his desire was tempered with compassion—the compassion of a decent man—it was no less wrong. He belonged with someone from his own world, not her.

Sipping her brandy while the fire danced in her eyes, Blaine thought of the woman Cal was to have married. The image that came to her mind was of a demure young woman with golden curls and an old-fashioned dress with a high collar and a long skirt. That seemed to be the sort of wife a young preacher should have, someone who hadn't seen the gates of hell, even at a distance.

"Blaine," he said softly in her ear, "you're not at all what I expected when I went to that casino tonight."

The statement surprised her. "What do you mean?"

"You're a decent, sensitive person and..."

"And what?"

"A lovely, attractive woman."

It was not what she wanted to hear just then, but somehow she expected it. It saddened her. She shot him a brief glance before lowering her eyes, not quite sure how to rebuff him.

"I hope it doesn't upset you that I tell you that," he said, as he pushed a strand of hair off her temple with his fingertip.

She fought back the tremor his touch evoked. "No, but I don't want you to misunderstand me, my intentions."

"What intentions?"

"To help Jason. To be a good mother to him...to get him back with me."

"After tonight, I understand that very well."

"That's all I want, Cal." She watched as he sipped his cognac, letting his gaze drift from her eyes to her mouth.

"You're trying to say you're not interested in me?" he asked.

"You're a very kind and generous person. You've helped me and I'm grateful. But I don't want you to have the wrong impression."

Cal sighed. It seemed more a sign of impatience than disappointment. Blaine turned her eyes upon him, hoping her expression would convince him insofar as her words hadn't. But if he noticed, he was unmoved.

He pushed at errant strands of her hair as he had before. The proprietary though gentle manner in which he touched her made the gesture all the more potent. Blaine trembled again. He seemed to be communicating directly with her desire, ignoring entirely her will.

Cal lightly stroked her cheek with the back of his fingers. "I don't want you to have the wrong impression either, Blaine. I regard our friendship as a totally separate issue from our joint concern for your son."

Rolling his words over in her mind, she decided that he meant to reassure her he was expecting nothing in return for his efforts. She wasn't quite sure whether to be grateful or offended.

Blaine drank her brandy, but decided that his proximity was too much to handle. She needed to escape, to move to where he couldn't touch her again. She got to her feet and walked over to the fire.

When she turned he was looking at her with brooding, masculine eyes. She yearned again for the compassion of the priest, because the man in him frightened her. "Tell me about your fiancée, the woman you were going to marry."

A little smile touched his lips and he reached for the bottle of brandy on the table. "What do you want to know?"

"Just what she was like—if it's not too painful."

Cal poured more cognac into each of their glasses then sat back, staring past Blaine into the fire.

"What can I say about Laura?" he said, more to himself than to her. "I loved her. I was devastated after her death. It was years before I found my equilibrium."

"What was she like?"

"She was surrealistic."

"Surrealistic?" Blaine said in surprise.

Cal laughed softly. "Yes, that's how I thought of her. She was a very real person, who saw the world a little differently from everyone else. Like that poem by Marianne Moore about the real toad in an unreal garden. She had a different vision."

Blaine could see the nostalgia on Cal's face and she felt sorry for him. It almost seemed to her that Laura must have been more an angel than a woman—surrealistic. The only toad she had known was in her biology class in high school. "Was she beautiful?"

"She was pretty, yes, but it was an unusual beauty. Maybe eccentric beauty. Laura was an artist, a painter. We met in England, strangely enough. It was the summer after I finished at Princeton, at the Theological Seminary. Laura was a friend of a cousin of mine, and she was studying art in London. I looked her up when I got to England. That was the beginning."

"Was she English?"

"No, she was American. Her family was from Connecticut. She grew up there."

"Vassar?"

Cal chuckled and looked up at Blaine. "No, she went to Bennington College in Vermont." He was grinning as he watched her. "You think I'm a snob, don't you?" he asked, amused.

Blaine felt as though she had been discovered. "No, I just thought Vassar and Princeton went together."

"It was her surrealism more than her pedigree that appealed to me."

"You were both made from the same mold," Blaine rejoined.

"We had many things in common, that's true. But there were also parts of me Laura didn't know or understand at all. I didn't realize that at the time myself, but I do now."

"Like what?"

Cal reflected. "She didn't care much for my father and the part of me that he represented—my sort of western heritage. Of course, that didn't bother me because I had rejected it myself."

"But you don't now?"

"I suppose at thirty-seven I'm a little more self-accepting."

"What if Laura had lived and you'd married her?"

"My life would be different, wouldn't it? There might not be a school. I might not be here...." He looked up at her. "I might not have met you."

His last words struck her as almost sacrilegious, coming on the heels of his comments about Laura.

They stared at each other for a moment in the firelight. Then Cal scooted forward to the edge of the couch and extended his hand toward her. "Come, sit by me."

"Please don't, Cal."

"Am I that offensive?"

"No, not offensive...."

"Then what?"

"I don't know," she lamented, suddenly feeling anguish. "It's improper. It's not right."

"There's someone else?"

"No, of course not."

"Why 'of course not'? You're a lovely woman. Surely other men have as much trouble keeping their hands off of you as I do." He reached for his brandy snifter and Blaine looked at his face, confirming the hint of sarcasm she heard.

"There's no law that says a woman needs a man," she retorted.

"And you don't?"

"No, not need."

"How about *want*?"

Their eyes met, this time clashing. Blaine's mind reeled, searching for the response she wanted. But before she could find the words, Cal's anger turned to amusement and he smiled. He put down his glass, then rose and stepped to where she stood.

Without warning Cal pulled her against him. His mouth descended toward her, and she gasped just as his lips touched her. Blaine was pressing against his chest with her hands, struggling to free herself, but the desire to surrender was stronger than the instinct to resist.

She let him kiss her, liking his strength alongside her feeling of frailty. But when her body began responding with desire for him she resisted again, pushing him away with newfound strength.

He wouldn't release her, though. He crushed her breasts against him, taking her mouth again and kissing her deeply. Blaine resisted at first, then permitted it, struggling only halfheartedly before kissing him as strongly as he kissed her.

Finally she forced her mouth away for air, clinging to the erstwhile priest, not fully believing what she had let happen to her. She abided his hands coursing her back and shoulders, fighting, without resisting, the pleasure of his mouth on the naked skin of her neck.

Stop him! Stop him! her mind screamed, but her body refused to respond, savoring instead the tongue on her flesh. Then, when her desire became a physical craving deep inside, she stiffened, knowing her own frailties were more to be feared than he was.

She wedged her hands between their bodies and pushed against his chest. "Please Cal, don't."

He gazed downward in surprise, but did not release her. "What's the matter?"

"I shouldn't have let you kiss me."

"Why not? Didn't you want me to?"

Blaine's eyes flashed with anger, knowing she had desired his kiss and that it would be absurd to deny it now. "I got carried away, that's all. This has been an emotional evening."

Cal loosened his grip on her waist and she managed to twist free, stepping away. Her back was to him and, when there was no sound, no words, she finally turned around. His face was sullen.

"I'm sorry, Cal. I obviously gave you the wrong impression."

He seemed at a loss what to say. Blaine felt sorry for him. He had read her correctly, but he didn't know her well enough to realize that her instinct for self-preservation was even stronger than her womanly desires.

"No, no," he said at last. "It was my fault, not yours. Hopefully it won't ruin what good was accomplished tonight." There was still disappointment on his face, but also concern. She was reassured by that.

After a moment's hesitation, Cal stepped forward and took her arm. "I know Jason means everything to you, but you've got a life of your own, too, Blaine."

She shook her head. "Jason is my life."

"I could see that."

She lifted her chin. "But you saw something else that wasn't me. I don't want you to have the wrong impression."

He sighed with exasperation. "Don't worry, I understand."

"Do you?"

"Of course."

"You saw what Agnes said you'd see. Is that what you mean?"

"Blaine! For God's sake, will you forget Agnes? I've told you she has nothing to do with me."

"So, what do you think of me now—now that you've tested me and I've failed?"

"Please stop this!" he shot back angrily. "There was no test, and I'm not judging you. I kissed you because I wanted to. It's that simple."

She turned away, wringing her hands anxiously. "I may not have gone to Vassar or Bennington," she said over her shoulder, "but I do have a certain amount of dignity. I would think that you of all men would understand that."

"Blaine, I do understand. I wish—"

She spun around and looked at him imploringly. "Please, let's not talk about this anymore. I'm very tired. This has been a difficult day."

He sighed. "I know it has. Come on," he said, stepping past her, "let me show you to your room."

THE DESERT WINDS BLEW all night, whistling around the eaves of the house, keeping Blaine from sleep. She thought about Jason, picturing him in a dormitory bed, listening to the same lonely wind, perhaps feeling dejected, perhaps afraid.

She worried that his ordeal was too much for him, that it would scar him. Only a few years ago he was a baby and now, at fourteen, he was going through a hell that many adults never see.

She remembered his face at the juvenile hearing, the tears running down his cheeks when the judge told him that he had caused a boy to be crippled, maybe for life, and that even though he was young he would have to pay for his actions. Blaine, too, had cried, sitting beside him, holding his hand, rubbing it, wishing with every fiber of her being that it was she, not her son, they'd send away.

The worst, she knew, was that he had been as much a victim as the other child. The boy had taunted Jason about Blaine being a gambler, calling her a hooker. At the time of the incident she was in Reno playing in a tournament, which compounded the guilt she felt.

"Unfit mother!" Agnes had screamed at her when she'd returned home. "Because of your evil ways, his life is ruined!"

Blaine didn't hate Agnes for that because she half believed it herself. Perhaps that was why she had given up so easily when the juvenile authorities asked if she would agree to send him to the Rutledge Ranch and School for Boys in lieu of further proceedings. Even though Agnes was behind it, and her motive was to separate Jason from her, Blaine was so consumed with uncertainty and guilt that she couldn't protect her child.

Now, thanks to Cal Rutledge, she had been able to hold her son in her arms again and share his sorrow. She knew she owed Cal a great deal. Still, she couldn't help feeling a little guilty at having hurt his feelings. He'd only wanted to kiss her.

But Blaine couldn't abide the notion of any man thinking she was his for the asking. The fact that she found Cal Rutledge attractive only made it worse.

She listened to the sounds of the desert night and wondered if her attitude toward Cal made her selfish. Was it pride that kept her from reciprocating his affection? Maybe that was the cause of all her problems. Maybe it was pride, and not Jason's welfare, that drove her to make money at cards—pride, and the desire to be somebody.

She thought about the way Cal Rutledge had looked at her, the way he had touched her, the way he had kissed her. She trembled, knowing it was a product of her self-denial and the passion that long lay dormant. But why did it have to be this particular man, and why now?

All night she wrestled with the problems pressing in on her. It wasn't until shortly before sunrise that her exhaustion finally overcame her, and she fell asleep.

RUTLEDGE HAD MADE the coffee and was mixing the pancake batter, wondering about the woman who still slept in his guest room. It had been a mistake to force himself on her, and he felt guilty about it.

But it was one of those rare instances in life where a person does something because they want to. He knew if he had stopped to think about it, he wouldn't have kissed her. And he had wanted to hold her in his arms as much as he had wanted to do anything for a long, long time.

Of course, there was a price, and Rutledge knew he'd have to pay it. He'd have to face her this morning, and every time she came to see Jason in the future. Letting his desires rule him had been selfish, though more inevitable than intended.

In truth, he had had no right to do what he did, and not just because of his position. Rutledge knew he had no more in common with Blaine Kidwell than a church has with a gambling hall. And he couldn't really blame her if she regarded what he did as bald-faced exploitation.

He was ready to put the batter on the griddle, but Blaine still hadn't appeared. Rutledge decided he'd better wake her. He went to her room and knocked on the door. It took several tries before he finally got a response.

"How about some coffee and pancakes?" he called through the door.

Blaine raised her head from the pillow and blinked at the strange surroundings, taking a moment to figure out where she was. She remembered Cal, and the night before. He was outside her door, offering her breakfast. "Okay. I'll be out in a few minutes." She rubbed her eyes.

"Thought I'd better wake you up if you'd like a tour of the school before I drive you back to Las Vegas."

Cal's words reminded her of her television interview, which she had completely forgotten about in the excitement of the previous night. "What time is it, Cal?"

"Almost nine."

"Oh, my God. I've got an interview back at the hotel at eleven." Blaine jumped out of bed and slipped on her bathrobe. Running her fingers through her hair she went to the door, but she couldn't bring herself to open it and face him.

"We couldn't make it by car if we'd already left. I'd better fly you down."

"You have a plane?" she asked, surprised.

Cal laughed. "Well, I don't have a broomstick."

"I can't let you go to that kind of trouble. I'll just call and tell them I have to reschedule."

"It's no trouble, I have some auxiliary radio equipment waiting to be installed down there anyway. This gives me an excuse to take the plane in and have the work done."

"Are you sure?"

"Scout's honor. Hurry up. I'll start your breakfast. We'd better be airborne no later than ten." He turned away from the door and headed down the hall.

There was juice waiting when Blaine came into the kitchen fifteen minutes later. She wore designer jeans that were tight enough to reveal the pleasant curve of her buttocks and the slender lines of her thighs. Her blouse was long-sleeved, simple white cotton. The opening at the V-neck revealed a thin gold chain. Her thick, luxuriant hair hung to her shoulders. She looked at Cal uncertainly.

"Well, good morning," he said, his eyes drifting down her body.

"Good morning." She wasn't sure what to think, but Cal seemed natural and friendly. She was glad.

He turned to the griddle and began pouring pancake batter onto it. "How many hotcakes can you eat?"

"A couple would be fine." She watched him moving expertly at the stove. It was an unfamiliar sight—to see a man so comfortable in the kitchen. Neither her father nor Frank had lifted a pan or broken an egg.

"Sleep well?"

"Yes, fine thanks." She couldn't admit she had lain awake half the night worrying about Jason, and thinking about Caleb.

"If I had known about your interview, I'd have gotten you up earlier."

"Yes, I'm sorry. I forgot about it completely. I was so excited about seeing Jason, I didn't think about the tournament at all."

"Well, I hope you didn't forget about all the money in your purse," he said, turning from the stove and pointing toward a counter where it sat. "I found it in the living room this morning."

Blaine's eyes rounded. "God, I've never done that before."

"Go ahead and check it, if you like."

"I trust you. I'm sure everything is there."

Cal looked at her for a long moment. There were obviously many things he wanted to say, but he finally turned back to his cooking without comment. Blaine wondered whether he was thinking about her refusing his affections the previous night.

A minute later he brought over a plate of pancakes for each of them and sat down across from her. "Oops," he said, "forgot the coffee." Cal climbed to his feet and got the pot off the stove and poured them each a cup.

Blaine looked at him with a mixture of amusement and admiration.

"What's so funny?" he asked, catching her wry smile.

"You're rather handy in the kitchen, for a man. I'm not used to being waited on like this."

Cal grinned. "You'll have to come for breakfast more often."

She poured syrup over her hotcakes. "Are you going to let me see Jason again?"

He grew serious. "I think so, yes."

"When?" she asked expectantly.

Cal smiled. "You aren't going to let me off the hook, are you?"

"Am I too pushy?"

"No. After seeing you with Jason last night, I understand completely." He sipped his coffee. "Whenever you feel the need to see him, you can call me and I'll try to arrange it."

Blaine beamed. "I'll try not to abuse the privilege."

He looked at her for a moment, thinking. "So you plan on moving to Las Vegas?"

"Yes, more than ever now."

Cal gave a little laugh. "Agnes is going to love me."

"You won't let her ruin this...interfere, I mean?"

He shook his head. "No, but I'll have to talk to her." His expression was pensive. "Perhaps you should avoid discussing this with her, Blaine."

"Don't worry, I have no desire to speak with Agnes, unless it's absolutely necessary. I'm going to wrap up my affairs in Prosser as quietly as possible. Not that she won't find out about it, though. There aren't any secrets in a small town."

"Will you keep me posted on your schedule and plans?"

"Sure."

His tone had resignation in it. Blaine decided he, too, realized that what had happened the night before was a mistake. She felt a touch of sadness at the thought, but also relief.

"Be sure and let me know if you need anything," he said. "I'll be glad to help, if I can."

"You've been very kind. Letting me see Jason was a wonderful gift."

He looked pleased. Neither of them spoke for a moment. They ate in silence.

"These are wonderful pancakes," Blaine enthused, trying to lighten the mood.

"Thanks. Years of practice in the out-of-doors. I have to admit my hotcakes are a favorite with the boys on packing trips and out on the trail."

"I can imagine."

There was an awkward silence. Cal finally poured some more coffee. They looked at the kitchen clock. It was nearly ten. Their eyes met. Blaine could sense his embarrassment. He seemed more a priest again. Father Rutledge. She was glad.

"You know," he said after a while, "I'm glad you asked me about Laura last night. I hadn't talked about her in years. Maybe it was something I needed to do."

"It's not easy to lose someone you love."

"No, and not easy to talk about it, either. But I felt I could with you. It was a gift."

Blaine sensed the emotion in him and tried to smile. "Maybe we both received something important last night."

Cal reached over and covered her hand. "Yes, maybe we did."

Somewhere in the house a clock chimed the hour. It was ten o'clock.

CHAPTER FIVE

CAL OPENED the baggage compartment and put Blaine's bag and a small case of his own into the plane, then closed the door securely. He glanced up at the cloudless, sunny sky and then at Blaine. There was a steady breeze, but it was warm, tossing the woman's raven hair around her shoulders and neck. She smiled up at him.

"You can board the aircraft while I inspect her, if you like."

"Whatever is easiest."

Cal stepped up onto the starboard wing of the Cessna 310 and unlocked the door to the cockpit. He leaned in to verify that the switches were in the off position, then helped Blaine up onto the wing. When she was comfortably in the copilot's seat, he walked around the plane to inspect each of the props for nicks and cracks, then quickly looked at the landing gear for loose nuts.

Finding everything in order, he removed the chocks then opened the caps to the fuel tanks to verify the levels. After he drained the gas tank sumps, he checked for water in the fuel.

Returning to the props again, Cal saw Blaine watching with curiosity as he pulled each propeller through to make sure the engines turned freely. He looked at the pretty face through the pale yellow of his aviator glasses, wondering if, despite their differences, there could ever be anything between them. He smiled at the thought. What a sensation that would cause in the church establishment: Father Rutledge and a poker queen.

Cal remounted the starboard wing and went to the cockpit door. "Just lean forward and I'll slip behind your seat," he said, as Blaine looked up at him. He squeezed behind her, took his seat, then reached over and pulled the door closed. "All set, copilot?"

Blaine smiled at him. "Does my Washington driver's license qualify me?"

Cal buckled his seat belt. "It'll be plenty—unless I eject and you have to take it in yourself."

She rolled her eyes.

Cal patted Blaine's knee affectionately. "Put on your seat belt, partner. It's buckled behind you.'' When she had done as he asked, he went through his checklist and turned on the ignition switches.

Looking out his window to make sure that the port prop was clear, he pushed the starter switch and the engine fired. Seeing Blaine flinch at the noise, he winked at her reassuringly. "How's your prop, co-pilot? Any personnel out there with an arm in the way?"

She looked out her window. "Nobody's out there."

Cal nodded and fired the second engine. After a moment and several adjustments of the throttles, the engines were nicely balanced. The vibrations in the plane had become sweet and Cal felt the familiar urge to take to the air. He smiled at Blaine, whose face looked somber. "Don't worry," he said. "I've done this before."

She shrugged a little sheepishly. "I was thinking of Jason, if something should happen to me."

"You're safer here than on the highway." Cal checked his instruments again and, when everything was ready, he looked up and down the landing strip. "See anything out there, Blaine?"

She peered out her window down the single runway, then into the sky beyond. "No. Just sagebrush."

"Good. Nobody uses this strip but me, but you can never tell." Releasing the parking break, he began taxiing toward the end of the runway.

Rutledge glanced at Blaine, who was still looking out the window, oblivious to his scrutiny. He saw the clear, smooth skin of her cheek, her glistening hair, the fullness of her breasts under the blouse. She was a terribly attractive woman, and she appealed to him.

A forbidden fruit, he thought. That probably explained the intensity of his desire. It was the old story of the unfamiliar and profane capturing a man's imagination—the fallen angel.

When Blaine turned and smiled, he could see the childlike excitement on her face, the innocence overlying the iniquity. It got him deep in his gut. He knew she would be a hard woman to resist. That was already apparent.

HALF AN HOUR LATER as they were making their final approach to the Las Vegas airport, Blaine listened to Cal talking to the tower. He had given her an extra headset so that she could hear both sides of the conversation, but everything both Cal and the impersonal voice on the ground said was gibberish. They were talking about wind direction and velocity, altimeter settings and other things that meant little or nothing to her, but with the static, most of what was said was not intelligible anyway.

Blaine looked out the side window at the dusty, barren checkerboard of the industrial area of town, then out the windshield at the broad runway in front of them. She had never seen an airport from that perspective, and the sense of landing was much stronger than in a commercial airliner where the ground simply rose up at the side to greet the aircraft.

Cal was so busy that he couldn't talk to her, so she contented herself with the unusual experience of watching a landing firsthand. She also found herself stealing glances at him, admiring the cool efficiency with which he worked.

He was different from the man who had accosted her at the hotel the previous evening, and different from the man who had kissed her. In the short time she had known him, she had learned that Cal Rutledge was many men, but the only one she dared know was the one who was guardian to her son. The others were fascinating, but too alien to belong to her life. And one was dangerous: the one she had submitted to, and kissed by the fire.

They were now just a few hundred feet above ground and Blaine leaned forward with expectation. Her heart was beating excitedly. She glanced at Cal, whose face was a mask of concentration. At that moment he had to be oblivious to her, lost completely in the critical function in which he was engaged. Strangely, the realization made him even more appealing and Blaine felt an urge to touch him, to express the feelings that she guarded carefully when he was in a position to reciprocate.

Moments later they were on the ground, and the excitement she felt ebbed into relief. After pulling off the runway onto the taxi strip, Cal looked at her. "Nice to fly with an angel on my wing," he said casually, and smiled.

It was the man who had kissed her sitting there now, and Blaine felt conflicting urges—she wanted equally to flee and to embrace him. Fortunately, in just a few minutes, she could escape the temptation. For there was only one thing that mattered: her son.

After they had parked the aircraft at the tie-down area and disembarked, he took the luggage from the cargo compartment and they walked in silence toward the gate. "Are you going to go to a bank and get rid of that cash?" he asked, nodding toward her purse.

"Yes. Even if I'm a few minutes late for the interview, I think I'll put it someplace safe. I don't like carrying this much around."

"I've got to see the fixed base operator and make arrangements for refueling the plane but, if you can wait a few minutes, I'll ride with you to the bank."

"Thanks, but that's not necessary. I'm safe now, and I've already been a burden to you."

His smile was warm under the mask of his aviator glasses. "It's been a pleasure for me, not a burden." They stopped at the door to the office.

"I'll just say goodbye here and let you take care of your business," she said, feeling conflicting currents of emotion. For some strange reason she hoped he would kiss her.

Cal looked down at the bags he was carrying. "You can catch a taxi just out front. I'll carry this out for you."

"That's not necessary...."

But he'd already started walking around the building. They stopped at the curb and Cal looked at her, his eyes partly obscured by his glasses, his mouth smiling, friendly.

"Thank you, Cal. For everything." She wanted to get away from him as fast as she could, but she also wanted him to take her into his arms.

"Call me," he said, taking off his glasses.

She nodded. "I will."

Then when she thought their farewell was over, Cal reached out, took her by the shoulders and kissed her softly on the lips. His pale blue eyes looked awfully serious, as though he was saying something with them, though Blaine wasn't sure what.

There weren't any words until he finally mumbled, "Take care, angel." And then he turned and walked away.

LATE THAT AFTERNOON Rutledge sat at his desk, Jason Kidwell's file open before him. There were court documents, school records from Prosser and correspondence—primarily letters from Agnes Kidwell. As he read through the file again the words took on a somewhat different meaning from the first time he had examined them.

References to Blaine now evoked the image of the raven-haired beauty he had kissed, the creature who had touched him so deeply, rather than a faceless woman of questionable repute. Now he felt personal involvement of the most sensitive kind. It was a very, very delicate situation.

The intercom buzzed and Rutledge picked up the phone.

"Rosemary's here," his secretary said.

"Send her in."

A moment later the door opened and a middle-aged woman in a plaid cotton blouse and slacks appeared. "You wanted to see me, Cal?"

"Yes, Rosemary, come in." He gestured toward a chair across the desk. "Sit down."

Rutledge smiled faintly at the staff psychologist and longtime friend. She waited, her benevolent face expressing her kindheartedness and wisdom, which had been so important to the school's success. He had relied heavily on her over the years, and considered their work at the ranch virtually a joint venture.

"Have you spent much time with Jason Kidwell yet?" he asked.

Rosemary Hodges touched her short, prematurely gray hair. "Only one session after the entry interview. Why, Cal, is something wrong?"

"His mother came to the ranch last night and I let her see the boy. I had an opportunity to observe them together and I was curious what your reading of the situation was."

"He's a quiet boy, and rather sensitive, too. I haven't seen any evidence of a severe functional problem that would explain his record."

"The assault might have been an anomaly."

"Quite possibly."

"It was apparent to me he's quite close to his mother."

"She's the card player, as I recall."

"Yes, poker champion. Queen of Hearts."

Rosemary smiled. "How colorful."

"She wasn't the hardened gambler I expected. Actually she struck me as a very responsible, caring woman." Rutledge was going to add "and attractive, too," but thought better of it.

"He talked about her quite a bit during the session," Rosemary continued. "I had the impression she was very important in his life."

"And he's very protective of her," Rutledge added. "Apparently he was defending her honor when the other boy was hurt."

"Yes, that's what I understand. At least his motives are unselfish. The key will be making sure he channels his actions constructively."

"Is he remorseful?"

"I think he's sorry the boy was hurt, but I get the feeling he wouldn't hesitate to fight for his mother again. Jason has developed a we-versus-them attitude toward the world, a siege mentality."

Rutledge shook his head. "His mom has had a pretty rough life. I suppose the notion of struggle has rubbed off."

"My concern would be that he might develop a belligerent, antisocial mind-set."

"Blaine...his mother, wants to see him regularly. Maybe we can involve her in some of your sessions with Jason."

"If she can be constructive, I think that would be a good idea. I'd like to meet her in any case."

Rutledge nodded. "I'll speak with her about it."

The intercom buzzed again. He picked up the phone.

"Cal, I found the station that did the interview with Mrs. Kidwell this morning. It's channel ten. They said there'd be a spot on the five o'clock news. It'll be coming on soon."

He looked at his watch. "Okay. Thanks, Barbara."

Rutledge hung up. "Blaine's going to be interviewed on channel ten. Care to watch?"

"Sure. What's the occasion?"

He got up from his desk. "She came in second in a poker tournament in Las Vegas yesterday." Rutledge went to the bookcase across the room, opened the cabinet door and turned on the set. He returned to his place and they sat silently watching the news. The spot on Blaine came near the end of the half-hour segment as a human interest story.

When her image came on the screen Rutledge felt a little twinge. She looked beautiful—poised, relaxed, engaging.

"Wow," Rosemary said, "she's attractive."

The interview only lasted a minute. Rutledge could tell it had been edited down to her more provocative comments about Bedrock Butler, an attempt to stir up a little controversy for the anticipated rematch at the National Championships. But her words were almost secondary. He was concentrating on the image, the woman. He was remembering her.

When the spot ended Rutledge felt disappointment, frustration with the brevity of his encounter with her. He stared blankly for a moment at the commercial that followed.

"Celebrity parent," Rosemary said.

"Huh?" He only half heard her, his mind still with Blaine.

"I said Jason has the added complication of a celebrity parent, though one with a shading of notoriety."

Rutledge nodded. "Too bad she plays poker."

Rosemary laughed. "You'd prefer bridge?"

"I doubt Jason would have gotten into a fight over a mother who plays bridge professionally."

The psychologist smiled at him.

"Am I wrong?"

"Who knows. They're from a small rural community. It wouldn't have happened here in Nevada, or in a big city—at least over that issue. The question is whether there's a systemic problem, or whether Jason has an adjustment problem that's behind the incident.''

"I think her chosen profession is the problem. Maybe for her as much as for Jason.''

"Having been born and raised in Nevada, I have trouble getting excited over gambling issues,'' Rosemary replied.

"I was born here, too.''

"Yes, but you still see the world through ecclesiastical glasses to some degree. It's only natural...part of your life's experience.''

"What are you trying to say, Rosemary? That I'm narrow-minded?''

"How did you feel about Mrs. Kidwell when you met her? Were you as accepting and open toward her as if she had been a nurse or an accountant?''

Rutledge thought about Blaine's thirty-eight-caliber revolver pointed at his gut, and the purse full of hundred-dollar bills. "I suppose not.''

Rosemary grinned. "Maybe I ought to involve you in the sessions, as well.''

THE SUN WAS STILL ABOVE the mountains as Rutledge jogged across the soccer field toward the boys. They were practicing penalty kicks and doing skill drills at one end of the field.

"You're late, Father Rutledge,'' one of the boys shouted.

The others laughed.

"Do a lap,'' another called. "We have to if *we're* late.''

"All right,'' he said good-naturedly. "Sauce for the gander. But I'm already in better condition than most of you.''

Several of the boys hooted.

"Don't forget, twenty bucks for anybody who thinks they can beat me at the mile. It's an open challenge.'' He started around the perimeter of the field.

"One of these days you're going to be old, Father Rutledge, and somebody's going to take your money.''

He looked back. "Who said that?''

The boys laughed and Rutledge eased into a smooth, graceful lope. Halfway around the field he saw a boy sitting in the small stand of bleachers. It was Jason Kidwell. Rutledge waved and the boy waved back. The man went on for a few strides, then stopped. He walked back toward him.

"How you doing, Jason?''

"Okay.'' He looked down, a little embarrassed.

"You must have your homework done already."

"Almost."

Rutledge came up to him and stopped. "Just out for some air?" The boy nodded.

"I guess it was good seeing your mom last night."

He nodded again.

"I imagine she told you she's planning on moving to Nevada."

"Yeah."

"Are you glad?"

Jason looked up at him. "Are you going to let me see her?"

"As long as it works out well for everyone, yes."

The boy smiled. "Really?"

"Yep."

Jason stood up, beaming. "Thanks, Father Rutledge."

The man shrugged. "I think it would be good for you and her both." He put his hand on the boy's shoulder. "And you could help the cause by studying hard and doing well here at the ranch."

"I will."

"Good."

The boys back at the end of the field began calling and waving their arms. Rutledge waved back.

"I'd better go or they'll make me do another lap." He squeezed the boy's shoulder and started to turn away.

"Father Rutledge."

"Yes?"

"Did Mom spend the night here?"

"Yes, I flew her into Las Vegas this morning. She had some business to attend to."

"Where'd she sleep?"

Rutledge looked at the boy soberly. "In the guest room at the house. It was too late to make other arrangements. Besides, lots of people stay there when they visit."

"Moms?"

The man sighed. "Well, I don't suppose I've had any come before under those conditions."

Jason gave a slight nod, then turned and walked away.

RUTLEDGE WAS BARELY in the office the next morning when Agnes Kidwell called. "What did Blaine say?" she asked eagerly.

"She didn't feel there was a problem coming to Nevada and, so far as I know, intends to make the move."

"Then you weren't able to convince her?"

"In talking with her, Mrs. Kidwell, I discovered the situation is more complicated than what I'd first thought."

"What's that supposed to mean?"

"I think this is something we should discuss in person."

There was a pause. "All right."

"I have to fly up to Boise for a meeting Monday, so perhaps I can swing by and see you on Sunday. Would that be convenient?"

"Yes, Mr. Rutledge. I'm anxious to hear what you have to say."

He hung up, feeling ill at ease. Jason's file was still on the corner of the desk, and he fingered it distractedly. Rutledge was concerned about the boy—he was concerned about all his charges—but he knew that what gnawed at him was not so much the son, as the mother.

Blaine Kidwell had insinuated herself deep into his soul. He couldn't blame her. Nor could he blame himself. It was one of those things that happened, and Rutledge could only hope that he had the strength to do what he knew was right.

SUNDAY AFTERNOON Blaine drove north out of Prosser, across the river and the flat-bottom land toward the Rattlesnake Hills where the Kidwell ranch was located. The house where her husband had grown up sat large and imposing on a bluff above the highway. There were cottonwoods for shade, and a garden that survived thanks only to the irrigation water that fed it. The surrounding hills were vacant, treeless grazing land and wheat fields, parched through most of the year.

The Kidwells' best land was farther up the Yakima Valley and included several farms where they raised apples, hops, alfalfa and some row crops. But Agnes liked the ranch and the barren land surrounding it. She stayed put there most of the time, letting the world come to her.

Blaine didn't like going to the ranch and hadn't been out in months, but Agnes said there would be an important meeting regarding Jason's future and that, if she wanted a say, she ought to be there. She couldn't imagine what Agnes was up to, but had decided it was better to find out firsthand, so she went.

As she drove up the long dirt road to the house, she began to worry that Agnes was up to no good. She suspected that her move to Nevada figured into the invitation, but she didn't know how. The housekeeper greeted her at the door and showed Blaine into the parlor, leaving her alone with the Kidwell clocks, antiques and knick-knacks.

After a while the woman brought in some tea and announced that

Agnes would be down shortly. Blaine was on her second cup before the old woman finally entered the room.

"Hello, Blaine," she said stiffly, and sat in her chair, waving off the housekeeper's offer of tea.

"What's this about, Agnes?"

"Let's hold off our discussion until the other participant is here, shall we?"

"What other participant?"

"You don't know? Well, you'll find out soon enough."

They sat in a stony silence, Blaine growing more and more suspicious until they heard a vehicle outside the house, then steps on the porch. The housekeeper answered the bell.

Blaine was surprised when Caleb Rutledge walked into the parlor. He looked at her with astonishment, as well.

"Blaine, what are you doing here?"

She glanced at Agnes, then at the man. "I suppose the same thing you're doing here. I didn't know you were invited."

"Please sit down, Mr. Rutledge," Agnes said. "I didn't see the need to mention my plans for this discussion with either of you, so you're on equal footing—equally unprepared."

Blaine and Cal exchanged looks.

Cal sat down in a third chair. "I have no objection to Blaine being here, but I was under the impression she was part of the subject of our conversation."

Agnes looked at her former daughter-in-law. "You have no problem hearing what Mr. Rutledge thinks of you, do you, dear?"

Blaine knew the invitation to come to the ranch that morning wasn't innocent. With the old woman, something like this was inevitable, but she was sorry now that she'd come. "I won't stand for any of your abuse, Agnes."

"I don't intend abuse. I'd like a frank, open discussion about the welfare of my grandson. What three people are more important to such a discussion than the three of us?"

Blaine glanced at Cal, who was staring at Agnes, his chin resting on his folded hands. She could tell he was no more pleased than she was.

"We may as well get to the bottom line," Agnes said. "I won't bother to express my views on the cause of Jason's problems. You've both heard them before. The question is, what is in his interest?

"I say he needs to be away from Prosser and the people who are responsible for the mess he's in. That's why I arranged for him to go to your school, Mr. Rutledge."

"You don't want me moving to Las Vegas," Blaine interjected. "Get to the point."

"Yes, that is the point. But my impression is you aren't convinced. And you, Mr. Rutledge, are pivotal in the matter. I want to hear what you think, and what's more I want Blaine to hear you tell me."

"I'm moving to Las Vegas whatever he says," Blaine shot back.

Agnes Kidwell gave her a level stare. "Whatever your faults, Blaine, I will give you this—you do care about Jason's welfare. If you are convinced it's better not to see him, I'm sure you won't." She turned to Cal. "Mr. Rutledge, will you give us your views on the matter?"

"It was wrong of you to have Blaine here, Mrs. Kidwell. It's manipulation and insensitivity of the worst kind. But since you have, she might as well hear what I have to say. It will hurt her far less than it will hurt you."

Agnes blinked at Cal's words. Blaine looked uncertain.

"It's no secret what you think of Blaine's profession," he continued. "And to be honest, I think it's an unfortunate choice myself. Based on what I've learned of Jason's history thus far, her career has created some problems for him. But at this point in time the issue is not her career so much as it is Jason's future.

"From my point of view their relationship as parent and child means a great deal. It certainly is critical as to whether they ought to see each other."

Agnes scoffed. "I don't see how you can disregard who she is."

"She's his mother, Mrs. Kidwell. That's who she is. The only question beyond that is, is she unfit? That's all that really matters. And I have to tell you that, based on what I've seen, Blaine and Jason have a very healthy, loving relationship. I think that her seeing him is not only acceptable, I believe it's desirable."

The old woman sat in stunned silence for a moment. "If what you say is true," she finally said, "why is it the boy gets involved in fights because of her?"

"I don't think it's that simple. Jason has difficulty reacting appropriately to problems facing him, that's true. At least there's been one instance of excess. To blame his reaction on the spark that set off the fight would be wrong, just as it would be wrong to blame the forest fire on the match."

"But this woman raised him!" Agnes said, pointing a quivering hand at Blaine.

"If faulty values, emotional abuse or an unhealthy environment were the root cause of his problem, you'd have a point. I see no evidence that that is the case.''

"But what kind of environment can a gambler—a creature of the casinos—provide for a child? Would you want that sort of woman raising your child? A woman who has to protect her earnings with a gun? Thank God, Jason is not a girl. What kind of role model would Blaine be for an impressionable little girl?''

Blaine bit her lip, holding her silence. She glanced at Cal Rutledge.

"My personal preferences and values are not at issue, Mrs. Kidwell," he replied steadily.

"Well, in a sense Jason is your child. And as far as I'm concerned you can't evade the issue. Would you want this woman to be the mother of your child?''

"The point is that Blaine *is* Jason's mother. She's committed no crime. She loves the boy and he loves her. She gives him the emotional support he needs. To deny him that would be an even greater wrong than to spare him the influence of her work.''

"The devil's work!" Agnes screamed. "You, of all men, should see that!''

"My personal values are not at issue," Cal replied, his jaw hardening at Agnes's insistence.

Finally Blaine could take no more. She rose to her feet. "There's no point in arguing with her, Cal. Agnes hates me. That's the reason for all this. Her opinion will never change, regardless of what I do or don't do.''

"Nonsense!" Agnes shot back. "Things were just fine until you became a gambler. Our relationship was civil, at the very least.''

"I know you don't approve of what I do, but my independence is as much a problem to you as my work.''

Agnes scoffed again. Then she turned her attention back to Cal. "You know, Mr. Rutledge, that more is at issue here than whether you permit this woman to see Jason. I think you should consider the consequences carefully before you decide.''

"I've made my decision. Blaine is aware that I can't prevent her from moving to Nevada, and I will permit her to see the boy regularly, so long as I decide it is not contrary to his well-being.''

The old woman bristled, her mouth drawing into a hard, thin line. "Then I consider this interview to be over.''

Cal stood and Blaine started for the door.

"But you both may as well know," Agnes said in a quivering voice, "that I don't consider this matter resolved.''

Blaine was climbing into her car when Cal signaled for her to wait.

She rolled down the window as he came over and leaned against the door.

"I'm sorry about that. I had no idea she'd do this."

"I know. I should have realized it'd be something like this when she invited me out here. I have less of an excuse than you. I've known her for more than fifteen years."

"Still, I'm sorry you had to endure it."

"Listen, I'm grateful for what you did. I know the easy thing would have been to let her have her way."

"I'm supposed to do what's right, not what's easy."

Blaine smiled. "You're sounding like a priest."

"Clergymen don't have a monopoly on morality."

She nodded. "I'm grateful, Cal."

He looked at her, and Blaine read the same sort of messages from him as she had before he kissed her. She wondered about his motives. "Did you mean what you said to Agnes about me being a good mother?"

"Yes, absolutely."

"And even though you don't approve of me, you want me to see my son?"

Cal's expression looked pained. "What I told Agnes is true. It's not for me to judge."

"But you don't approve of what I do."

"It would be a lot easier for me if you didn't gam...if you didn't play poker. But I'm the first to admit you have no obligation to make things easy for me."

Blaine smiled faintly. "You take your sinners as you find them?"

"It's not a matter of sin."

"Well, I'm not going to argue theology with you, but I really don't think you understand what I do. The poker I play is a contest of equals. We compete, just like businessmen. I don't think you would turn them away from the church door."

"Blaine, I don't have a church, but I wouldn't turn you away from my heart, either. That's what matters."

She sighed. "Somehow that strikes me as a qualified admission. I'm not going to apologize for what I do—ever."

"Am I sounding morally superior to you, or is it in your head?"

"That's a good question. More suitable for a psychologist than a clergyman, however."

Cal leaned closer, his pale blue eyes engaging her intimately. "I'm a rancher and I run a school for troubled boys. I won't deny or renounce my past, but I'm not a clergyman anymore, Blaine."

Her lips bent with amusement. "I seem to have trouble with my present, and you with your past. Maybe we both need a shrink."

He nodded, smiling. "I wasn't going to bring this up until later but, since we've been discussing psychology, I should tell you we do have a staff psychologist who works with the boys. She and I discussed Jason's case the other day, and the fact that you'd be visiting regularly. We considered the possibility of involving you in his sessions occasionally. What do you think of the idea?"

"Sure. I'd be glad to. If it gives me more opportunities to see him, why not?"

"Fine. Let's discuss it, then. By the way, I'm flying over to Boise for a meeting tomorrow morning. If you'd like a lift back to Las Vegas, I'd be happy to swing by and pick you up tomorrow afternoon."

"Thanks, Cal, but I've decided to make this a permanent move. I'm putting my house on the market and leaving Prosser for good. It'll take me a week or so to close up my affairs here, so I'm going to stay and get it done."

"Will you be looking for a place in Las Vegas?"

"I'll rent an apartment until Jason is up for review at the end of his first year. What you decide then is critical to my plans."

"The state of Washington still has jurisdiction, you know. It's up to them whether he stays longer."

"Yes, I'll deal with that when the time comes." Blaine glanced up at the house and saw Agnes's face between the curtains of an upstairs window. "She's watching us and getting paranoid, I'm sure. I'd better go."

Cal stood upright. "When will we see you?"

"I guess that's up to you. I'll come out to your ranch as soon as you'll let me."

"Why don't you stop off on your way down? You'll be driving right past the place."

"Could I?"

"Sure." He rubbed his chin. "In fact, plan on staying a few days. We have an old foreman's house out on a corner of the ranch that we use for guests from time to time. It's modest, but furnished. You're welcome to use it until you've found an apartment."

"That's very kind, Cal, but I couldn't impose like that."

"Think of it as an opportunity to see Jason."

"You do know how to hit a woman where she lives, don't you?"

Cal shrugged, then patted her hand. It was a friendly gesture, but his fingers lingered an instant, and Blaine felt something more than pastoral warmth. She looked up at him and, as she did, saw the curtains in the upstairs window close.

CHAPTER SIX

BLAINE KIDWELL GLANCED OUT the window of her Pontiac Grand Prix at the Nevada wastelands. To the west were the White Mountains, snowcapped and majestic, ahead a ribbon of pavement undulating across the arid countryside. She was nearing the place where she would be turning off for the Rutledge Ranch, and she grew excited at the prospect of seeing her son.

The last time she had come it had been different, a stolen minute with the boy at the pleasure of an unknown man who the law and Agnes Kidwell said was his keeper. Now Cal Rutledge was an ally of sorts. He had stood up to Blaine's longtime nemesis and flatly told her it was good for Jason to see her.

But the ex-priest was also troubling. Cal had kissed her, and he was sending messages in contradiction to his role.

If Blaine considered Cal offensive she would have found a way to rebuff him, despite his position. Unfortunately he wasn't offensive—to the contrary, he was appealing and attractive. That made it much more difficult.

Whenever she was in his presence her convictions, values, conditioning went right out the window. Even Jason faded from her mind, and she constantly had to remind herself of Cal's relationship with the boy. Why was the man having such an effect on her?

Blaine had thought about it a great deal since leaving Las Vegas a couple of weeks earlier, and hadn't come up with an obvious explanation. Except for the trauma of Jason's being taken from her, she was less vulnerable emotionally than she had been in years.

Clergymen were safe, normally, for a woman to have a crush on, but Cal wasn't really a clergyman. He was single, and as attracted to her as she was to him. But he was dangerous—not because of his character, but because of his position.

Worse even than the complication of having her son between them was the disparity of their lives. Their attraction was futile because of who they were. Whether Cal had a church or not, he was a creature of his training. His views toward her and what she represented were clear. There was nothing to be gained by mutual titillation, and Blaine could only hope that Cal had the decency and integrity to recognize that fact.

She also hoped he had the strength to resist temptation because she wasn't sure she had, though God knew she had long since learned the importance of self-reliance. Cal Rutledge might have affected her like no other, but she wouldn't let her weakness destroy her life, no matter what.

Blaine glanced in the rearview mirror and, seeing the highway empty behind her, stepped harder on the accelerator. She was growing more anxious by the minute. She felt anticipation, but also a sense of freedom. Blaine's work and her travels had taken her from Prosser before, but she'd never made a clean break. This time she was leaving the town and the past for good.

Her clothes filled the back seat. The trunk was full of her personal possessions and everything else was in storage, ready to be shipped to Nevada. She was starting over, in every sense of the word.

The sign for the Rutledge Ranch soon came into view, and Blaine decreased her speed. She would be there before long. Excited, she blinked back tears of pure joy.

WHEN RUTLEDGE CAME OUT of the staff meeting there was a note from his secretary, Barbara, taped to the door. Rutledge opened the handwritten note. "Cal, Blaine Kidwell has come to see her son. I told her she'd have to speak with you. She's waiting in your office."

He folded the paper, put it in his pocket and headed out of the building, bidding his colleagues goodbye as he hurried across the compound toward the ranch house. Blaine was sitting in an easy chair in the corner of his office when he entered.

She was sitting upright, seemingly a little nervous, her hands folded on her trim, jean-clad knees. Her eyes reflected a touch of wariness, but she smiled weakly anyway.

Rutledge had the same feeling he'd had as a minister when he was about to meet with a parishioner for counseling or advice. Looking at Blaine's lovely face he felt inadequate, spiritually bankrupt, without the extra strength to shore them both up.

"Hi, Blaine," he said, knowing the mutual silence had to be broken.

She whispered a greeting, her dove-gray eyes full of the same awe he himself felt.

"I didn't know exactly when to expect you."

Blaine rose, though it wasn't really necessary. She stood looking at him, unconsciously fiddling with her fingers. Rutledge had an urge to go to her and give her a hug, a brief friendly kiss, but he didn't trust himself. "Please sit down," he said, and walked behind his chair to the desk.

Blaine sat again. "I wouldn't have bothered you, but they said I needed your permission before I could see Jason."

Cal bit his lip. "You're going to kill me, but he's up in the mountains on our spring camp-out. I didn't think about it when we spoke in Washington." He saw Blaine's shoulders sag.

"How long will he be gone?"

"Only a week. But unfortunately they just left yesterday."

She looked terribly disappointed.

"I don't know how adventurous you are," he said, trying to be cheerful, "but I usually go up to the lake for a day or two. You're welcome to come along." He glanced down at Blaine's booted feet. "Are those an affectation, or do you ride?"

"I ride."

"That's the only reasonable way to get to the camp, short of a two-or three-day jaunt on foot."

"You wouldn't mind?"

"I wouldn't, no. The only reservation I have is how Jason would feel about it. I suppose you could answer that better than I."

"You mean, because of the other boys?"

Rutledge nodded.

"Are they difficult with one another over this sort of thing?"

"Well, I don't run a nursery school here, and these are not your basic shrinking violet sort of kids."

"I wouldn't want to create a problem for him."

Rutledge was having difficulty denying her. "Maybe if we're discreet about it, it'll be all right."

Blaine beamed.

"I didn't see a rental truck outside. Where's your stuff?"

"Most of it's in storage. My clothes and personal things are in the car."

"Well, do you want to see your quarters?"

She nodded, though there was skepticism in her eyes.

"Come on," he said, getting up, "I'll show you." He walked around the desk, taking Blaine's arm as he went past, unable in the end to resist touching her.

BLAINE FOLLOWED Cal's four-wheel-drive vehicle along a dirt road leading from the main compound to the foreman's place a mile away.

The house sat in a little draw under a big cottonwood tree. In all directions were sagebrush-covered hillocks, giving the impression the small structure was completely isolated, though it wasn't.

A small cloud of dust slowly drifted away after they came to a stop at the front door. Blaine got out of her car and walked to where Cal waited at the foot of the steps.

"You'll have privacy, but it's safe. We don't have problems out here," he said easily.

"I'm used to taking care of myself."

Cal gave her a half smile and climbed the three steps to the porch. He pulled the screen door open, braced it with his foot and opened the front door. "There's no keyed lock, but you can bolt it from the inside."

They stepped into the house. Blaine immediately noticed the musty, stagnant smell, and saw that the place was sparely and plainly furnished, like a cheap motel room. She could tell no woman had been in residence recently.

"It needs airing out," Cal said, and went to a window.

He had to knock the frame several times with the heel of his hand, but managed to slide the window open six inches. The front door slowly squeaked closed so Blaine opened it again, propping a rock, which was obviously there for the purpose, against it.

"I haven't been out here for a while," he said apologetically. "I'd forgotten how plain it is."

"It'll do just fine. I wasn't raised with a silver spoon in my mouth."

"You deserve better."

Blaine looked at him, not quite sure what he meant. Cal turned away, and she decided he was as uncomfortable as she was.

"The bedroom and bath are back here," he said, pushing open another door.

Blaine glanced in at the high double bed on an iron frame. There was a nubby pink cotton bedspread on it, hiding a single pillow at the head. The spread was badly faded from numerous washings, but the bed was neatly made. "It looks comfortable."

"Except for the dust, the place is clean. I should have had one of the cleaning people come down."

"No problem. A couple of minutes with a rag and a mop and it'll be fine."

Cal stepped over to the open door leading to the kitchen and Blaine followed him. It was Spartan, like the rest of the house, but it somehow looked a little more hospitable to her. The oilcloth on the small table looked faded but cheerful, as did the year-old calendar with a picture of a puppy on it.

The place reminded Blaine of her childhood, evoking a touch of sadness, although the familiarity was also comforting. She decided that she liked it.

"There are dishes—pots and pans and utensils—in the cupboards," Cal said, stepping back into the main room, "but you're welcome to eat with us, so there's no need to cook."

"Thanks, but I'll be just fine once I settle in." Having said it, Blaine realized the remark must have sounded strange because the house was to be just temporary quarters—perhaps only for a couple of days. Still, it represented being reunited with her son, and she didn't want to view that as temporary.

"There can't be much here in the way of food, so plan on coming up to the house for dinner tonight."

Blaine felt uncomfortable at the suggestion, perhaps because she was uneasy about the prospect of being alone with Cal. He had kept things proper. She didn't want to change that.

He saw her hesitancy and commented before she could respond. "Maybe Rosemary Hodges, our staff psychologist, could join us. I want you to meet her. She's been working with Jason, and I'm sure it would be helpful for her to get some input from you."

"I'd be happy to meet her."

"Rosemary has a place up in Tonopah, but she stays here at the ranch much of the time, so hopefully she'll be available."

"That would be nice."

Blaine and Cal stood staring at each other, half the small room between them. His hands settled on his hips. "Why don't I help you unpack the car."

"That's not necessary, Cal."

"I'm here. Why not? How about if I carry things in. You can put them where you want."

"Okay."

"The keys are in the ignition?"

"Yes."

Blaine watched him walk out, pushing the screen door open, letting it slam behind him. For a while she watched him outside at the car, wondering who he was, which Caleb Rutledge he was being. She hated to admit it but, whoever he was, he was affecting her just as he had before. She finally turned away, her insides trembling like jelly.

AFTER CAL HAD GONE, Blaine had unpacked a few of her things. But she deliberately left most of the car packed, as a signal to herself, if not to Cal. She bathed and put on a violet cotton dress that accentuated her thin waist. Once the sun had set she knew it would be cool, so she took a sweater and went out onto the porch, trying to decide whether to wait inside or out until it was time to go.

The desert air was nice, fragrant with sagebrush and spring wildflowers. The vastness of the open landscape gave Blaine a sense of peace, and it beckoned her to leave the house. Walking would be good for her. She decided to go to the main compound on foot, rather than driving over later.

Looking down at her high-heeled sandals, Blaine realized she wasn't really dressed for a walk along a dirt road, but there was plenty of time and she would go slowly. Heading off, she picked her way up the rutted track, alternately feeling the excitement of an adventure and the uncertainty at seeing Cal.

He seemed a lot more in control of himself than he had at their previous encounters, and she was glad for that. But she was definitely developing an obsession with him. Blaine knew it had a sexual impetus, but his attraction was only part of it.

He was forbidden and untouchable like the social studies teacher she had had a crush on in high school, and yet, like the teacher, he seemed as aware of her as she was of him. The flattery implicit in that added to the allure.

Caleb Rutledge bore no similarity whatsoever to any other man she had known. The only other preacher she had really been acquainted with was at the church where her mother had taken her as a child. But he had been old, and the last thing Blaine would have associated him with was physical attraction.

No, Cal was different. He wasn't like the men she interacted with in her work, even the casino executives. He wasn't like the lawyers, doctors, judges, professors or other professional men that she had encountered in life, either.

There was an otherworldliness about Cal. He seemed akin to the sort of man you'd run into at some exotic, remote place. Yet, he was surprisingly familiar, remarkably comfortable to be around.

Blaine decided it was that strange combination of familiarity and uniqueness that drew her to him, compelled her even. But hidden in the feeling was weakness, something to beware of. She knew nothing good had ever come from her frailties—only from her self-reliance and strength. And yet something other than her will always seemed in control when she was around Cal.

By the time she reached the ranch house the sun was low over the mountains, and the air had begun to cool noticeably. Cal greeted her at the door, smiling and taking her in with his eyes, looking at her longer than was appropriate. Blaine immediately felt the weakness he inevitably induced with his presence.

He took her arm and they stepped into the parlor where a woman with gray hair, though seemingly still in her forties, sat waiting.

"Blaine, this is Rosemary Hodges, the staff psychologist I told you about. Rosemary, Blaine Kidwell."

The woman rose to her feet and she and Blaine shook hands. "Happy to meet you, Mrs. Kidwell."

"Please, it's Blaine."

Rosemary gestured for Blaine to sit next to her on the couch.

"Either of you care for a drink?" Cal asked.

"I'm fine," Rosemary replied, touching the empty glass on the table beside her.

"No thanks," Blaine said, looking up at the blue eyes that always seemed so aware of her.

Cal shrugged and dropped into the chair opposite the women.

"I've gotten to know Jason," Rosemary volunteered. "He's a fine boy, a fine young man."

For some reason the comment brought a lump to Blaine's throat. It was a validation, a sign that things were all right. "I think so, too," she managed.

"We haven't spent a tremendous amount of time together yet, but I think what happened to him was an anomaly. I don't see evidence of a major underlying problem."

"That's what I've felt all along. I'm glad you agree." Blaine's eyes misted so suddenly it surprised even her.

Rosemary reached over and patted her hand. "You and Jason have both been through quite an ordeal. I just want you to know we understand and care."

Blaine bit her lip and looked at Cal, feeling embarrassed at the sudden rush of feelings. His face also was clouded with emotion, his expression sympathetic. She felt like a child being reassured by two adults. "Thank you," she said fighting to maintain her composure.

"Has Cal mentioned our idea to include you in some of our sessions with Jason?"

Blaine looked at him.

"I've mentioned it in passing, Rosemary. But I thought you could elaborate."

The woman smiled. "It's nothing earthshaking, really. I'd like to involve all the parents, but it just isn't possible, normally. What we had in mind was meeting with the two of you. It will help me evaluate the dynamics of your relationship. It might even help me recommend some things to do.''

"Do you think I might be the problem?''

"I have no reason to think that you are, but every relationship has a character of its own, and relationships evolve, especially where children are concerned. My observations might prove helpful to both of you, if only to say everything looks fine, keep up the good work.''

Blaine tried to smile. "Has Jason said anything that makes you think—''

"That there's a problem between you? No, to the contrary, you seem to be one of the pillars of his life. I can tell you have a very close relationship.''

"Then that's good.''

"Yes, but we wouldn't want to see the same degree of closeness when he's in his twenties, for example. A young person needs to develop independence and establish an identity of his own.''

Blaine glanced at Cal, then at the woman next to her. "Do you think I'm too protective?''

"I have no reason to think so,'' Rosemary replied. "But you're closer than most mothers and sons. That's understandable, though. There are just the two of you, and you've been through a lot.''

Blaine smiled ironically. "Yes, you could say that.''

"Don't worry about the sessions,'' Cal said. "Rosemary is very good, and the intent would be a constructive one. Our feeling was that Jason might be less resistant and more open with your participation.''

"Whatever you say.''

"I don't know about you two, but I'm getting hungry,'' Cal interjected. Blaine could hear the forced heartiness in his voice. "Did you have lunch on the road?''

"A sandwich.''

"Well, there's prime rib tonight. Hope you like beef.''

Blaine nodded. "Yes, I do.'' But she was still thinking about Jason, wondering if there wasn't more going on than what she was hearing.

THE CONVERSATION during dinner was easy and comfortable. Blaine began to relax and decided that Rosemary Hodges was what she appeared: an open, good-hearted and caring person. By the time the meal was over, her misgivings were pretty much laid to rest. They had coffee, chatted about the school, and Blaine even answered Rosemary's questions about her work without feeling defensive, as she often did.

It wasn't until Rosemary looked at her watch and begged her leave that Blaine realized she had spent the evening hiding from Cal behind the psychologist's presence. When he returned to the dining room from having walked Rosemary to the door, Blaine suddenly felt an acute awareness of him. Cal's grin was a little crooked as he slipped back into his chair.

"Want another piece of pie?"

"No, thanks. I've had plenty." Blaine wiped the corners of her mouth with her napkin, looking up at him shyly.

"More coffee?"

"No. But thanks."

He chuckled and Blaine didn't know whether he was laughing at her, or the circumstances. She looked up questioningly.

"I guess there's only an after-dinner drink left."

"I'll pass on that, too. Thanks." She remembered the brandy by the fire, and felt the need to escape. Just being alone with him was too intimate. "Actually, I think I'd better be getting back myself. It's been a long day and I'm tired from the drive."

"I understand." He got to his feet.

Blaine rose and he escorted her to the parlor where she grabbed her sweater and purse. They went to the door. Cal looked out, searching the drive.

"Where's your car?"

"I walked," she replied, going out onto the porch. It was dusk and she was aware of the deep shadows on Cal's face, giving it a brooding sensuous appearance. She couldn't help staring a bit, though she forced her eyes away. He smiled, and she could see his teeth gleaming in the semidarkness.

"Maybe I should walk you back."

"No!" Blaine realized it had been more a protest than a reply. "It's not necessary, really."

"You still packing your piece?" he asked, gesturing toward her purse.

Blaine laughed. "You mean Old Betsy?"

"Yeah, Old Betsy."

"No, it's in my makeup case."

"With the bullets?"

She chuckled. "Yes, with the bullets."

"Then there's no one to protect you from the coyotes. I'd better come along."

Blaine didn't see any point in protesting further. She wasn't afraid, but the company would be welcome—as long as he didn't try to traverse the distance she had managed to keep between them.

Cal stepped inside to get his jacket and Blaine waited on the porch, looking at the full-colored sky to the west. Her son was out there in the mountains somewhere, unaware she had arrived, though she had written him she'd be coming down soon. She worried, even though she knew Jason was better off with people like Cal and Rosemary than he had been at the correctional institution in Washington. Perhaps Agnes's maneuver in getting the boy to Cal's ranch was a blessing in disguise.

"Nice sky, isn't it?" Cal remarked, as he came back out.

"Yes, it is."

They went down the steps and headed across the compound toward the road leading to the foreman's house.

"When will you be going up to where the boys are?" she asked.

"I was considering leaving tomorrow morning, unless you'd rather wait a day."

"Oh, no. The sooner the better."

"We'll go tomorrow then."

The road was a little rough and Blaine had trouble with her heels in the dark. After she nearly stumbled Cal took her elbow. They walked in silence, she acutely aware of his touch.

"Air's nice," she said to the silent man beside her. "More deserty than what we have in Washington."

"We're not far from Death Valley, you know."

Blaine's heel slipped on a rock and she stumbled, Cal holding her from falling. "Maybe it's a good thing I let you come along. I'd be flat on my face if it weren't for you."

"All part of the service," he said with a little laugh. His fingers dug more deeply into the soft flesh of her arm.

Blaine felt on edge, helpless. She was figuratively and literally in his hands—equally liking it and fearing it. They were nearing the bottom of a little draw when Cal stopped dead in his tracks. Blaine listened in the darkness, sensing danger. She felt his hand tighten on her arm. "What is it, Cal?"

"Water. I hear water."

Blaine listened. She heard a faint trickling sound. They inched forward, it being darker there than it had been on the higher ground. Then Cal released her and walked a few paces ahead.

"Damn," she heard him mutter.

"What's the matter?"

"There's water running across the road. Up above there's a well to water the stock. The tank must have overflowed."

"What are you going to do?"

"I'll go up and turn the thing off. Do you mind waiting here for a minute or two?"

"No, go ahead."

Blaine watched Cal's vague figure move in the darkness up the draw. Then she heard what sounded like him climbing the slope of the bank. A minute later she could see his silhouette against the lighter sky on the bluff above. He soon moved on out of sight, and she stood still, listening to the faint purr of the breeze through the sagebrush.

Five minutes later he returned. "All fixed."

"Good. I don't imagine you like to waste that water."

"No, but we've got a more immediate problem."

"What?"

"There's a twenty-foot span of mud up ahead and I don't have a coat that'll cover it."

"How chivalrous of you to think of it."

"Just so you know I didn't plan this." Without warning Cal reached down and swept Blaine from her feet and, with her in his arms, started plodding ahead in the darkness.

She was startled by his initiative but said nothing. Her arms settled around his neck, but she didn't have to cling to him, he held her effortlessly.

"This wasn't necessary. I could have taken off my shoes."

Cal was stepping gingerly through the water. "I got muddy up above. There's no sense in us both getting messed up."

Blaine heard the squishing sound of his boots in the mud, but she was even more aware of the press of their bodies and his musky, masculine scent. His face was just inches from hers, but he was concentrating on the precarious crossing. The smell of sage, his cologne and the cool desert air all touched her nostrils at the same time and she felt her body respond. She softened in his embrace.

When they had finally traversed the water and were again on dry ground, Cal turned his attention to the woman in his arms. Blaine had been watching him, fascinated by the experience, yet fearful.

His blue eyes were just a whisper of gray reflecting the faint night sky, but she saw them studying her. He made no move to return her to the ground. Rather, he held her possessively.

Blaine was accustomed to the nearness of his body and the protection of his arms, and felt no immediate need to escape, though the uncertainty of what was happening made her uneasy. His face was very close, his warm breath caressing her.

She became aware of his mouth moving incrementally toward hers. Then, in the darkness, their lips touched, the contact light and uncertain, like a blind man's fingers in the obscurity. But, when their mouths melded into one, the kiss became more sure and intentional. Blaine knew she was reacting to the moment, but could do nothing about it. She permitted the kiss as though she had no choice.

When their lips finally parted, she did begin to question what had happened, her head moving back from his shadowed face. Cal slowly released her legs, and she slid down the front of him, her skirt bunching between them. The friction of their bodies was an unexpected sensation, as erotic as any she had ever felt.

Once her feet were firmly on the ground, Cal released her. She stood looking up at him, her legs quivering. He was silent. Blaine could not see his face clearly, but she didn't need to. She knew it was full of desire. Without a word she turned, and stumbled up the road.

CHAPTER SEVEN

THE NEXT MORNING Blaine was up and dressed when she heard a vehicle in the distance. She went over to the window and saw Cal's four-wheel drive coming over the rise, the windshield reflecting the first rays of the sun. When he had stopped out front, she opened the door and stood watching him through the screen. He was in jeans, a western shirt and boots.

"Morning," he called, seeing her at the door.

Blaine could see he had put the incident of the night before behind him, but she hadn't. It had worried her all night.

Cal raised a paper sack he was carrying. "Brought you some breakfast."

"You didn't have to do that."

He grinned at her as she pushed the screen door open. "Couldn't have you fainting on the trail." He went to the table and unpacked the bag, setting a thermos of coffee, a banana and some doughnuts on the table.

The coffee smelled delicious as he poured it into the lid of the thermos. Blaine looked at him, but didn't hold the gaze for long. His eyes were the danger.

She sat down at the table and reached for the cup, her hand trembling slightly. She took a sip and glanced up at him, but he was busy putting the doughnuts on a paper plate he had brought along.

Blaine considered saying something about the night before, but it somehow seemed forced just then. Undoubtedly there'd be plenty of opportunity for that later. But something would have to be said—they couldn't go on titillating each other at every opportunity.

"It's a great morning for a ride," he said cheerily. "It'll be good to be on the trail."

"I'm awfully anxious to see Jason."

"I'm sure he'll be pleased to see you."

Blaine took a bite of a doughnut, then another quick look at the man who was settling in the chair opposite her. He looked so hand-

some, so good. Why did she have to fear him like the devil himself?
It seemed so unfair.

She had wondered why he insisted on kissing her, interjecting sex
into a relationship that couldn't, by any standard, be more than friendship. What was his motive? Sex? Surely he could get that anywhere.
Maybe it was the same feeling she had had—the lure of forbidden
fruit. They were as unlikely a pair as any man and woman alive.
Perhaps that made the attraction all the more poignant.

Blaine glanced at him again as he sat watching her, looking like
anything but an ex-priest. She doubted he felt the slightest shred of
remorse. Maybe that was why he was no longer in the church. Maybe
he had no conscience. Maybe he couldn't deal with temptation.

"Why haven't you apologized for last night?" she asked, letting
loose the irritation that had been building.

"You were offended?"

She was surprised at the question. "Of course I was."

"Then I apologize."

Blaine blinked. He didn't seem remorseful in the least. "Don't you
understand why I would be?"

"Yes, certainly. I'm sorry I offended you."

She still wasn't satisfied, but could see that to pursue it would only
make matters worse. Perhaps it would have been better to wait and
talk about it later, as she had planned.

Blaine popped the last bite of doughnut in her mouth and took a
final sip of coffee. She eyed the banana.

"Want to save it for the trail?" Cal asked.

She nodded, still chewing.

"Then come on, partner," he said, climbing to his feet, "let's go
see your son."

They went outside and Cal put his hand on her waist as they strode
to the jeep. Blaine looked up at him, uncertain, but not really dis-
pleased, though she wouldn't admit it—not even to herself.

THE RUTLEDGE RANCH extended into the foothills to the boundary
of the Inyo National Forest, where the pack trips were held. To save
time, Cal had established a station to stable the horses at the western
edge of the ranch. It saved several hours' ride across the desert, and
enabled the boys to get into the mountains more quickly.

They arrived at the station an hour after leaving the compound.

Cal helped the wrangler saddle the horses while Blaine waited on
the porch of the station shack in the shade. By the time Cal had

finished he was perspiring. He led a small black mare with white points over to Blaine.

"She's spirited, but a good little horse," he said, lifting his hat and wiping his brow.

Blaine rubbed the horse on the forehead and patted her affectionately on the neck. "What's her name?"

"Midnight." He watched as her mouth curved with amusement.

"At least it's not Black Jack."

The wrangler led a larger sorrel over to where they stood. Cal took the reins, thanking the man.

"What's yours called?" Blaine asked.

He grinned. "It ain't Reverend."

She twisted the stirrup, lifted her left foot into it and swung up onto the horse. "I could say something, but I won't."

Cal looked up at her, sitting on her mount. It was hard to tell whether she was being playful or was truly annoyed. The only thing he was sure of was that she had wanted him to kiss her last night. That was probably what was irritating her. "You aren't still mad at me, are you?"

"About what?"

Cal smiled sardonically, thinking it was obvious enough. He looked at her slender jean-clad leg. "Looks like you could have those stirrups shortened a notch."

Blaine slipped her boot out and Cal adjusted the leather. He went to the other side and repeated the procedure.

"Mad at you about what?" she asked, when she saw he wasn't going to respond.

"About last night."

"No, I'm not." She looked at him thoughtfully. "Well, yes, maybe I am."

Cal went to his own horse. "Yes and no?" He swung up onto the saddle.

Blaine definitely looked annoyed now. "I wish you'd act more like a preacher."

"Is that what you want?"

She gave Midnight a nudge with her heels and the horse stepped away smartly. "Where's the trail?" Blaine asked over her shoulder.

"Back this way," Cal replied with a laugh. "You're headed for Las Vegas."

Blaine wheeled her horse around. "I'd be better off *there*." Her eyes flashed as Cal watched her go by. He smiled to himself, then headed after her.

They rode up a rocky canyon for several miles, then climbed to a ridge line where they encountered the first scrubby pine. The mountains ahead were covered with conifers, and the air was cooler at the higher elevation. They stopped in the first heavy stand of pine to rest the horses.

"Want to stretch your legs a bit?" he asked.

"All right."

Cal got down off his horse and stepped over to Blaine's mount. "Need some help?"

She immediately swung down from the saddle. "No, thanks."

He slipped the strap of the canteen he had been carrying off his shoulder and handed it to her. Blaine unscrewed the lid and took a long drink. Then she wiped the mouth of it on her sleeve and handed it back to Cal.

"You're a regular trail hand."

"I told you I wasn't born with a silver spoon in my mouth."

"You say that a lot. Is there something I do or say that makes you feel defensive?"

"Is that what it is, defensiveness?"

He could plainly see she was unhappy with him. "Sorry, I didn't mean to be judgmental."

Blaine let her hands settle on her hips. "I just wish you'd be consistent."

"What do you mean?"

"Playing preacher or psychoanalyst or whatever you are one minute, and lover boy the next." Her eyes flashed again. "Just because I'm not the product of an eastern finishing school, doesn't mean I'm your plaything. And just because Agnes told you I'm a whore, doesn't mean that I am!"

"Blaine." He reached out, but she pulled her arm away. "I don't want you to think that's what I had in mind."

"Well, what is it you have in mind?"

"Do you really believe I'm using my position to take advantage of you?"

Her eyes locked with his in an angry glare. "You're not being consistent."

"Yes, that's what you said. Would it be better if I just forget about my job, Jason and you, and took you to bed?"

Blaine's mouth dropped. She spun around and walked away. Cal knew it was more than indignation—he'd hurt her, and he was sorry.

She was standing by a tree ten yards or so from the horses, her back to him. He slowly walked over.

"Blaine, I'm sorry I said that."

She didn't reply.

"It was my own frustration speaking."

"What frustration?" Her back was still to him.

"I'm obviously attracted to you. And I thought you were to me, as well."

"I am. But so what? A person could be attracted to anyone. The only thing that could be worse is if you were married."

"I'm not married and I don't see what's so horrible about being attracted to each other."

Blaine turned around. "You may not see it, but I do. If you didn't have my boy, I'd light out of here faster than you can imagine."

"Why? Then it wouldn't matter."

"No, it wouldn't matter, would it? You could take me to bed and not feel guilty a bit. No conflict with your responsibilities, no guilt over taking advantage of a woman beholden to you...just free sex!"

Cal's anger boiled at the accusation. "Dammit, Blaine, that's not it at all. I don't regard you as a sexual object."

"Well, what am I then? Do you plan to marry me and put me on display for all the Agnes Kidwells of the world? 'Here, Mrs. Smythe, I'd like you to meet my wife, the Queen of Hearts.' Is that what you've got in mind, Cal?"

He was left speechless by the intensity of her feelings. He just stood staring at her, unsure what to say.

"You see, I'm not as dumb as I look. I might falter when you snuggle up to me with those baby-blue eyes, but I haven't survived all these years by throwing caution to the winds."

Her eyes started swelling with tears. "My desires never made me a nickel or gave me a moment of happiness, but my common sense has. And I don't see any reason to change that for you or any other man." Blaine's face began to crumple and she turned away again.

Cal stared at her, dumbfounded. Her shoulders shuddered as she silently sobbed, and he wanted so badly to take her into his arms. He wanted to comfort her because he cared. Her happiness was truly important to him, but where was the line between compassion and affection? When would his embrace be an expression of his humanity, and when would it become an indication of his desire?

Cal knew there were two kinds of love—he had lived and experienced both. Neither would permit him to turn and walk away. So he became a priest again. He reached out and laid his hand on her shoulder. "Don't worry, Blaine," he said softly. "Everything is going to be all right."

THE LAST MILE OR SO of the trail went through a heavily wooded forest of sugar pine and fir. Blaine's anxiety had been replaced by a longing to see Jason—the only constant in her life. Her son meant everything to her; he was all she really had.

Midnight plodded along at a leisurely pace, apparently enjoying the cool air in the woods, but Blaine kept squeezing her with her legs, urging the animal on. In her mind it almost seemed as though reaching Jason would mean escape from Cal. Emotionally, the boy was her protector, though he'd never know.

Finally the glimmering blue of the mountain lake shone through the trees and Blaine grew still more excited. Cal must have noticed because he urged the sorrel up beside her. They hadn't spoken since the rest stop, and Cal had ridden behind most of the time, his silent presence disturbing after the words they had exchanged. She turned and looked at him as he spoke.

"It might be a good idea if I go find Jason and bring him to you, so you can see him in private," he said soberly.

"All right. But I won't embarrass either him or you, if that's what you're worried about."

Cal's expression was pained. "I just want the visit to go well for both of you."

Blaine realized she had been more caustic than she had intended. "I'm sorry, I didn't mean it that way. I'll do whatever you wish."

"The other boys might not understand your coming up here, and I don't see any point in putting Jason under needless pressure. He'll find a way to work it out with the others if we give him the opportunity."

"I appreciate your concern, Cal. Please don't take anything I've said to be a lack of gratitude."

"No, of course not." He smiled, seemingly to reassure her.

Blaine smiled, too.

"I'll ride on ahead. The camp is just a few hundred yards down the trail."

She watched him gallop off, worrying for the first time about embarrassing Jason. Having his mother visit him on a camp-out couldn't be the most macho experience for a boy. She was glad now that Cal had been sensitive to the issue.

By the time Blaine reached the camp, Cal was in the midst of a conversation with one of the counselors. The men walked over to greet her.

"The boys are all out on a survival training exercise," Cal explained. "I've asked Tim to go get Jason."

Blaine got down off her horse and Cal introduced her to the young man, who looked to be in his early twenties. He shook her hand, then turned to head off around the lake to fetch the boy.

"He knows not to embarrass Jason?" she asked, when the counselor had gone.

"Yes, I explained the situation."

Blaine nodded and looked around at the camp, which consisted of a small, canvas-roofed cabin, a corral and lean-to for the horses and half a dozen tents. It was neat and quiet. The only sounds were from the blue jays darting among the trees.

"We try to keep it basic, close to nature," he said. "About the only concession to civilization is a privy down there in the trees," he added, pointing. "If you need to avail yourself, feel free."

Blaine smiled at his euphemistic turn of phrase. "Sometimes I *can* picture you in a black coat and collar."

"You're a hard woman to please."

"Oh, I wasn't complaining. As a matter of fact I feel safer with Father Rutledge than I do with you."

"Ah, I'm lover boy again."

Blaine colored, spun around and began marching off toward the privy. "I think I *will* avail myself." She heard him laugh behind her and turned even brighter red.

When she returned, Cal had tended to the horses and was at the door to the cabin, looking inside. He turned as she approached. "The fellas will move out for the night and you can sleep in here."

"I don't want to upset things."

"I think there'd be less disruption if you take the cabin. The boys are in the tents, the counselors can put up another or sleep under the stars."

"What about you?"

"I like sleeping under the open skies."

It would have been an opportunity for some sort of suggestive remark and Blaine was glad he hadn't taken it. She walked over and sat on a nearby tree stump, aware after a moment that Cal was watching her. Even when nothing was said she felt the threat of their attraction.

A minute later he brought over a Sierra cup of cool water, offering it to her without saying anything. Blaine took it and drank eagerly, not realizing how thirsty she was.

"They've all eaten," Cal said, "so I'll have to rustle up lunch. I'm sure I can find some beef jerky or dried fruit if you'd like to munch on something right away."

"I'm really not hungry. But thanks." She looked up at him standing over her. His face was solemn, but it wasn't the solemnity of a priest. It was that awareness again. Blaine got up and strolled slowly away, knowing his eyes were on her, probably tracing the lines of her tight-fitting jeans.

"Mom! Mom!"

Blaine heard the familiar voice echoing through the trees and looked up to see her son running toward her. She ran to meet him and they embraced at the edge of the camp, clinging to each other.

"Jason, darling, it's so good to see you."

"How come you came all the way up here? Are you all right?"

"Sure. I just wanted to see you so bad I couldn't wait. And Cal said I could ride up with him."

Jason looked toward the cabin where the man was still standing. "Father Rutledge?"

"Yes," she replied, running the back of her fingers along the boy's cheek, "Father Rutledge."

They were about the same height and looked into each other's eyes. "Gee, Mom..."

"I think you've grown," she said happily. "I've got on boots and you're just as tall."

Jason looked down at their feet, then over again at Cal. "How come he let you come up?"

"He knew it was important to me. And he knew you'd be glad to see me."

The boy nodded.

"You *are* glad, aren't you?"

He smiled, then nodded more enthusiastically. He gave her another big squeeze.

"Oof," Blaine groaned. "You're getting stronger, too."

Jason laughed and they turned and walked toward where Cal stood waiting.

WHEN HE HAD FINISHED arranging his gear, Cal wandered down toward the lake, taking in the refreshing scent of the pine forest and the mountain air. Blaine and the boy had headed off toward the lake earlier, to be alone and talk.

Cal intended to give them as much space as possible, but even so he was drawn to them, by concern and a desire to protect. He worried about the tension on the ride up.

She had gone right to the heart of the matter when she asked him what his intentions were. It was an obvious enough question, but one

Cal himself hadn't really addressed. The truth of the matter was that he didn't know what he intended, except that he wanted to hold Blaine Kidwell in his arms, and refused to fight the opportunity to do so when it presented itself.

When he was just about at the lake, Cal saw the woman and the boy sitting on a log at the water's edge farther up the shore. They were side by side, Blaine's arm around Jason's shoulder, both looking down thoughtfully, apparently deep in conversation.

For a while Cal watched them, realizing that he cared a great deal for them both, but quite differently. It was Father Rutledge whom the boy knew and Father Rutledge who cared about his well-being.

But Blaine had touched a different part of him, a different man. That was what prompted the confusion in his feelings and in his behavior. She had bitingly referred to him as "lover boy," but the sarcasm was misplaced. It wasn't sex that motivated him, it was a very deep feeling for her, a feeling he hadn't experienced since Laura.

Clearly it was more than just physical attraction, but love? Surely, it couldn't be what he had felt for Laura. For one thing he hardly knew Blaine Kidwell. For another they were such different people, with such totally different lives.

Laura had fit his life like a glove. She was everything he needed in a woman: refined, cerebral, cultured. She had understood him and his intended life's work and was prepared to be his helpmate, sharing what she so deeply understood.

He looked over at the woman on the log, hugging her adolescent son. Cal was moved at the sight of her, her image affecting him in a way that even Laura hadn't. Why was that so? Was there something he himself didn't see?

Cal's rambling thoughts returned to the question she had posed. What were his intentions? She had mentioned marriage, but only to illustrate the absurdity of any serious relationship.

But was it really that absurd that he should care deeply for her, even love her? If the prospect of a serious relationship was out of the question, then what the hell was going on in his head...and probably hers, too?

Snapping a twig off a dead branch next to him, Cal turned and headed back for the camp. He was beginning to understand Blaine Kidwell's frustration.

CHAPTER EIGHT

THE MORNING SUN'S RAYS angled through the trees, bringing a little warmth to Blaine as she sat on the stoop of the cabin. Breakfast had been at first light, but she hadn't eaten with the others, listening instead to the chatter and noise of the group from the cocoon of her sleeping bag in the canvas-roofed cabin.

Jason had asked her the night before not to make a big deal in front of the other boys in saying goodbye the next morning, so she had waited until she heard them organizing to leave on their day-long hike before she came out. He had been lined up with the other boys and had smiled at her, finally risking a little wave just as they marched off with the three counselors, leaving her and Cal alone at the camp.

The boy's sensitivity proved that Cal had been right to be careful about the way she had been presented. When the other boys had returned the previous afternoon, Jason had joined them immediately, keeping his distance, though he often smiled at her.

At the camp fire that night Blaine sat with Cal and the three counselors, though a few of the boys, including Jason, were interspersed among them. She could tell he wanted to be near her without being too obvious.

As the camp-fire gathering was breaking up Cal called Jason aside, took him into the cabin, then a few minutes later discreetly came to get her. She and the boy had a few more minutes alone before saying their goodbyes.

Blaine looked up at the sun, which had moved behind a large tree branch. A stump nearby was in a bright patch of sunlight so she stepped over to it, cheered and soothed by its warmth. She glanced around the deserted camp, but Cal was not in sight.

Blaine's thoughts returned to Jason and she worried that coming might have been a mistake. She had watched the faces of the other boys at the camp fire to see if she could detect a problem, but could sense none. Maybe the teasing, if there was to be any, was done in private.

What a shame, she thought, that the male fraternity should make such a big deal of a boy's relationship with his mother. Men, it seemed, had to measure their masculinity by being independent of women, though to have a woman dependent on *them* was a badge of honor.

Blaine knew it had been that way for time immemorial, so why did it particularly annoy her? Maybe she was clinging to Jason too much, if only emotionally.

Blaine heard the sound of footsteps in the woods and looked up to see Cal coming through the trees from the lake.

"Good morning!" he called to her, vapor billowing from his mouth in the cold morning air. "Ready for some breakfast?"

"I'd love some coffee. Anything hot, actually."

"Cold?" He headed toward the fire where a coffeepot still sat at the edge of the grill.

Blaine got up from the stump and walked over, too. She waited as Cal poured some of the steaming liquid into a Sierra cup. His eyes seemed to twinkle over his ruddy cheeks as he offered her the cup, holding the rim with a gloved hand.

Blaine took it, wrapping her bare fingers around the cup for warmth. She took a sip and sighed with pleasure. "Funny how the simpler pleasures become so much more important out here, isn't it?"

"At least you aren't one of those women cursing the deprivation of her hair dryer."

"I do feel deprived," she replied, touching her hair self-consciously. "I'm just less vocal than some."

Cal picked up another cup and poured himself some coffee. They stood near the fire, liking its warmth, watching each other as they drank the steaming liquid.

"Do you think it was a mistake for me to come?" she asked after a while.

"Because of the other boys?"

"Yes."

"No. It was handled discreetly. You didn't do anything to embarrass Jason."

"Will they tease him?"

"Maybe, some. I wouldn't worry about it. There's always something, and everybody has their turn eventually."

"What is it about you men? Sometimes you're more like a band of hunters, or something."

"That's what we were once, I suppose. The transition into manhood is not an easy one."

"Too bad you can't go about it in a more civilized fashion."

"Seems to me there's a precept about that.... Something about civilization being perpetuated by women."

"Yeah. The idea has new meaning for me."

Cal chuckled, and she found herself engaging those blue eyes of his again. She looked up at the trees and took a deep breath of air. "What's the plan for today?"

"They'll be hiking till late, so we can leave whenever you like. If you want to lounge around for a while and fish, or something, we can. As long as we're on the trail by midafternoon, we'll be all right."

"Do you want to fish?" Blaine asked.

"I enjoy it occasionally, but it's not essential."

"Well, we're here. You might as well take advantage of the opportunity."

"How about you?"

She shook her head. "When it warms up a little I might clean up and wash my hair—whether I've got a hair dryer or not."

"Okay, and what will madame have for breakfast?"

"How about eggs Benedict?"

"How about eggs period?" He laughed, then reached over and tweaked her on the cheek.

BY TEN O'CLOCK it had warmed up and Blaine had taken off her jacket and sweater, but still sat in the sun, enjoying its soothing rays. After breakfast Cal had taken a fishing rod and headed off for the lake. She had spent a quiet time alone, thinking.

Though tension remained between the two of them, there was something about being out in nature, alone with Cal, that had desensitized her somewhat. Everything was more elemental in a place like this, including relationships. She felt more at ease.

Blaine thought about Cal's hair dryer remark and wondered if he was thinking about her comment that she wasn't born with a silver spoon in her mouth. But she could hardly complain about not being thought of as ladylike, because she didn't strive to project a refined image, though she'd always thought of herself as proper and wellmannered. And just because a woman could keep up with a man didn't mean she wasn't feminine, either.

Thinking about it, the remark did annoy her a little, though she knew she shouldn't let it. After all, it didn't really matter what Cal thought of her, except insofar as Jason was concerned. Still, Blaine wasn't the type to make statements about that sort of thing. She decided it was important to present a respectable image for herself, if not for him. Feeling her hair with her fingertips, she decided she would bathe and shampoo.

Blaine found a large pot, filled it with water and put it on the grate over the fire, which had burned down to red-hot coals. She might appreciate nature, but there wasn't a woman alive who'd use cold water if hot was available, and she was no different.

When the water had heated, Blaine carried the pot into the cabin and set it on the floor. There were no windows, so she had to prop the door open for light. Working quickly, she stripped off her clothes and gave herself a sponge bath, drying herself with a towel. Then she slipped her jeans back on, but left her blouse off so that she could wash her hair without getting it soaked.

Kneeling over the container, Blaine let her hair drop into it, then added a few drops of shampoo. When she had lathered it she dipped her head into the water, rinsing the nape of her neck and her temples to get out all the soap. It wasn't the most elegant way for a lady to wash her hair, but it was better than going without.

With all the rinsing and splashing she didn't hear him enter, or walk across the plank floor. But when Blaine was hanging over the soup kettle, groping around for the towel, she saw his booted feet on the floor beside her out of the corner of her eye. She looked up.

Cal's face was the most solemn she had ever seen, his eyes intense, almost frightened. In his hand was the towel. Without a word, he extended it toward her.

Blaine was still on her hands and knees, her hair dripping. She was frozen with shock at his intrusion, her eyes locked on his. Finally she became aware of the towel he was offering, and she grabbed it with one hand, clutching it to her breast.

Cal's expression hadn't changed. He looked more shocked, more awestruck than she. There were words in Blaine's head, but she couldn't find them. She was frozen there, kneeling on the floor, looking up at a man she didn't know, a man who at the moment terrified her.

Slowly she rose to her feet, the towel clutched to her bare chest, her wet hair dripping down her back, face and neck. He was only a couple of feet from her, and she was sure he was going to take advantage of her.

"I'm sorry," he whispered. "I had to."

Blaine wasn't sure what he meant, but she still couldn't speak.

There was a lump in her throat that felt like a pine cone. Cal blinked a few times and the expression on his face began to soften. He didn't take his eyes off hers. He didn't smile or sneer. He didn't look at anything but her eyes. Blaine's lip trembled, but she couldn't speak, she couldn't move.

"Lord," he mumbled, barely audibly, as though it was a miracle he was witnessing.

Blaine heard a tiny whimper emerge from her throat as he slowly extended his hand toward her face. He touched her wet cheek, then her hair, taking the dripping strands gently between his fingers. His eyes didn't quit hers.

Cal took a half step toward her and Blaine felt her body start to quiver. One of his hands went to each of her naked shoulders and she moaned with fright.

"I'm sorry," he whispered into her ear, and gently drew her against him, his face touching the side of her head.

Blaine shook from fear and cold, and Cal's arms tightened around her. His body was warm and as enticing as it was threatening. She prayed he wouldn't hurt her, and knew somehow now that he wouldn't.

"Oh, Blaine. Oh, Blaine," he murmured.

She knew then he was there out of weakness, not aggression. He was a moth, and she the flame. Chills ran through her body and she leaned against him, strangely drawn to the body that only seconds earlier had seemed dangerous.

Cal began rubbing the goosey flesh of her back with his warm hands. They were hot—fire on ice. She moaned, but this time more with pleasure than fear. The rhythm of his caress quickened, and the fingers began biting into her skin. He turned his mouth against her cheek and kissed her.

Her arms and the towel were clutched between them. Blaine trembled, her body pressing into his. She began shivering again and Cal massaged her skin vigorously, wrapping as much of himself around her as he could.

Then he took the towel from her and with one hand began rubbing her hair, holding her close to him with the other arm. When he finally stopped, her tresses were a tangled web of ebony thread, her gray eyes pools of apprehension.

A sensuous lip dropped and he kissed it through the snarl of damp hair, pressing his chest against her taut breasts. Blaine raised her mouth and he brushed the hair aside, taking her mouth deeply, drinking in all of her he could.

"Oh, Cal."

It was almost a whimper, a submission, and it fired him. He took her head in his hands and possessed her with his mouth. Blaine's knees buckled and he grabbed her, half carrying her, half dragging her to the cot.

She lay on the smooth nylon of the sleeping bag. Cal stood over her, unbuttoning his shirt, the canvas roof above him speckled with sunlight and shadow. She was on her back, her arms submissively at her sides, the firm mounds of her breasts exposed to his eyes, her nipples turgid.

She waited motionless, her eyes round. When he had bared his chest, he paused, undecided whether to fall on her or remove more clothing. In the end he reached down with one hand and slipped several fingers under the band of her jeans. Fumbling to unfasten the heavy brass button, he nearly lifted her from the cot, but managed to undo her pants. Without hesitating he pulled down the zipper so that the jeans lay open.

Then Cal grasped the waistband with both hands and peeled the tight pants from her body, throwing them aside. He removed her panties with the same determined haste.

Blaine swallowed hard, feeling totally exposed and vulnerable with the cool nylon under her, the fresh air all about her, and the fire of Cal Rutledge just inches away. Outside the wind rose irrelevantly and rippled the canvas above them. She waited as he slowly, hypnotically, undid his pants.

When he was as naked as she, he put one knee against her thigh, a hand on the edge of the cot at her shoulders and swung himself over her. He looked down into her eyes, only their legs touching.

Blaine reached up, locking her hands behind his neck and pulling him down upon her, her clammy flesh sizzling under the fiery warmth of his body. Their mouths engaged, and she surrendered.

For long minutes he kissed her face and neck, his mouth and tongue tracing down her chest several times to her breasts. He sucked her nipples until they stood throbbing and swollen. Then he fell upon her mouth again, probing and penetrating its recesses, possessing her.

Blaine permitted the wash of sensation to claim her. Her body was making love to the man without her intending it—it was just happening. There was no reason or justification but the sensation itself, and her weakness. Desire could not be denied.

"Oh, Blaine, I want you so much."

Apart from his words, his breathing and the swell of him against her proved it was true. She shuddered with expectation, her body trembling so hard it shook them both. It had been so long, so terribly long since she had known the feel of a man, that her dread was as strong as her desire.

"Ohh...ohh..." she murmured incoherently, her brain full of sensation, but not words.

Cal lifted himself slightly, enough to let his hand slip between their hips. His fingers found the moist mound between her legs and he began stroking the nub of her.

Blaine moaned, her consciousness suddenly indifferent to everything but the exquisite feeling between her legs. She had always thought that if she were ever to have a man again, finding herself would take time and patience. She was sure that her sexuality was as dead as her heart, and that only gentle coaxing could unchain the woman in her again. But Caleb Rutledge's kisses and his touch had belied that, in just minutes.

He kissed the corner of her mouth, groaning with desire. His finger tested her moist depths. Preorgasmic tremors passed through her.

"Take me, now," she whispered, and as he shifted she opened her legs to him.

Cal slowly eased into her, slipping incrementally deeper with each tiny thrust of his pelvis. Blaine gasped at the terrible and wonderful sensation, and locked her legs around his buttocks, pressing him more deeply into her.

Even before his undulations had begun she felt the first waves of her climax. It came so quickly and unexpectedly that it shocked even her. "Oh God!" she exclaimed. "Now! Please, now."

Cal responded instantly, slipping in exquisite rhythm first out, then deep inside her. Her body caught the tempo and they pulsed together, at first slowly, then faster and faster as the storm built. Then, when she could wait no longer, he exploded.

Blaine cried out with joy, unaware that her screams of pleasure echoed in the nearby woods. Then lesser sounds—those of inner contentment—emerged quietly from her throat. And in the passing of only several minutes, she fell from a stupor of exhaustion to a sweet and timeless sleep.

THEY DOZED TOGETHER until the discomfort of Cal's weight brought Blaine into consciousness. He lessened the pressure of his body, kissing her neck, permitting the air to touch their moist skin. For long minutes she toyed with the locks of his hair, nearly as wet from the heat of lovemaking as her own. She stared at the fabric ceiling overhead and the dappled pattern of light and shadow, knowing that something awful, yet monumental, had just happened.

The forbidden and impossible had occurred. Blaine knew it was as wrong as it was inevitable, but most important she knew she was now powerless to do anything but retreat. Cal Rutledge was in command, because he had had her. There was nothing left for her to give but more of the same. Only he knew if that mattered, or if he had already gotten what he wanted.

She closed her eyes as if to fend off the reality that began closing in. She longed to return to the world of sensation, but who she was, and where she was, were as undeniable as consciousness after a dream.

Caleb Rutledge was a stranger again, but one she'd rather hold against her in total nakedness than look in the face. Blaine wished with all her heart that she could evaporate into the mists of the mountain peaks.

Outside the jays cawed and barked their warnings, the wind sent pine needles and twigs against the canvas, but there was another sound, too. It was faint, but Blaine heard the titter of voices, young voices.

Cal must have heard it, too, because he lifted his head and turned toward the door. They heard the sound again, this time more distinctly.

"There's someone out there," Cal whispered, and lifted himself off of her.

Blaine peered out the door, but could see nothing from where she lay on the cot. Cal moved across the wooden floor and looked out. He silently pushed the brace away from the door with his feet and closed it. Then, in the semiobscurity of the cabin, he dressed.

Blaine, too, sat and groped for her clothes. But she had barely gotten them turned right side out when Cal, in shirt and pants, opened the cabin door and stepped outside.

"Tommy, Brent," she heard him call out, "what are you two doing back here?"

"He got a bee sting, and I fell and scraped my leg bad," she heard a young voice reply. "Tim and Randy sent us back."

Blaine's head fell into her hands. How much had they heard?

"Are you all right?"

"Yeah. It ain't bad. They just didn't want us climbin' no mountains."

"I'm glad to hear it, but I wish you hadn't sneaked around the camp like this."

There was a tittering from the boys, and Blaine groaned.

"We didn't know what you was doin', Father Rutledge, honest."

"Well, never mind. If you feel up to it, why don't you go on down to the lake and throw some rocks in the water or something. I'll have a look at your injuries in a little while."

There was more giggling. After a moment Cal stepped back inside.

"A couple of the boys—"

"Yes, I heard."

"I'm sorry, Blaine."

She looked up at his face in the obscurity. "Oh Cal, do you suppose they'll tell Jason?"

He sighed and shook his head. "I don't know, but I'm going to have to talk with them. You'd better get dressed. After my little chat I'll saddle the horses and we'll leave as soon as you're ready."

Cal turned and stepped outside. Blaine's heart sank. All at once it didn't matter what Cal thought or what had happened between them. She and her son were suddenly thrust into another crisis.

CHAPTER NINE

CAL MADE HIS WAY BACK through the trees toward the camp. He'd told the two boys to wait at the lake and that he would come down for them shortly. Their injuries were minor, and it was doubtful that they'd even needed to be sent back from the hike, but they had and there was nothing he could do about it now. He dreaded telling Blaine that they were well aware of what had gone on in the cabin, but he knew she was probably expecting the worst, anyway.

As he neared the camp he saw her standing outside the cabin, looking anxiously in his direction, rubbing her hands together. When he was still a dozen yards away, he could see the concern on her face.

"They know what we were doing," she said, reading him.

He nodded. "Yes."

Her face twisted with pain. "Poor Jason. I've let him down again."

"You haven't."

"What would you call it?"

"You have your life, too. He's got to understand that."

"This is a hell of a way to tell him."

"I know it's embarrassing, but—"

"Embarrassing? Think how humiliated Jason will be. His mother and...and...Father Rutledge!"

"Blaine, don't torture yourself. I'm as responsible as you—more so."

"No, I wasn't thinking."

"We had no way to know we weren't alone."

"Cal, don't try to whitewash it. I had no business making love with you. Not under the circumstances."

He grew irritated. "It's unfortunate, of course. I'm not pleased, either. But we do have our own lives."

"Don't you see, I have a son virtually in jail! And now I've added to his burden! Imagine what this will do to him."

"It's regrettable, unfortunate, a damn shame even. But it's not a tragedy, not life-threatening. He has to face the fact that someday you may develop an interest in a man, that he won't have you to himself forever."

Blaine looked at him with dismay. "Is that what you think bothers me?" She waited. "Well, it's not. The problem isn't that I'd be interested in someone else, or sleep with him. The problem is I was caught in bed with you!"

"Good Lord, it's not a crime, Blaine."

"But think of Jason—what he'll go through, the teasing, the ridicule. Children can be cruel. I shouldn't have to tell you that!"

"Yes, that will have to be dealt with. But the problem is that Tommy and Brent intruded, not that we made love."

She gave a derisive laugh. "That serves your purposes, I understand, but it doesn't solve the problem."

"*We're* not the problem!"

Blaine's eyes narrowed. "Yes, we are! Jason's mother was caught in bed with Father Rutledge."

"Blaine, please."

"We can stand here arguing all day, Cal, but there's one thing I'm adamant about," she said, shaking her finger. "My son's not going to learn about this from someone else. He's going to hear it from me."

Cal stared at her for a long time, realizing that Blaine was only seeing one side of the issue. "All right," he said after a while, "we'll stay until they come back from the hike and you can talk with Jason. But I hope you don't give him the impression what you did was wrong. If we were guilty of anything, it was being indiscreet. That's all."

Blaine searched his eyes, not really trusting his words. Then she turned, and walked away.

THE BOYS RETURNED from their hike late in the afternoon. Cal immediately took Jason to Blaine, who walked off with him into the woods. Cal waited impatiently, unsure what to think but feeling powerless to interfere. He knew he was more to blame than anyone else, and hated to think that the incident should be permitted to harm so many relationships.

He was sure Blaine was taking the wrong course with her son, though it was obvious she already felt responsible for his problems and couldn't bear the thought of causing more. The question was, what impression should Jason be left with?

After fifteen or twenty minutes Jason returned and somberly rejoined the group, avoiding Cal entirely. Blaine walked over to him. She looked up mournfully, but without accusation.

"He wasn't pleased, obviously. I asked if he wanted to return to the ranch with us, but he said he didn't want to run from the other boys. He'd face them."

"Was he angry?"

"I don't know. He was rather stoic, but that doesn't mean he wasn't hurting inside."

"Should I talk to him?"

"No, I don't think so. He heard about it from me. He's prepared...for whatever happens. I think that's all that was necessary."

"I have no problem with any of that, Blaine, but I've got to talk to him eventually. After all, I do have responsibilities to him."

"Just let him try to work it out on his own for a while first, will you?"

Cal nodded. "If that's what you wish."

Blaine bowed her head, not wanting to look him in the eye.

"Do you want to stay the night?" he asked.

"No. If we have time to get back, I'd prefer to go."

"We'll have to hurry, but we should be able to get to the station before dark."

Blaine picked up her bag, and Cal grabbed the rest of their gear, following her toward the corral.

THE NEXT MORNING Cal paced the floor of his study, stopping every once in a while to look out his window or to drop into a chair for a moment before rising to pace again. Rosemary Hodges would be arriving at any time and he was still undecided how, exactly, to present his dilemma to her.

There were so many people to consider, so many aspects to the problem, that he wasn't even sure what the priorities ought to be. The only thing he was certain of was that he wasn't going to bother worrying about himself.

Blaine concerned him more than anyone—more even than Jason. The ride back to the ranch had been one of the more painful experiences of his life. He felt horrible about the situation he had put her in, and his agony was compounded by the fact that she had refused to blame him.

Cal had driven her in the dark to the foreman's house and she had gotten out of the jeep, thanking him for letting her handle Jason the way she wished. It had been as though they were returning from a funeral, and he couldn't help asking himself if it had been their brief but wonderful love affair that had been buried that day.

The intercom buzzed on the desk and Cal grabbed it.

"Rosemary's here."

"Send her in, Barbara."

Rosemary Hodges was the picture of serenity, as always. Seeing her, Cal realized how much he needed her guidance and wisdom. "Sit down," he said, pointing to a chair. He went around and sat next to her.

"Jason Kidwell?"

He nodded. "And Blaine Kidwell. And Cal Rutledge."

Rosemary's eyebrows rose.

"I'm afraid I'm in a pickle. We all are."

After he had explained what had happened, the psychologist sat for a moment in contemplation.

"So what do you think, Rosemary? That I'm a horse's ass?"

"No, not if you care for the woman."

"It wasn't frivolous."

"I wouldn't think so, considering the ethical issues. Mrs. Kidwell could certainly raise a stink if she were so inclined."

"She's not the type. That's not what concerns me."

"What does concern you, Cal?"

"I'm worried about Jason, naturally. But I'm especially worried about Blaine."

"I assume your feelings were mutual."

"She wasn't disinterested, let me put it that way. But we didn't exactly decide to make love. It was spontaneous. She's already blaming herself. And I'm afraid that she'll let the incident harm her relationship with the boy, and with me."

"It's not the best way to begin a romance," Rosemary said ironically. "However, I doubt Jason would reject her because of this. She *is* his mother, and a child will forgive a great deal."

"Does she need forgiveness? I tried to tell her there was nothing wrong in what we did. It was an accident that those boys came along. *That* was the problem, not us."

"She's obviously sensitive about the way her son perceives her, especially in light of what they've both been through. I think she reacted naturally under the circumstances. The question is how it will affect the dynamics of their relationship."

"Yes, and that worries me, too. I tried to tell Blaine that she shouldn't give him the impression that what she did was wrong, or that she didn't have a life of her own."

"You're right, but I'm not sure you're the one to tell her that."

"Who is?"

"Obviously she'll have to come to that conclusion on her own, if it's to mean anything. If I end up working with the two of them, I may be able to plant some seeds. Jason has to learn to deal with the way his mother lives her life, and this just might prove an opportunity for a lesson."

"That's fine, Rosemary, but I've got to tell you, yesterday morning a lesson was the farthest thing from my mind."

The psychologist grinned.

"I take it you're getting a kick out of me being caught with my pants down—literally."

She laughed. "To be honest, I'm glad to see you out of your cocoon, living a little. Everybody needs to be jolted occasionally."

Cal looked at his friend thoughtfully. "That woman has done something to me, I'll admit that. Maybe she has given me a jolt, as you put it."

"Is it too personal to ask if you care for her?"

"Yes, it's too personal, but I'll answer it anyway. I do care for her, though I don't really understand why."

"She's very attractive."

"This is not just glandular, Rosemary."

"Then perhaps you've got something to learn about yourself, too."

BLAINE CAME OUT of the ranch house and walked around the building toward the soccer field. As she approached, she saw Cal amid a group of boys on the far side, jogging around the perimeter of the field. She waited while they came toward her, everybody in the group looking at her with curiosity as they passed. Cal dropped out and jogged over to her.

"Hi," he said, trying to sound cheerful through his heavy breathing.

"Hi, Cal. Do you have a minute? Your secretary said I'd find you out here."

"Sure. I was going to come over to your place after practice and see if I could interest you in dinner out someplace this evening."

"Thanks, but I can't. As a matter of fact, I've come to tell you that I'm leaving."

He took a couple of deep breaths. "Leaving?"

"Yes. I'm going to Las Vegas to find an apartment."

"I thought you were going to stick around for a few days."

"I was, but after yesterday, I can't."

He looked at her. Blaine felt the accusation in his eyes.

"What about Jason?"

"I thought I'd come back and see him when the camping trip is over...if you'll let me."

"I'll let you, but I don't see why you can't stay. We have some things to talk about."

"Everything's been said."

"Nothing's been said."

She saw his anger. "Please, Cal, don't make this any harder than it has to be."

"But Blaine, what about us?"

"There can't be anything between *us*. I know you don't understand. It's just the way I feel. Please accept that."

The boys had almost made another circuit of the field and were nearing the couple. There were a few hoots and whistles as they ran past.

Blaine watched them. "Do they know?"

"About us?"

She nodded.

"No, of course not."

"They will."

"Yes, maybe so. Eventually."

"You see what Jason will be living with?"

"Look, you're right to be concerned. I want to do everything I can to make things right. And I think Rosemary Hodges is the key. Maybe you and Jason should discuss this with her."

"He'd die."

"She's a professional. Leave how it's handled up to her."

"Have you told her?"

"Yes."

Blaine lowered her head. "Maybe it's just as well."

"Will you talk to her?"

"I promised I would. If Jason will be seeing her, I will, too."

"Good."

"Well," she said, extending her hand, "I'll be going then."

Cal looked at her hand, noticing that it trembled slightly. He took it in both of his, pulling her half a step closer.

Blaine lowered her eyes with embarrassment, uncomfortable with her hand trapped in his.

"Will you call Barbara and let us know where you'll be?"

"Yes, I promise."

He still held her hand, unwilling to release her. "I don't want it to end like this."

"I'll be back," she said, biting her lip.

"To see me?"

She shook her head, emotion suddenly welling inside her. "I've got to go," she whispered.

He hesitated, then finally released her. She glanced into his eyes one last time then turned away, quickly walking back toward her car. When she reached the corner of the ranch house, she glanced back. Cal was still standing there, looking after her.

BLAINE WALKED in the front door of the Chaparral to the sound of a jackpot bell coming from one of the dollar slots. There were shrieks of joy several rows into the ranks of one-armed bandits. She hardly paid any attention, heading purposefully toward the poker parlor at the back of the casino.

Walking through the crowd, her arm tightened on her shoulder bag. She was carrying two thousand dollars in crisp one-hundred-dollar bills. One of the assistant managers, an extremely thin man whose name Blaine had forgotten, saw her coming and beamed.

"Evening, Blaine. You lookin' for a game?"

"Have any high-stakes tables tonight?"

"There's a hundred-dollar Texas Hold 'em," the man said, looking over his shoulder at a corner table, "but it's full at the moment. Would you like to have a drink in the lounge until there's an opening?"

Blaine looked through the smoke to see if she recognized any of the players. One heavyset older man looked familiar, but she didn't recall his name. "Anybody else around?"

"What kind of action you looking for? I might be able to chase up a few fellas, if you give me a while. There's more 'n a few who'd jump to play with the Queen of Hearts."

Blaine repressed a smile. Her ego didn't need strokes, so she always ignored PR drivel. "I'm not looking for expensive action, just some solid poker to shake off the rust." *And to occupy my mind,* she thought. But she didn't add that.

"What game?"

"I don't care. Seven-card Stud, if you've got some takers."

"Joey Parnell was around earlier. And I think I seen Milt Day. Give me a few minutes, Blaine." As he started off, the man snapped his fingers and a cocktail waitress with huge breasts overflowing her brief costume came over.

"Drink, ma'am?"

"Club soda. Lots of ice."

The woman's ruby lips widened into a reflex smile and she left. Blaine leaned against the railing and peered out over the casino. Behind her she heard some whispering and the murmur of voices. Word was getting around that the Queen of Hearts had come to play.

When the cocktail waitress returned with her soda water, Blaine slipped a silver dollar on the tray, and the woman mumbled her thanks and withdrew. A few minutes later a little old man with just a few crooked teeth in his mouth and a good-natured grin came up to her.

"Excuse me, ma'am, I understand you're Blaine Kidwell."

"Yes, I am."

He beamed. "I hear you're going to play, and I...er...just wanted to say I wish I could set at the table with you, but I'm on social security and my wife's got limits on me."

"Never play a table richer then you can afford," she replied. "The first rule of poker."

"Oh, I know," the man agreed. "I just wanted to say I admire your playin' and wish I could be in the game."

"Thanks." She smiled. "Maybe another time."

The man started to leave, then stopped. "And I hope you beat Butler real good at the Nationals."

"I'll do my best." She winked at her admirer and he shuffled away.

Blaine stared idly into the crowd and, in spite of herself, she felt a little depressed. Images of Caleb Rutledge flashed into her mind. She saw the look on his face when he had walked in on her at the cabin.

The sensuality of his eyes and his full lower lip never seemed far from her mind. She didn't want him there, constantly in her thoughts. She had come to the casino to try to clear his image away, but he had pursued her, even here.

"Blaine," the assistant manager said, approaching her, "I've got a Seven-card Stud game, thousand-dollar buy-in, two-hundred-dollar limit. That okay?"

"Sure. Which table?"

"Number two, in back."

Blaine looked where he was pointing. "Okay, I'll go buy my chips."

SEVERAL LONG NUMB HOURS had passed, and Blaine had worked her stake up to about twenty-five hundred dollars before she lost three hands in a row and was down to only nine hundred. It was not a particularly interesting game, and her mind kept wandering. Except for Milt Day, who was sitting on most of the money, none of the players was noteworthy—a couple of local pros of no particular distinction, and two out-of-town visitors.

Blaine suspected that the visitors—one of whom claimed to be from Minneapolis, the other from Amarillo—were a team, but if they were, they were either very cautious or inept. She wasn't sure which.

After one of the locals bet everything on a low straight and lost to Day, there was an empty chair. The other local cashed in a few hands later, leaving just Day, Blaine and the two out-of-towners.

She sensed a shift in mood at the table, and Day, who was flush, suggested doubling the stakes. The two visitors agreed immediately, and Blaine wavered for a minute, knowing her head wasn't fully into the game, though she finally agreed.

She took two small pots in a row, picking up a couple hundred, then folded on the next two hands, Day taking one, the man from Amarillo the other. Watching the action, she started getting more and more suspicious about the Texan.

After two more hands, observing him closely, she picked up a subtle tell: a giveaway mannerism. Every time Amarillo had an ace in the hole, he stacked his hole cards neatly. Otherwise, he left them scattered on the table.

After they traded several small pots, Blaine sensed that Day had picked up on the tell, too. Amarillo's cards were always spread, unless he had an ace. Her curiosity aroused, Blaine started getting more into the game.

The next hand she got into a battle with the two visitors. The betting was heavy. She held a flush and, at best, Minneapolis only a straight. Amarillo had raised the limit on the final round, but Blaine figured it was a bluff. She and the other visitor both stayed in the game.

Minneapolis showed his straight, Blaine her flush, and Amarillo threw in his cards. He *was* bluffing! She picked up another five hundred dollars.

Blaine was about even and ready to cash in, but the Texan's mannerism when he had an ace in the hole still had her curious. Day was still sitting on a majority of the table stakes, and seemed a little impatient. She figured he was uneasy about the tell also.

Several hands later Blaine was dealt another flush—all four show cards were hearts. Minneapolis had folded, but Day and Amarillo were both betting heavily. Amarillo had a king, queen, jack and ten showing. All he needed was an ace for an ace-high straight. Blaine glanced at the hole cards, they were all neatly stacked. If the tell was true, Amarillo had an ace in the hole. Blaine felt the perspiration on her brow.

Day, too, saw the implications. If the visitor wasn't baiting them, he had a straight. Blaine had him beat, but Milt Day, who had the bet, went to the limit to open the final round, pushing in a large stack of chips.

Amarillo sat fidgeting, staring at the pot. If he had the straight his tell indicated, Blaine figured he knew Day would have to have a full house or better to beat him. After the long hesitation, he raised Day the limit.

Blaine blinked. Neither of them was intimidated by her apparent flush. Either they figured she was bluffing, or their hands were pat. Day worried her the most, because he was betting against a flush and a straight. Smelling something, she folded.

Now the pressure was on Day. Blaine knew he had to have a full house to even be in the game at this point, but the question was whether the tell was a trick and the Texan had been baiting them all evening.

After hesitating, Day raised the limit again and Amarillo called. As Blaine suspected Day had a full house—eights over sevens. But to his surprise the visitor called a full house, too—queens over jacks.

Milt Day's mouth dropped open. Amarillo was a huckster, having set them up with the fake tell. His neatly stacked cards had said he had an ace in the hole. If that were true his best possible hand was a straight. Day would have had him beat. But in fact the visitor had a pair of queens and a jack in the hole, giving him a superior full house to Day's.

Milt had been had, but there wasn't a thing he could do about it. It was all perfectly legal. The Texan's tipping his hand had been a trick.

Day got up sheepishly as Amarillo racked in his winnings. Blaine got up, too, only having lost a couple of hundred dollars. She walked with Day to the cashier.

"Damn bastard," Day mumbled under his breath.

"We both bought a lesson," Blaine said. "Mine was just a little cheaper than yours."

"I feel pretty stupid."

"Don't. If I had been in your shoes, I'd have done the same thing.

You betting against a probable flush is what made me fold, not the chance of his tell being a con."

Day shook his head. "Still hate to be taken like that."

"Just be glad it didn't happen in a real high-stakes game."

"Damn," Day said, leaning against the cashier's counter as Blaine waited for her money. "Hear you're moving to town, Blaine. Is it true?"

She looked at the man and nodded. "News sure travels fast."

"Want to live closer to the action?"

"No, my son's down here. I just want to be nearby."

"How old is he?"

"Fourteen."

"You have a son fourteen? Oo-ee. You must have been a child bride."

Blaine laughed. She took her eighteen hundred dollars, put it in her purse next to Old Betsy and winked at the man. "Good night, Milt." She headed toward the door.

Outside the casino Blaine waited for the valet to bring her car. She looked up at the black sky and took a deep breath of the balmy desert air. As she expected, Caleb Rutledge popped immediately into her mind. For a long time to come, whenever she stepped outdoors, Blaine knew she'd have to contend with memories of him.

She got into the car and headed off for the motel she was staying in temporarily. As she drove, Blaine looked out the window at the false gaiety of The Strip. It had never particularly appealed to her, but tonight it seemed unusually shallow and triste. And loneliness bothered her for the first time in a long, long time. There had been something added to her life...and something lost. Cal.

Although the ex-priest had come to mind in the casino, while at work she could be relatively free of him. At a poker table she survived by her wits. There was nothing to fall back on there but her skill and mental toughness.

Outside, or anyplace she was alone, Cal haunted her. That was where she was vulnerable. And Blaine knew, if she was to survive, the vulnerability he had created was something she'd have to conquer.

CHAPTER TEN

TWO DAYS LATER Cal Rutledge walked out of the office of the fixed base operator at the Las Vegas airport, through the gate to the rental car parked outside. The agent handed him the papers, which he signed on the fender of the car. She gave him the keys and Rutledge jumped in and drove away.

The address that Barbara had given him was on the south side of town, at the intersection of two wide boulevards. The bright afternoon sun shone down as Rutledge turned into the entrance of the Twin Palms, past a large sign indicating that furnished studio apartments were available for rent.

Slowing to ease over the speed bump, he continued ahead, passing the swimming pool, a small kidney-shaped pocket of water that looked hopelessly ineffectual against the blazing Nevada sun. He found Building C and parked in a space designated by a Visitors sign, tilted askew on a rusty metal stake.

Rutledge looked again at the number Barbara had written on the scrap of paper, slipped it into his shirt pocket and got out of the car. He went to the stairway leading to the open balcony of the second floor, climbed the steps and walked along until he came to Unit Twelve. He knocked. There was no answer so, after a minute, he knocked again. He heard a voice inside.

"Who is it?"

"It's Cal, Blaine."

The door opened a crack—to the extent of the safety chain—and her face appeared. There was a white towel wrapped around her head like a turban, accentuating her lovely porcelain skin and the dark lashes around her gray eyes.

"Thanks for the warning," she said, after staring at him for a second.

"I wanted to talk to you."

"Did you consider that it might not be convenient? Or that I might not be here?"

"I decided to take a chance."

She gave a look of irritation and closed the door enough to unfasten the chain. She opened it again, then turned away and walked into the room, pulling the towel from her head so that her wet hair dropped to her shoulders.

From the doorway Rutledge scanned her body. She was clad only in a T-shirt and cutoffs. Her feet were bare. The sight of her nicely rounded buttocks brought him an instant recollection of their intimacy, and it stirred him.

Blaine plopped down onto the cheap Swedish-modern couch. Then she folded one shapely leg under her as she ran her fingers through her hair, fluffing it.

Rutledge closed the door, cutting off the bright sun that had been streaming in. Only the muted rays filtering through the curtained windows lit the room.

He glanced around. Everything was plain, cheap and worn. The panel on one wall obviously concealed a Murphy bed. Sitting on the Formica table were open cartons of Chinese take-out food, an empty plate with a fork lying across it and a soft-drink can.

"Sit down," she said, gesturing toward a matching armchair opposite the couch.

"Sorry to drop by like this, but I came on an impulse."

She watched him ease into the chair. "What is it you wanted to talk about?"

"I've been worried about you. I wanted to see how you were."

Blaine saw him looking at her hair as she unconsciously fiddled with the wet ends.

Rutledge remembered her kneeling over the container of water at the cabin, and felt a lump in his throat.

She self-consciously picked up the towel and rubbed the side of her head, as though she was aware of the image in his mind and wanted to erase it.

Rutledge let his eyes drift down her, noticing the peaks of her braless breasts rising against the thin fabric of her T-shirt.

"You needn't worry about me, Cal. I've gotten along fine for years. There's no reason why I won't in the future."

"It doesn't matter that we made love—that we shared that?"

She looked at him uncertainly for a moment, then her face grew sober. "You've come to titillate me. Is that it?"

"No. I haven't been the same since that afternoon. I've sat at my desk the past couple days knowing that you were here, and I was there. It didn't make a whole lot of sense to me, so I got in my plane and flew down."

She almost smiled. "You don't have a lot of self-control, Father Rutledge."

"No, Blaine, I don't. Not when it comes to you."

"What does that mean, that it was my fault?"

"No, I wasn't implying that at all."

"Then what were you implying?"

"That I care about you."

"If you cared, you wouldn't have seduced me...put me in the position you did."

Rutledge knew she was protecting herself, but he couldn't tell what it was she feared. Was it him, or herself? "What are you afraid of, Blaine?"

"Nothing."

"Then why are you so hostile?"

"I have no desire to be used by you."

"Is that what you think, that I used you?"

"Either intentionally, or out of weakness. It doesn't matter a whole lot which."

"Then I suppose it was weakness. I didn't fight my desires, anyway."

"Well, I admire your candor, but that won't undo the damage."

"I meant no harm, believe me." He looked at her smooth bare legs and felt a wave of desire. His gut felt like jelly.

Blaine must have read his feelings. She turned her head away. "I was weak, too," she confessed. "So I'm not blaming you. If I'm hostile, it's because I don't want to make the same mistake again."

"But was it really wrong, Blaine? What we shared wasn't meaningless. It was something very special. You've got to care about yourself, too."

"You're not thinking, Cal, unless a moment of bliss is all you care about. You know as well as I do we've got no future, nothing to look forward to. Living for the moment is fine, but it's not very smart."

"And total abnegation is?"

"Do I look like a nun? Do you think I didn't enjoy being with you? Do you think I don't have the same desires you have? Of course I do."

Rutledge felt his frustration starting to boil. "Then why don't you just accept your feelings?"

"You mean why don't I just throw caution to the wind and jump in bed with you? I'll tell you why. Because when you're through, I won't have anything left but a few memories, that's why!"

"It doesn't have to be that way."

"Cal, oh Cal," she lamented. "You're blind—blinder than the sinners you once tried to save. Didn't you tell *them* to look past temptation?"

"What makes you so sure I'm not looking past it?"

She shook her head, disbelieving. "Only you know what's in your heart. But I know who I am, and who you are. All we have in common is a mutual attraction. I'm not stupid, Cal. I know that you don't approve of who I am and what I do. How could any relationship work under those circumstances?"

Rutledge just stared at her, feeling defeated, not because of her fervor but rather because of her wisdom. He didn't want to believe what she was saying, but he couldn't deny it.

"I don't know what you intend in your heart of hearts, Cal, but we couldn't last long enough to get bored with each other. Look at me! Look at my life," she said, pointing around the room. "This is the way I live by day. And by night I'm in the casinos, trying to make a buck."

"It doesn't have to be like this."

"No, I could be setting my hair to look pretty for some fella coming home from work, instead of setting it to head for the poker parlor. And maybe that'll happen someday, I don't know. But the problem I'm talking about is not just cards and casinos."

"What is it, then?"

"It's who we are, Cal!"

"So you can write us off, just like that?"

"This hasn't been any easier for me than it has for you. If you want to know the truth, I've lost as much money the past few days as I've made. Partly it's because I've been worried and upset over Jason. But it's also because of you."

"What do you mean?"

"You've been sitting at your desk thinking about me, and I've been sitting at the poker table thinking about you. And it hasn't done either one of us a damned bit of good."

Rutledge was at a lost for words. All he knew was that he wanted to kiss her, to hold her, not to think about anything she'd said. Her narrow shoulders, her mouth, her hair hanging in ringlets, her slender, voluptuous body all called to him in utter contravention with her words.

"Just go away and leave me be," she said beseechingly. "Please."

He rubbed his fingers distractedly, not accepting what she'd said, but unable to protest. If nothing else, he'd learned her feelings were much the same as his. Only her conclusions were different.

"Please go," she whispered.

Rutledge got to his feet, staring down at her, hating the pain inside him. He went to the door. "I know you're right, Blaine," he said, looking back. "But I also know you're wrong."

AT THREE IN THE MORNING Blaine walked out of the Oasis Palms casino toward her Grand Prix in the parking lot. She didn't need a security guard to escort her to the car, her purse was empty. She'd lost nearly twenty-five hundred dollars that evening—her worst night of poker in five years.

She wasn't surprised, she'd played long past when she should have quit. But she had preferred to lose money than to go back to that apartment. Weakness.

She cursed herself. She cursed Cal Rutledge, too, but not with much conviction. Blaine couldn't blame him for what had happened any more than she could blame the cards or the dealer. The Queen of Hearts had bought herself a lesson in life, but what had she learned?

Blaine got in her car and drove out of the lot faster than she should have. When the tears began streaming down her cheeks, she didn't even care.

She climbed the stairs of her building, hearing a telephone ringing somewhere, and wondered if it could be hers. She hurried along the balcony, the brisk desert wind tossing her hair and drying her tear-streaked cheeks. At her door, she could hear the phone ringing inside. She fumbled with her keys, hurrying to open the lock.

Inside she ran across the dark room to the telephone, taking the receiver breathlessly. "Hello?"

"Blaine, it's Cal."

"What's happened?"

"Jason's been hurt. It doesn't appear too serious, but I wanted to let you know."

A pain went right through her heart. "Oh no! What happened?"

"He hit his head on a rock this evening up at the lake. It's a concussion, but we think he's okay. He was taken to the hospital and released. We've got him here at the ranch, in the infirmary, now. He asked for you, and I promised I'd track you down."

Blaine tried to steady herself. "How did it happen?"

There was silence on the line. "It seems he was involved in a fight," Cal finally said.

Blaine's strength seemed to drain right out of her. "A fight? Over me?"

"I don't know yet. Our first concern was Jason—getting him to a doctor."

"I'll leave right away."

"You won't get here till morning. Why don't you wait and get some rest?"

"I'm awake, and I won't sleep, so I may as well drive."

"I hate to drop this on you in the middle of the night, but I've been trying to reach you all evening. I tried the Chaparral, but they said you weren't there."

"No, I was at the Oasis Palms tonight."

"Sorry. I didn't know."

"Thanks for calling, Cal. I'm sorry you had to stay up for this."

"Look, why don't you let me fly down and get you? It'll be much quicker. I can have you here in an hour and a half."

Blaine considered his offer, the image of Jason in a hospital bed at the forefront of her thoughts. "You wouldn't mind?"

"Of course not. Pack a bag and meet me at the airport in forty minutes or so."

IT WAS STILL DARK when Cal's plane slipped from the black sky to the landing strip at his ranch. As they taxied to the tie-down strip, Blaine turned her face to the window. Far to the east, above the low ridge line of desert mountains, the first signs of day appeared. It would be light in less than an hour.

She glanced at Cal, whose face bore the eerie glow of the plane's instrument panel. In mood the trip had been much like that first night when they had driven to the ranch in his car.

They hadn't talked much then, either, but there had been the same tension—though now it was more deep-seated. And she was concerned for Jason, just as she had been before.

Having talked with Cal in person, she was less preoccupied with Jason's health. But the fact that he had been in another fight, and had asked for her, made seeing him all the more urgent.

When they had come to a stop and the twin engines of the plane had sputtered dead, Cal climbed out, then helped Blaine down the wing and to the ground. She stood aside as he finished securing the aircraft, the cool wind fluttering the sleeves of her blouse and tossing her hair.

The only light was from a single bulb atop a pole next to the nearby aviation shed. The jeep was parked under it, waiting.

When Cal had finished, he took her arm and they walked to the vehicle. Though Jason would doubtless be asleep, they moved with a sense of urgency, if only because Cal sensed her single-mindedness. At that moment, all that mattered to her was that she be at her son's side.

An additional nurse had been called in, which was customary whenever someone was in the infirmary overnight. The woman greeted Blaine when she and Cal entered the building.

"He's sleeping, Mrs. Kidwell. But I've been looking in on him and he seems just fine. Jason's resting very comfortably."

The words were reassuring, and Blaine felt for the first time that things would be all right. "Where is he?"

"I'll show you."

Blaine glanced at Cal, who was sitting on the corner of the desk, her bag at his feet.

"I'll wait here," he said.

She nodded and followed the woman into the adjoining room. A blue night-light illuminated the small ward containing just four beds. Only one was occupied. Blaine crept to Jason's side. The boy was sleeping peacefully, a small bandage in his hair on one side of his head.

She looked down at him, feeling a sense of relief that he had evaded disaster, though the thought of him fighting worried her. The nurse brought over a chair and Blaine sank into it, realizing for the first time how weary she was.

SHE FELT WARM FINGERS on her face, then blinked awake realizing her head was on Jason's bed, and she had fallen asleep in her chair. Blaine lifted her head and looked at her son's smiling face.

"Hi, Mom."

She got up and leaned across the bed to embrace the boy. "Honey, I was so worried." She kissed him on the cheek and pulled back to get a good look at him. "How are you feeling?"

"Okay," he replied without enthusiasm. "I still got a headache."

"I'll bet you do. Did the clunk knock you out?"

"I guess, sort of. I was pretty dizzy."

Blaine patted his cheek and smiled.

"How'd you get here, Mom? Drive?"

"No, Cal came and got me in his plane."

Jason looked vaguely annoyed, but didn't say anything. They looked into each other's eyes.

"Is that what caused the fight, honey? Cal and me?"

He looked away.

Blaine waited. "Maybe we ought to talk about it."

"There's nothing to talk about. You already told me what happened."

"But if your feelings are strong enough that you fight over it, maybe there's more that needs to be said."

"Don't worry, Mom. It won't happen again."

"I'm not chastising you. I want to help."

"I don't need help." He looked at her plaintively. "Can't we just forget about it?"

"We can if it was just a passing incident. But if there's a problem, we have to deal with it, honey."

"It was a passing incident."

"But this is the second time."

He looked at her impatiently.

"Why don't you tell me what happened?"

He wasn't pleased, but seemed resigned. "This kid was just teasing me about you and Father Rutledge. That's all."

"He teased you, then what happened?"

"I said something, and he said something. Then we started fighting."

"Was it like the last time, or was it different?"

"What do you mean?"

"You told me last time you couldn't stop hitting Brian, remember?"

"Naw, it wasn't like that. This kid was bigger than me. He pushed me down, that's all."

Blaine rubbed his cheek again with her fingers. "What did he say?"

"I don't remember...exactly."

"Tell me, Jason."

He looked pained. "He asked me if you were a nun."

"And what else?"

"That's all. I told him to shut up and he shoved me. I shoved him back, then he shoved me real good. That's when I fell and hit my head."

Blaine studied him for a long time. "You know it's not your head I'm most concerned about. I'm afraid I've hurt you, let you down."

He could see her emotion. "Naw, Mom, don't worry about that."

"But I do worry. I don't want to let you down. I don't want you to be ashamed of me."

Jason didn't reply, and Blaine felt as though a knife had been plunged into her heart.

CAL RUTLEDGE suppressed a yawn, listening to the boy sitting across the desk from him. It had been more than twenty-four hours since he'd had any sleep. After leaving the infirmary he'd shaved and showered, but there wasn't time for even a brief nap.

"Nobody's accusing you of anything, Kevin. Right now I'm just trying to gather the facts, find out what happened."

The tall, lanky boy pushed his hair off his forehead with his fingers. "I was just kidding around, and he got pissed off. It's not my fault, Father Rutledge. I was defendin' myself."

"Did Jason strike you—punch you?"

"Not exactly."

"What did he do?"

"He shoved me."

"He shoved you or you shoved him?"

"I don't know, a little of both."

"What was this teasing, that would get him so upset?"

"Oh, nothin'. Just the usual stuff."

"I don't buy that, Kevin. What was it about?"

The boy hung his head.

"Was it about Mrs. Kidwell, Jason's mother?"

"Yeah, I guess."

Rutledge could see talking about the problem was as hard for Kevin as it was for himself, but he knew it wasn't an issue he could run from. The best way to deal with it was to face it straight up.

"In other words, you were teasing Jason about his mother and me."

The boy looked up in trepidation. "I didn't mention your name, Father Rutledge, honest."

"That's not the point, Kevin. The question is whether you said something hurtful to Jason. If that was your intent, you were wrong. My feelings aren't at issue."

"It was just teasing."

"What strikes you as amusing may not seem that way to another person. If nothing else, I hope you gain a respect for another's feelings because of this incident."

"I have, I have. I won't do it again. Honest."

"But do you understand how Jason might be hurt by what you said?"

"Yeah."

"Kevin, you're considered a leader by many of the boys, and that gives you an extra measure of responsibility. I hope some of the others will learn from your experience, as well as you. You need to realize that Jason is not responsible for what his mother does, what I do, or anyone else for that matter.

"He was embarrassed by the talk going around, and that's particularly unfortunate, because what Mrs. Kidwell does, and what I do, is nobody's business. And if you find it amusing, that's your privilege. But to hurt someone by flaunting it is not right."

"I said I was sorry, Father Rutledge."

"I'm not the one to apologize to, because I'm not the one who was hurt."

"I'll tell Jason I'm sorry, if you want."

"I'd prefer that you feel the need to tell him you're sorry yourself."

"Okay."

"I'll leave it to you to handle it as you see fit, Kevin."

"All right."

"But remember, the knock on the head is not what hurt Jason most."

"Yeah, I understand."

"And one last thing, Kevin. Mrs. Kidwell happens to be a very nice person, and a very good mother to Jason. That's why your teasing was particularly hurtful to him."

The boy nodded.

"Okay, you're free to go."

Rutledge watched him leave, wondering if his own moral influence had been irreparably damaged. Was it enough that he was sincere and well-intentioned? He didn't know the answer.

CHAPTER ELEVEN

THE NURSE TOOK JASON'S TRAY and glanced over at Blaine, who'd hardly touched her lunch. "You're not setting much of an example, Mrs. Kidwell."

Blaine smiled weakly. "No, I suppose I'm not."

"We'll want Jason to have a nap to rest that noggin of his. And to be honest, you look like you could use a little sleep yourself."

"I am beat."

"Why don't you go and get some rest? You can come back this evening and see us."

Blaine felt too exhausted to object.

The nurse picked up her tray. "I'll call the office and tell them you're ready, if you like."

"Okay."

When she walked out of the infirmary a few minutes later, Cal was sitting at the door in his jeep. "Taxi, ma'am?"

"You can take me to the cemetery. I think I'm ready for it."

"What kind of a service do you prefer? I've got one for every budget."

Blaine couldn't help laughing.

"Come on, jump in."

She took the seat next to him. Cal looked tired, too, but he was trying to be cheerful. She knew he was doing it for her. "Where's the nearest motel?"

"About thirty-five, forty miles."

"You're kidding."

"No. Nothing between here and there but prairie dog burrows. But you can stay at the foreman's house. There's no need to leave the ranch." He started the engine.

Blaine wearily acquiesced.

As they drove across the compound, a group of boys turned to watch them pass by. Blaine felt conspicuous. "They all know who I am, don't they?"

"Some do, I suppose. But don't let it bother you. What these kids think doesn't matter."

"It does to Jason."

"He can handle it."

"Yes, he can." She smiled softly. "I learned that this morning."

"Oh? What happened?"

They had left the main compound and were headed down the road toward the foreman's house. She turned to Cal. "It was rather touching, actually. The boy Jason got into the fight with came by the infirmary."

"He did?"

"Yes. I was in the back corner of the room looking out the window and he didn't see me at first, but I heard him apologize to Jason for what he'd said about me. He told Jason he was sorry he hurt his feelings."

"What did Jason say?"

"Well, he was a little embarrassed, because I was there and the other boy didn't realize it. When the kid turned around and saw me, he went as red as a beet."

"Poor Kevin."

"I tried to put him at ease by introducing myself. He hummed and hawed for a second and said, 'I hear you're a real good mother, Mrs. Kidwell.'" Blaine chuckled. "Poor thing. I would have given him a hug, but he was already embarrassed to death."

"Well, it was probably good for everybody."

"I certainly felt better." Blaine looked at the fatigue lines at the corners of Cal's eyes. "Did you get a nap this morning?"

"No. After I drop you off, I'll go back to the house and lie down for a while. I've got a meeting at four."

"I feel terrible about what you've been through because of me."

"We've all had our ups and downs, so don't worry. The main thing now is to get Jason squared away."

"Do you think there'll be more trouble?"

"I was thinking about you and him."

"Jason and I get along just fine," Blaine replied, feeling a little defensive.

"I wasn't referring to your feelings for each other."

She started to ask what he did mean, but withheld comment. She knew. "You're talking about Rosemary."

"She'll be working with Jason. It might be good for you to get involved, like we discussed."

Blaine held on to the hand grip to steady herself as they bumped along the road. Perhaps things were even worse than they appeared. A little wave of self-doubt went through her, and she glanced at Cal.

"Well…"

"I imagine you'll want to stick around for a few days…until Jason is on his feet," he said. "It might be a good time to get started."

"All right."

A few minutes later they stopped at the foreman's house. It looked rather lonely and forlorn. Cal turned off the motor and the dust settled in the hot, still air. A small lizard scampered across the porch and ducked under the stairs. Blaine looked at Cal, who was sitting pensively.

"We're in a mess, aren't we?" she said.

He smiled benevolently. "It's part of life."

"You're Father Rutledge again," she whispered.

He reached over and took her hand. "I am who I am, Blaine, just like you are who you are."

She looked down at the large hand on hers. His touch was neither rough, nor aristocratically fragile. It was both. She let him squeeze her fingers, though she didn't know why. "You know," she said with a little laugh, "you're the first person since Frank who's made me wish I was somebody different from who I am."

"What do you mean?"

She felt embarrassed for having said anything. "I wish I was somebody else, that's all."

"Why?" He pressed his hand more tightly around hers. She pulled it away, gently.

"I don't know. Maybe I'm just feeling inadequate or something."

"There's no reason why you should. You're a remarkable person."

Blaine was as amused as she was saddened by his words. "I have to say, Frank never said anything like that to me."

"I'm not Frank."

"No, you aren't."

"Why the comparison, then? Why do you feel the compulsion to mention us in the same breath?"

She looked into his eyes. "I suppose because you make me feel inadequate, just like he did."

"Why? Is it something I do, or say?"

Blaine felt closed in by his questions. She swung one leg out of the jeep, but Cal grabbed her arm. Their eyes locked, hers flashing with a touch of anger.

"I want to know what's bothering you, Blaine."

She hesitated, but her eyes didn't quit him. "It's not what you do or say. It's who you are." With that she pulled her arm free, stepped out of the jeep and walked briskly to the house. At the door she stopped and turned around, sorry she had stalked away.

Cal was looking after her with concern. She started to say something, but thought better of it. She turned back to the door.

"Blaine, we both need to clear our heads a bit. After you see Jason this evening, I'll take you out someplace for dinner."

She looked down, thinking about his invitation. The skin of her face and neck suddenly felt damp from the heat. She shook her head minutely, but was having trouble saying no.

"I'll pick you up at five-thirty and take you by the infirmary. Then we'll go out."

Unable to deal with it just then, she went inside without replying.

HOGIE'S ROADSIDE INN was just a diner sitting at the edge of the highway and sharing a couple of shade trees with a gas station and a small store. Its principal virtue was that it was the second-closest place to the ranch to eat—the first being unreliable.

The proprietor, who was also the chef, was named Hogan. He greeted Cal with a wave from the kitchen as they came in the door. Blaine had put on a dress and heels and felt more relaxed in Cal's company than she had expected. His hand touched her waist as they made their way through the crowd to a booth in the corner.

"Your friend does a pretty good business," Blaine said, as they settled in.

"Hogie gets all the traffic off the highway. Heaven knows, there aren't enough people in the area to keep him going." His eyes drifted over her.

Rather than making her feel uncomfortable, his glance made her feel attractive. They had had a pleasant conversation on the ride over, mainly about Jason. The boy had been in a good mood when she visited him, and they hadn't talked about Cal, though Blaine suspected her son knew she hadn't dressed up that way just to come to see him. His only comment had been about her perfume.

"I suppose, though," Cal said, glancing around the rather ordinary surroundings, "that you're not used to much more than this in Prosser."

"We had a couple of nice places," she observed. "It was easy enough to tell by how crowded the parking lot was with cars and pickups."

"Guess it's the same everywhere."

The awkward silence that followed was broken by the arrival of a calmly efficient waitress who wore a dark brown wig, though she looked to be well into her sixties. "Evenin', Cal," she said, as she slid two glasses of water onto the middle of the table, and dropped a menu in front of Cal and Blaine.

"Hello, Fran. Looks like you're busy tonight."

"Better 'n not, I suppose." Her eyes lingered only a second on Blaine before she left, saying she'd be back in a minute for their order.

Cal flipped open the plastic-covered menu. Blaine did, as well.

"Chicken-fried steak is reliable...if uninspired," he said. "The chops and chicken are usually okay, and the liver, too, if you like it."

Blaine groaned.

"I can't recommend the spaghetti—Hogie's not Italian—and I'll have to ask how freshly unfrozen the fish is before I comment on that."

She laughed. "Sounds like you know this place pretty well."

"Let's just say one's options are limited."

Blaine was studying Cal's masculine, yet sensitive face. "But you like it, don't you?"

"What?"

"Living out here on your ranch, running your school."

"Yeah. I suppose I wouldn't do it, if I didn't."

"Don't you miss cities, people, churches—all the things you had back east?"

"Sometimes, maybe."

"I think I would. Of course I haven't been farther east than Colorado and Texas, let alone England and Europe and all the places you've been, but it's hard to believe you'd be happy with nothing but all this sagebrush and sky."

"I can travel, if I like. And I have. But I'm basically content living out here."

Blaine toyed with her spoon, aware of Cal's particularly calm mood. She felt less threatened than before, wanting to reach out a little and satisfy her curiosity about him.

"Why is it you haven't traveled more, Blaine? Your income is pretty good. You could afford to pamper yourself once in a while."

"I don't know," she said, spinning the spoon. "Habit, I guess. I've always been so used to hanging on to what I get. Spending it— except on things for our home—never seemed quite right. Besides, I was away from Jason too much as it was. But the two of us made some little trips. Last summer we went to Yellowstone, and on up to Canada for the Calgary Stampede." She beamed. "We had a ball."

Cal could see that her delight at the recollection was genuine. Strangely he felt a little deprived at not having shared in the experience. As he watched her expressive face, he imagined himself together with her and her son.

The thought of togetherness with her had struck him previously, but it had always been inspired by a protective urge. This was different. He almost felt as though he were on the outside looking in.

"What are you thinking about?" Blaine asked with a laugh. "You had the funniest look on your face just now."

Cal colored some, having been caught. But he felt bold. "If you want to know the truth, I was thinking what fun it might have been to be along with the two of you on your trip."

Blaine sat mute for a second, as though she were really surprised by his remark. "You have a whole school of boys you could take on trips."

"I wasn't thinking so much about Jason as I was about you."

"Me?"

"Yes. Why the surprise?"

The waitress, Fran, came up from nowhere, her order pad and pencil at the ready. "Ready to order?"

Cal looked up, and Blaine could see he was censoring a whole series of comments. But he acquiesced to the circumstances, looking at her. "You know what you want?"

"Yes. I'll have the chicken-fried steak, since it came so highly recommended."

Fran jotted down a few words. "You haven't had that in months, Cal," she said, without looking at him.

"Maybe memories improve with time, just like good wine."

Blaine repressed a laugh as Fran looked over her glasses at Cal.

"First you come in here with a beautiful young lady, then you start spoutin' poetry. What's happened to you, Caleb Rutledge?" She glanced at Blaine as if to confirm she was on the right track.

"If it's gossip you want, Fran, you won't get it from me," Cal teased.

"Pick up!" came Hogan's voice from the kitchen.

Fran half turned with annoyance. "What'll you have, Cal?"

"After this beginning, what else but chicken-fried steak?"

Blaine and the waitress both chuckled.

Cal rolled his tongue in his cheek, pleased with himself.

"And to drink?"

"Ice tea," Blaine said.

Fran looked at Cal.

"Same."

The waitress scratched a final time on her pad. "You're certainly compatible," she said before hurrying off.

Blaine and Cal smiled at each other. Then his grin turned quirky. "Maybe she knows better than we do."

She studied him with an equal measure of suspicion and discomfort, aware of his masculinity: the soft mat of hair under the open neck of his shirt, the vague yet familiar hunger in his eyes. She remembered the exquisite way he made love, and realized she was seeing Caleb Rutledge in a role she didn't want to see.

"That's silly," she said, more disdainfully than she had intended. After an awkward silence, she scooted to the end of the banquette. "Excuse me for a second, I'm going to the ladies' room."

Cal watched her make her way through the crowded little restaurant. Though she had gone, the conversation was continuing in his mind. *Where's your sense of romance?* he thought, but he wouldn't have said it to her face. He knew he had no right to.

He was the one who kept straying from the straight and narrow. Blaine Kidwell was fire and, like a foolish child, he insisted on playing with her. Mixing her with his feelings was tempting the devil, but he kept doing it, as though nothing else in this world, or any other, mattered.

He could tell himself a hundred times that it was enough just to be friends with her, that they should try to rectify the trauma they'd all been through, but even his own counsel went unheeded. Blaine enticed him in a way that gave new meaning to all those biblical stories of the power of a woman over a man. He felt weak, yet driven at the same time.

A few minutes later Blaine returned. "I'm sorry," she said, sliding into the booth opposite him. "I didn't mean to be flip."

"No, I was out of line. I'm aware of your feelings. I ought to respect them." Cal sipped his water because he didn't know what else to do. He watched a slight smile move across her lips. "What's so funny?"

"You're the other guy, again."

"Father Rutledge?"

She nodded. "It's like those masks that children have—wear it one way and there's a smiling face, turn it upside down, the face frowns."

"Which one is the smiling face?"

Blaine started to say "the priest," but she wasn't sure it was true. "I don't know."

"It sounds suspiciously like the problem is more with your confusion than my split personality."

She smiled wanly and avoided his eyes. At a nearby table a couple of truck drivers were drinking coffee and talking quietly; next to them four ranch hands were sipping beer and laughing. She contemplated them—all familiar types—the kind of men she had known most her life.

When Blaine looked at Caleb Rutledge's quietly simmering eyes again, she saw him a little differently than she had before. Maybe, in some perverse way, the notion of their similarity wasn't so silly, after all.

THE NEXT DAY one of the maintenance men drove down to take Blaine to see Jason. Cal had said he would be leaving at first light for Oregon, where he would be negotiating to trade timberland to a lumber company for grazing land in the eastern part of the state.

Earlier that morning, while she was in that twilight zone between sleep and wakefulness, she'd heard the sound of an aircraft taking off, and had known it was Cal. When he had mentioned his trip during the drive back to the ranch the night before, she had been glad for the reprieve. But hearing him flying off had sent little pangs of regret through her. Even during the hour or so she sat with Jason, Cal frequently came to mind.

The boy had had about all of the hospital bed he could take, and ended up sitting with her in the infirmary lounge during most of her visit. The nurse said he could be released as soon as the doctor came to examine him, so when they had run out of things to talk about, they had occupied their time by playing checkers.

Blaine let her mind wander. She had lost three games in a row when Rosemary Hodges came into the clinic. She greeted Blaine.

"Guess what, Jason?" the woman said, turning to the boy. "After they let you out of here you can have the pleasure of coming to see me."

"Oh, great," he said under his breath.

"Jason..." Blaine cautioned, eyeing him.

Chastened, he looked at the psychologist sheepishly.

"Don't worry," Rosemary said cheerfully. "Your mom can have the pleasure first." She turned to Blaine. "How'd you like to come by for a chat?"

Blaine looked at Jason, then at the woman. "Sure."

"Are you going to talk about me?" he asked.

"Of course," Rosemary replied. "Can you think of anything more interesting to talk about?"

He shrugged. "I guess not."

Both women laughed.

Half an hour later Blaine went to the building that Rosemary had directed her to. She found the office and knocked on the door. The psychologist greeted her warmly and they sat down.

"How's it going with your son, Blaine?"

"Maybe I should be asking you."

"No, your perception is more important than mine."

Blaine thought for a moment. "Things seem fine in a way, yet underneath I sense something is wrong."

"What do you mean?"

"I don't think Jason's feelings for me have changed. I feel he loves me like he always did, and yet there's something...."

"Do you know what it is?"

Blaine looked at her. "I suppose it's Cal."

"Your relationship with him?"

She nodded, then lowered her head, knowing what they both were thinking. She felt uncomfortable.

"How do you feel about it?"

"Our relationship?"

"No, about the fact that it appears to bother Jason."

Blaine shrugged. "I guess it's understandable. He's just a boy. And, since there's just been the two of us, it's natural that he'd be jealous."

"That all may be true, but how do you *feel* about it?"

"I'm not pleased, naturally. I feel terrible."

"Why?"

"Look at the unhappiness it's caused Jason."

Rosemary contemplated her. "We all know about the unhappiness for Jason. How about for you?"

"I'm not pleased that my son is hurt."

"No, but is your unhappiness just empathy for him, or is there more to it than that?"

"I don't understand."

"Blaine, I've asked you about your feelings, and you've defined them in terms of your son's emotional state."

"I'm his mother."

"Yes, but you're your own person, too."

"I hurt if he hurts. Isn't that true of most mothers?"

"To some degree, yes."

"What are you trying to say? That I go overboard?"

"No, I'm just trying to understand *your* feelings, and they seem to get tangled up with his when you talk about them. It may not be critical that I understand how you feel, but I think it would be good if you did."

Blaine thought again. "I get the feeling you're telling me I ought to be looking out for myself."

"What do you think?"

"I have looked out for myself, Rosemary. I've taken a career that fulfills my needs, not necessarily his."

"Do you think that's all you're entitled to?"

"What do you mean?"

"Career involves money, life-style, time available and other factors that impact a family. I'm curious about your emotional needs."

"You're referring to Cal again."

"Cal happens to be topical, because of your involvement. But whatever we say about him could be said about anyone you might become friendly with."

"Men in general."

Rosemary shrugged. "That's one topic with emotional significance, but there are others."

"The question is how I would choose, if it came down to a question of my child, or a relationship?"

"Possibly. It might be just as important how you draw that line, as it is which side of it you step on."

"What do you mean?"

"I've known women who say their children come first, no matter what. I've known others who say their relationship comes first. Taking Cal as an example, you might say anything involving him that's a problem to your son is bad by definition. Or you might ask yourself whether Jason's problem transgresses a fundamental right of your own."

"You're saying it does, obviously."

"Only you can say, Blaine. There's no right place for that line to be drawn. It depends on your feelings. That's why I asked how you felt about what's happened, how you feel inside. Guilt, resentment, anger are all indicators."

Blaine felt uncomfortable, but her mind began working. She tried to focus on what she'd been thinking and feeling during the past week or so. "I do feel torn," she said.

"Well, that's something to think about. Ask yourself why, and try to get in touch with your feelings."

"Is that a homework assignment?"

Rosemary ran her fingers through her gray hair and laughed. "You might say so."

"Sounds like you're more worried about me than Jason."

The psychologist shook her head. "Not at all."

"How's this going to help him?"

"Kids take their cues from their parents. Your attitude will help him define his own interests and rights."

"Am I screwing him up, Rosemary? That's what I want to know."

"No, of course you aren't. But I think there are some areas of your relationship that need some defining and redefining."

"Like what?"

"Like those areas of your life in which his interests don't necessarily come first—rights that you have that are independent of him. You see, Blaine, when he sees that you have your own life in addition to what the two of you share, he's going to read a message in it— namely that he must develop some independence emotionally and make a life apart from yours."

"I need to shove him out of the nest, in other words."

"Well...you can't protect him his whole life. Part of growing up is establishing a separate identity, a healthy self-image. And Jason's got to develop the skills to handle setback and conflict, particularly when the issue involves you."

Blaine sat staring for a long time. "I guess I'm having trouble realizing he's not my baby anymore."

"A good mother cares and fears for her child. But love is manifested somewhat differently at different stages of a parent-child relationship."

Blaine was nodding. "The funny thing is, you aren't telling me anything I don't already know. But knowing it and doing something about it aren't necessarily the same thing."

"That's normal."

A devilish smile crossed Blaine's mouth. "Do you know as much about men as you do about kids?"

"People are people."

Blaine's eyes narrowed. "Men are different."

Rosemary laughed. "Only to women."

Blaine laughed, too.

"If it's my dear friend Caleb Rutledge you're thinking about, I'll tell you a little secret about him."

Blaine's breath wedged in her throat. "What?"

"He's having the same problem with his past that you're having with Jason."

"What's that?"

"Feeling comfortable about letting go."

CHAPTER TWELVE

THAT AFTERNOON Blaine learned that Jason had been given the okay by the doctor to return to the dorm. She was pleased, but it meant she wouldn't be able to see him again until a visitors' day, or until Cal made special arrangements. Alone again, she spent a quiet afternoon at the foreman's house thinking, reading and waiting for Cal to return.

The long, hot hours passed slowly, and Blaine found herself listening to the distant sounds of vehicles, wondering if any of them might be a Cessna 310. Her thoughts about Cal came more easily, and she realized it was due, at least in part, to her talk with Rosemary Hodges. The conversation had given her permission to think about Cal without feeling guilty, but the fundamental problem hadn't changed: he was still who he was, and she was who she was.

At four o'clock the maintenance man came back down with a message from Cal's secretary that he was due in from Oregon at five and, if she was packed and at the strip, he would take her directly on to Las Vegas. Hurriedly Blaine threw her things into a bag, closed up the house and went in the truck to wait for Cal at the field.

When the aircraft finally made its approach, Blaine grew excited. She watched it touch down, tiny puffs of smoke visible as the tires struck the pavement. In a few moments the plane had taxied to the apron where she waited. Cal, wearing his aviator glasses, waved as he killed the starboard engine.

The maintenance man escorted Blaine to the aircraft, carrying her bag. The port propeller kicked up a swirling wind, blowing her hair across her face as she climbed onto the wing and through the door that Cal held open.

"Hi," he said, leaning across her to secure the door. They looked at each other and Cal reached up to pull a last wisp of hair from her face. The feel of his fingers on her skin made her tingle. Then he leaned closer and kissed her softly on the lips before settling back into his seat.

Blaine was surprised. It was almost as if he knew that she had relaxed her vigilance against his affection. But he said nothing, turning his attention immediately to the aircraft. She busied herself by fastening her seat belt and watching the maintenance man securing the door to the baggage compartment.

Cal was flipping switches and checking dials. "How's Jason?" he asked, as he went about his routine.

"Doctor said he's fine. He was back in his dorm this afternoon." She smiled to herself. "His only complaint was that it didn't happen during school."

"He'll learn to time his illnesses and injuries. They all seem to." He looked out the window. "How's it look out your side?"

"All clear."

He released the brake, eased the throttle forward, and the plane started moving toward the taxi strip. Moments later, when they were airborne, Blaine looked out the window at the barren landscape. Below she saw the school buildings clustered around the ranch house. Out at the end of a stretch of dirt road she saw the foreman's house.

She felt a real sense of leaving, of separation. Though her time at the ranch had been brief, Jason and Cal had made it a home of sorts. She was leaving the only two people in her life she could honestly say she cared about.

Blaine tried not to let her emotions get to her, but she couldn't help it. She felt sentimental. Perhaps because she wanted to.

LAS VEGAS SEEMED BIG, unfriendly and foreboding to Blaine as she drove with Cal to her apartment. He had rented a car and insisted on driving her home, not wanting to leave her at the airport to take a cab. She was glad in a way, because she wasn't ready to say goodbye, but she didn't like dragging it out, either. Still, she wondered if he was going to kiss her. Blaine hoped he would, yet dreaded the awkwardness at the same time.

Cal tried to say something cheerful now and again, but he seemed reflective, hiding a mood of some sort. She thought about what Rosemary had said about his having trouble with his past, and wondered if she was a problem for him. Maybe it wasn't easy for a man like Cal to be attracted to a woman like her.

"A week from Sunday is visitors' day," he said after a long silence. "Are you going to come up?"

"Probably. I miss him already."

They were almost at the Twin Palms. Blaine felt nervous.

"I never asked you how your meeting in Oregon went."

"Fine. We closed the deal."

"Is it a good one for you?"

"You always like to think so, especially right after you make it. But on a trade like this, you don't know for a while. Sometimes, it takes years."

"I can imagine." Blaine didn't really understand, but she felt the need to talk. "How many ranches and things do you own, anyway?"

"Five major spreads, and some smaller ones. Nearly three hundred thousand acres all together."

"Three hundred thousand!"

"A lot of it's sagebrush. The quality ground is a small part of the total."

Cal turned into the entrance of the complex and eased over the speed bump. Blaine felt very tense. He stopped at her building, pulling into the same visitor parking space he had before. The sign was still crooked.

He got out of the car and she did, too, not waiting for him to come around. He took her bag from the back seat, and Blaine waited on the walk. As he approached she reached for the bag, but Cal took her arm instead.

"Come on, I'll carry it up for you."

She went along compliantly. They climbed the stairs in silence. Blaine was agonizing when they came to the door. There was a note taped to it. She took the slip of paper and read.

"Oh, no. Somebody broke in."

"Broke in?"

She showed him the manager's note. As she fumbled through her purse for her key, Cal ran his fingers over the metal door frame that showed signs of having been jimmied.

"Did you leave anything valuable here?"

"Just my clothes and things. The furniture belongs to the complex." Her hands were trembling and Cal took the key from her and opened the door.

The inside of the unit was a mess. Cupboard doors and drawers were open. Clothes were scattered all around, though it appeared someone had gathered most things up and piled them on the couch. Blaine gasped.

"Looks like vandals," Cal said as they stepped inside. "Probably kids."

"Look at this mess," she groaned. "Why did they have to do this?" She noticed that the television was missing. Though it didn't belong to her, she felt an empty feeling in the pit of her stomach.

Blaine went to the dresser, stopping to pick up some of her underwear on the floor. Her jewelry case was lying open on top of it. A couple of odd pieces of costume jewelry were still in the box, but everything else was gone.

"What'd they take?" Cal asked, stepping up beside her.

"I didn't have much. Gold chains, some earrings, a broach and a pearl ring my mother left me." Blaine heard her voice crack with the last words. Her throat tightened. She repressed a sob and stepped to the bath to look in.

The medicine cabinet was open, as was a makeup case sitting on the back of the toilet. She peered inside. Old Betsy was gone. She felt her body tremble.

"What's missing here?" Cal asked from the doorway.

"My gun."

Blaine's eyes flooded and she felt the sobs start to well. She tried to stifle them, covering her face with her hands. Cal stepped in and put his arm around her shoulders.

"The gun's easily replaced," he said soothingly.

"It's not that," she said between sniffles. "It's the fact that someone was in here. I feel so...so violated."

"You shouldn't be staying in a place like this."

She reached over and took a tissue, first blowing then wiping her nose. "It was just temporary, until I found a decent place and could have my furniture shipped."

"You should have stayed at the ranch."

She blew her nose. Cal went back out into the other room. Blaine dabbed her eyes and looked at her face in the mirror, groaning at the sight.

"Where's your suitcase?" he asked.

"The two big ones are in the closet."

She heard him fumbling in the other room.

"There's nothing in here but a couple of boxes."

Blaine spun around and hurried to where Cal was standing at the closet. She poked her head in past him. "Oh, no. I bought two brand-new Vuitton bags just a month ago!"

Cal pulled the empty cardboard boxes out and began filling them with clothing.

"What are you doing?"

"Packing. You're coming back to the ranch with me."

"No. I can't."

"No arguments, Blaine. There's a house for you there that's safe, and has privacy. You can stay until you have a decent place to live."

For some reason his earnestness amused her. She smiled at him through her tears. "That's pretty dumb."

He looked perplexed.

"How can I find a place here if I'm a hundred miles away at the ranch?"

He gave her an embarrassed grin. "Oh."

She looked at him sympathetically.

"Well, that's easy enough. We'll stay the night in town, find a place for you in the morning, then head back to the ranch."

"No, Cal, I'll be fine. I can stay here for that matter. It'll only be for a week, or two at the most."

"I won't have it."

Blaine laughed. "You'll have to, because I'm not letting you have your way."

He abruptly reached for her, first taking her by the shoulders, then gently pulling her against his chest. Blaine melted into him, luxuriating in the protective warmth of his body. He put his cheek against the top of her head.

"We'll see about that," she heard him whisper.

THE TUXEDOED WAITER PLACED a demitasse of aromatic coffee in front of each of them, then withdrew. Blaine looked at Cal in the candlelight. His full lower lip seemed particularly sensuous, his sandy-blond hair was glittering with golden highlights. She studied eyes that seemed dark and more penetrating than usual in the shadows. He lightly ran his fingers along hers.

"We're not going back to the apartment until morning," he murmured. "We'll get your things then."

Blaine knew what he intended, yet she didn't have it in her to protest. She wanted Caleb Rutledge. There was no more pretending.

"We'll stay at a nice hotel. Someplace safe and secure."

"No place seems safe."

"You'll be with me." He sipped his coffee, still toying with her fingers.

She watched his hand caressing hers and remembered a big doll she had gotten when she was five. She had played with its fingers the same way, loving it as though it were as alive as she. Blaine wondered if maybe she was like a doll to Cal, a special plaything—one you loved because it was different, having entered your life unexpectedly.

In her loneliness she realized it didn't really matter. She was no less compliant than the doll. His solemn, hungry eyes possessed her. She felt she had no choice.

Twenty minutes later she sat in the car outside a pleasant-looking inn while Cal registered. She was calmer than she expected, but there was a nagging feeling of uncertainty. She was headed along a path, but she didn't know where it was leading.

Cal came out of the office and got back in the car next to her. On his face was a devilish grin. "Where'd you go on your honeymoon?"

"I didn't have a honeymoon. We ran off to Oregon and got married over Christmas."

"Ever stay in a honeymoon suite?"

"No..." She saw a funny look on his face and suddenly understood.

Cal threw up his hands in mock innocence. "Totally unplanned. Believe me. It's all they've got available."

"What's it like?"

"This is Las Vegas. Use your imagination."

Blaine closed her eyes and told herself he was an ex-priest, but it didn't help.

Cal opened the car door, got out and walked around to her side. He helped her out rather ceremoniously, obviously having fun with the situation.

"Where is Father Rutledge now that I need him?" she mumbled.

Cal laughed.

They went up to the room, Blaine holding her breath as he opened the door. She stepped inside. The place was everything she expected, and more. There was a canopy bed on a platform with red satin flounces, red carpet and drapes, white satin wall covering and gold fixtures everywhere.

"My God." She turned to Cal, who seemed a little shocked himself. "I feel guilty already."

"You're the Queen of Hearts. What could be more fitting?" He looked up at the plump cupids on the foot of the canopy.

Blaine looked at them, too, thinking how insincere their smiles seemed. "I don't think I could have taken this even at seventeen."

There was a knock at the door and Cal went to open it. A man came in carrying an ice bucket with a bottle of champagne and some glasses. "You're paying for it," he said with a shrug, "you may as well have it." He saluted them and left the room.

"Maybe that's the secret," Cal said. "You have to see the place through a champagne mist." He smiled at her. "May I interest you in a little bubbly?"

She sat on the bed. "Why not?"

Her common sense told her it was all really very funny, but Blaine felt a little overwhelmed anyway. She fell back on the bed and, as she stared up, her mouth dropped open.

"Good Lord."

Cal was removing the foil from the champagne bottle. "What's the matter?"

"Come and look at this," Blaine said, still staring.

He walked over and peered up under the canopy. There, on the ceiling, he saw her lying on the satin bedspread. "Hmm," Cal said, "a mirror."

"Have you ever done...slept in a bed with a mirror over your head?" she asked incredulously.

"Don't you know that the first rule is never to ask a man about his past?"

"But you were a priest!"

"That was a long time ago."

Blaine sat up, staring at him in disbelief. "Cal, you haven't!"

"No comment." He went back to the champagne.

She shook her head. "Are you sure they didn't throw you out of the church?"

He was loosening the wire around the cork. "Absolutely."

"I think I've been seeing you through the wrong color glasses."

The cork popped, thumping against the ceiling and bouncing once or twice on the thick red carpet. Cal smiled.

"I feel horribly decadent," she confided.

"I think that's one of the objectives of these places. Brides are supposed to find it inspiring."

"I'm not a bride."

"But are you inspired? That's the important question."

She laughed. Cal began pouring the wine. She watched him, realizing she was with the man who had taken her in the cabin at the lake. That day there had been a haunted look in his eyes. Tonight he was more relaxed, lighthearted.

"Are you sure you want to be here with me?" she asked. "I somehow feel responsible for this."

"You *are* irresistible." He walked over, carrying two glasses of champagne.

"I don't want to be irresistible."

Cal sat on the bed next to her, then handed her a glass. "Why not?"

Blaine reflected for a minute. "I don't like to appeal to a man's weakness."

He touched her glass and they both sipped the wine. "What makes you think it's weakness?"

Blaine took another sip and wiggled her nose because the bubbles tickled. Cal leaned close and kissed the tip of it. With him so near, she could smell his masculine aroma. Without thinking she took a deep breath, savoring him.

She looked into his eyes. They were smiling, unlike the first time when they had frightened her a little.

"Aren't you going to answer the question?"

She blinked. "What question?"

"Weakness. Why is this weakness?"

"I don't know."

His mouth curled with amusement. "You were implying that it was, weren't you?"

Blaine took another sip of champagne, then another. "Yes, I guess I was."

"Why?" He leaned close to her, softly rubbing his cheek against hers. Nowhere else did they touch.

The sensation mesmerized her. "I don't know," she said dreamily. Cal chuckled. Then he slid his lips along her jaw to her ear, letting his breath scorch the skin of her neck. "You aren't making much sense."

His moist lips touched her ear, then he took her lobe between his teeth, gently nibbling it.

"About what? What were we talking about?"

He slid closer, burying his face into her neck as he slipped an arm around her waist. More than anything she was aware of his warm breath bathing her neck and flowing down the collar of her blouse.

"It was something about weakness." He kissed her cheek and his hand dropped from her waist to the curve of her hip.

Chills passed through her body, and she knew he was torturing her on purpose. But he had answered a question, and in her distraction she'd missed it. Still, she managed to catch the echo of his words— weakness, something about weakness.

Cal's finger was at the opening of her blouse, caressing her exposed skin. His cologne was faint, but it flooded her because of his proximity. He opened the gap of her blouse wider, leaned over and kissed the naked flesh of her chest. Blaine trembled.

He looked up and she smiled as if to tell him she liked it. There was only a splash of champagne left in her glass. She tossed her head back, downing the wine in a swallow.

Cal took her chin in his hand and kissed her mouth. "How's the mist? Want some more?"

Blaine nodded, so he got up and went over to pour more of the frothy liquid into their glasses. She watched him, wondering how she ever could have thought they shouldn't be together this way.

When he walked back to the bed Blaine was on her back, staring at the mirror overhead. He sat down next to her, but she didn't get up. Her smile bore a touch of euphoria. As he watched her, she moaned softly and threw her arms over her head, still looking happily into the mirror.

Cal was aware of her sexual vulnerability just then. Her mounded breasts lay under her blouse, inviting him to expose them, to kiss and suckle them.

But as he studied her she turned her gaze from the mirror overhead to him and, seeing the refilled glasses, she sat up, taking the one he offered her. Blaine took a long drink.

"You're getting me tipsy. Is that your plan?"

"I don't have a plan."

"Just flying by the seat of your pants?" She giggled, but then realized it really wasn't that funny. She drank again, and watched him over the rim of the glass.

Her softness and vulnerability were more obvious than they'd ever been. She had put herself in his hands, trusting him to do what was right, leaving caution to the wind. Cal took a drink. In a way he didn't like that sort of responsibility.

"Tell me the truth," she said, "have you done this often?"

"More than you."

"How do you know?"

"Intuition. A sixth sense, I suppose."

"If you've done it once before, you've done it more than me. This is the first time I've gone to a place like this with a man."

Cal studied her. He believed what she said. "Why is that?"

"Oh, I've been asked."

"I'm not surprised. But why didn't you go?"

"I didn't want to. Sex never seemed a good enough reason."

"But you want to now?"

Blaine took another long drink. "I'm here, aren't I?"

He touched her cheek. "Why is this different?"

"I don't know. It's just that now I want to. I haven't thought about it past that.'' She looked straight into his eyes. ''Why did *you* do it before, and why are you doing it now?''

''Maybe I have done it for sex, out of need, in the past.''

''And now?''

''I want to be with you.''

''Because you feel sorry for me?''

She was slurring her words a little and Cal realized she wanted to get drunk. ''Not because I feel sorry for you.''

''Then why?''

''Does there have to be reason beyond it's what I want?''

Blaine shrugged and drained her glass again. She extended it toward him, smiling a little crookedly. ''You only go to a honeymoon suite once...or twice...or three times.''

Cal went to fill her glass again.

''Poor Cal,'' she said, as he came back to the bed. ''You didn't get to have a honeymoon with the woman you loved, did you?''

''No.''

''Poor Cal.'' She sipped her wine, watching him with sad eyes. ''Do you come to places like this with other women and pretend?''

''No.''

''It's okay to tell the truth. It won't hurt my feelings.''

''That is the truth.''

''Poor Cal.''

''There's no need to say 'Poor Cal,''' he said a little harshly. ''I'm quite content. I'm exactly where I want to be.''

''Yeah,'' she said, her voice maudlin, ''every man's dream—to score with the Queen of Hearts.''

''Blaine, don't.''

She took another drink and lifted her chin. ''You're right. I shouldn't worry about tomorrow when it's still tonight.''

''Is that what you're doing—worrying about tomorrow?''

''No, can't you see?'' she said, lifting her champagne glass. ''I'm living for the moment, for myself, just like Rosemary said.''

''Rosemary?''

''Yes. We talked. She told me I ought to have a life of my own, do what I want. Live.''

He saw that her eyes were brimming with tears.

''And here I am, living!'' She took a hasty gulp.

Cal took the glass from her and set it with his on the nightstand. ''I don't want you to have to drink to be able to be with me.''

A tear rolled down her cheek. ''It doesn't have anything to do with you.''

"That's reassuring."

Blaine smiled through her tears. She wiped her eyes with her sleeve. "Nothing personal."

"Even worse."

She laughed and leaned against him, letting her head settle on his shoulder. "At least I'm not a hostile drunk. A little weepy maybe, but not mean."

He caressed her face with his hand, his desire for her rising again.

"I don't think we belong here...either one of us," she said a little sadly.

"Maybe that's why you were gulping down that champagne."

"What's your excuse?"

Cal thought, taking the question seriously. "Maybe deep down I'm a little afraid."

"Of me?"

"Of myself *and* you."

She lifted her head from his shoulder. "Do you know something that I don't?"

"Just that I want to hold you in my arms."

Blaine turned her face up and he kissed her, long and deeply. When the kiss finally ended she looked into his eyes. "Now I'm afraid, too."

"Don't be." He took her hands and they stood by the bed. He began unbuttoning her blouse. When it was undone he kissed her again on the lips. Then he unsnapped the waistband of her slacks and let them slide over her hips to the floor. Blaine stepped out of them, her eyes never leaving Cal's.

"You have the same look as that day at the lake," she said.

"I want you like I wanted you then."

He pushed her blouse off her shoulders. With her arms behind her back, she pulled the cuffs over her hands as Cal leaned down and breathed fire on her throat. His tongue skittered across it. She moaned, and her blouse dropped to the floor.

His fingers moved lightly along the edge of her bra, gingerly testing the fullness of her bosom. Then he grasped the clasp between her mounds and unsnapped it, letting the undergarment fall open to reveal the naked whiteness of her breasts. When the bra, too, fell to the floor, Cal bent over and lightly kissed her nipple, causing it to engorge instantly.

The excitement of the disrobing left Blaine light-headed. Between the champagne and the aching throb of desire, she felt unsteady. But Cal wasn't ready to hold her yet. He stared at her breasts, cupping them with his hands, tracing the rosy edge of her nipples with his thumbs. Her head rolled back and she took a deep breath, arching her breasts toward him.

He gently squeezed her nipples, then abandoned them, letting his hands slide down her sides to her hips. Hooking the band of her panties with his thumbs, he pulled them down to the floor, leaving her entirely naked.

When he stood and ran his hands down her arms, she trembled. He responded by embracing her, gathering her closer.

Blaine held him, but without much force. Her insides quivered. "I feel shaky," she whispered.

Cal whipped back the satin bedspread and helped her onto the bed. Looking up, she was taken by the startling vision of her own naked body. She had never seen it like that before, and it looked alien to her, almost as though it were another woman there on the ceiling.

Out of the corner of her eye she realized Cal was undressing, but she didn't look at him, partly out of shyness, but also out of a fascination with her own body in the mirror. She lay staring for a while, but when Cal climbed in next to her, his body warm against her cool flesh, she forgot the woman on the ceiling.

All at once she was with the man at the cabin, but this time she was unafraid, this time there was love even more than desire. She touched his face, awed by her feelings as much as by him.

He kissed her and ran his hands over her body, arousing her with his touch. She watched his eyes worshipfully follow the progress of his hands over her breasts, down her waist, and across the flat of her stomach. There was a hunger in his gaze, but it was restrained, quiet.

Blaine felt his love and she wanted to merge herself into him, not just her body, but her being. For so long her soul had been isolated from involvement that her desire to be one became unstoppable.

When his fingers trailed down her thigh, across it and up her inner leg, Blaine's skin tingled. She craved his intimate touch.

Looking overhead she saw the man with the other woman. She saw his hand moving incrementally toward the place between her legs. She saw her limbs part and the hand draw nearer. She felt the dewy reservoir of her femininity moisten. She saw and felt the touch, saw and felt her hips lifting to meet his hand.

But Blaine turned away from them, closing her eyes and giving herself totally to Cal. His finger took command, its gentle rhythm dominating her awareness. Her body began undulating, lost to her control. She gave a tiny cry and, despite everything, looked up to see herself in pleasure, fascinated by the other woman's joy. The vision aroused her even more, and suddenly she wanted the man on the ceiling, even as she wanted Cal.

The storm of her climax began gathering and she craved more than just his touch. She wanted him.

"I love you, I love you," she mumbled incoherently into his mouth, feeling in her excitement the blending of herself with him, the abandonment of her separateness.

Along with Blaine, the woman in the mirror pulled him closer, and she saw the masculine body with its broad shoulders and golden hair cover the image in the glass. She felt him hard and swollen. Oh, how she wanted him, wanted to surrender to the love she felt.

The woman's legs enveloped the man, and Blaine felt him at her opening. Then, as he started to enter her, she gasped, startled by the sensation and by the terror and joy she saw on the face above.

His body felt wonderful both inside and out, drawing her building storm closer with each movement. But Blaine was drawn with fascination to the other couple, too, taking pleasure in their pleasure, excitement from their excitement.

It was then that she understood her two joys: the love of the man in her arms, the excitement of the man overhead. One was melded to her soul, the other to her body. She loved them both, but had surrendered only to one.

Cal's feverish embrace ignited her, loosening the last tethers of control. The sight of him crashing into her with his lean, muscular frame sent her screaming into ecstasy and the final, blind delirium of joy.

CHAPTER THIRTEEN

THE NEXT MORNING the sun shone brightly from the clear sky as they walked hand in hand along the wide boulevard. Blaine felt Cal squeeze her fingers and she was exhilarated by the affection. She took a deep breath of the cool air, liking the sting and crispness of it in her lungs.

She squeezed his hand back and bumped her shoulder against him to be close. They glanced at each other and smiled simultaneously.

"I've decided I like that place," Cal said. "Maybe I'll remodel my bedroom at the ranch."

Blaine laughed. "You'll need a permanent champagne mist, if you do."

"Seriously, it kind of grows on you, don't you think?"

"They say people will adjust to anything eventually."

"I think last night speeded up the process of adaptation."

Blaine poked him with her elbow.

"You didn't like it?"

She smiled. "No comment."

Cal put his arm around her shoulders and gave her a big hug. "You can't fool me. I could tell."

"Cal! You're not very polite! You may be an ex-priest, but you're no gentleman."

He chuckled and they turned up the walk to the pancake house. Inside they had to wait a bit for a table. They stood against the wall, Cal's arm around her neck. Blaine rubbed her cheek against his hand and thought how natural and wonderful it had seemed awakening in his arms that morning. It was the next day all right, but still not tomorrow.

The hostess, a heavy woman with vibrant makeup, finally called their name and they went with her to their table. Cal pushed aside the syrup tray and sugar bowl so he could hold Blaine's hands. He studied her for a moment. "Do you feel like a bride? You're as radiant as one."

"I feel happy. I enjoy being with you, Cal."

"Now *that* was my plan."

"Why?"

"Because I enjoy being with you. And I've found these things work so much better when it's mutual."

She gave him a look of mock derision. There was a serious issue in what he'd said, but she wasn't in the mood to think about it. She felt too good, too happy just then.

The waitress brought some coffee and they ordered. The pancakes came fairly quickly and they ate, not saying much, but feeling content. When they had finished and were waiting for the bill, Cal looked at his watch.

"I think we ought to go by the police station. I'm sure they'll want to know what was taken in the burglary. Afterward we can get a paper and start looking for a place for you to live."

It was the first concession either of them had made to the realities waiting for them. "Okay."

They walked back to the inn, holding hands as before, but Blaine had started thinking about the problems ahead. Cal had wanted her back at the ranch, but now she wasn't so sure it was the right thing to do.

She wondered why she felt the hesitation. After the previous night, it seemed she would have jumped at the chance. But on reflection it was no great mystery—what they shared was only temporary. It couldn't go on.

She wasn't even sure the experience was what Rosemary had in mind when she had encouraged her to think of herself. Blaine decided she might simply have jumped at the excuse. But why did it bother her? Was it guilt? Maybe the problem was that she had a tendency to think of selfishness and weakness as the same thing.

She glanced up at him as they walked, hating the thought that the good things she felt should in any way be weakness, but she knew they were. Being out of control—as she had been—was to open oneself to disappointment. Her marriage to Frank Kidwell had proved that.

After picking up the car they stopped at the police station, and Blaine gave a clerk the information required. She described the jewelry her mother had left her but, judging by his reaction, there didn't seem to be much prospect of ever seeing it again. The loss of her revolver was of greater interest, and Blaine was asked for specific information on its registry in Washington, which she provided.

Cal bought a paper and, while they drove back to the Twin Palms to pack her things, Blaine glanced through the rental section.

"I'd get a house, but until things are clear with Jason, I'm probably better off renting a condo or town house—something nice, but without the worry of upkeep."

Cal didn't comment. Blaine looked at him.

"What do you think will happen after this year? Will your report carry much weight with the juvenile authorities?"

"We haven't had a lot of experience with Washington, but, if they're like the others, I'd say so."

She looked at him expectantly. "That's good, isn't it?"

Cal reached over and patted her leg. "If the rest of the year is like last night, absolutely."

There was a deadly silence.

He turned, and saw she had taken the comment wrong. "I was just kidding."

"It wasn't very funny."

He felt his heart drop. "No, you're right. It was insensitive. I'm sorry."

She didn't say anything. After a while he looked at her again. "You aren't mad at me, are you?"

"I know you didn't mean it seriously, but what you said does raise an issue."

"Whether I'd let us affect my evaluation of Jason?"

"No, not that exactly. I trust you to do what's right."

"Then what, Blaine?"

"The impossibility of the whole situation."

"What impossibility?"

"You and me. You and Jason. Jason and me. The authorities in Washington. Agnes. None of it goes very well with what happened last night, or at the lake. Let's face it, honeymoon suites might work for a night, but they don't fit into either of our lives."

"Maybe they don't. Not yet."

Blaine wasn't sure what he meant, but she didn't feel inclined to ask. He'd taken her point, and that was what mattered at the moment. She didn't want to destroy the mood any more than she already had.

They entered the apartment complex, and Blaine decided she was glad to be moving out. Returning to Cal's ranch might not be ideal in some respects, but she knew she didn't want to be alone in this place. On reflection, she thought that maybe she didn't want to be alone at all.

RUTLEDGE SLOWLY walked down the pathway to the sidewalk and turned to look at the house. It was small and plain, but neat. The subdivision was pleasant—a place of family homes, not ostentatious, but respectable.

Blaine had decided against a condo after all, so they had looked at several rental houses before she picked one. She was inside now with the agent, signing the lease. In a little more than a week she'd be able to move in.

Cal strolled along the sidewalk, stepping around a tricycle and a wagon attended by a towheaded little girl of about four. A small dog yapped at him from the porch of the neighboring house for a minute, then quieted down when he moved on.

He thought of the husbands and fathers who would be coming home from their labors in a few hours, home to waiting families. It was not a familiar way of life, but it touched his emotions anyway. A part of it, perhaps the implied sense of being needed and loved, called to him.

As he walked along Rutledge thought of another dwelling, one he had occupied a long time ago on the other side of the continent, the rectory of his church in Massachusetts. It would have been his and Laura's first home together, and he had so looked forward to sharing it with her.

Since then Rutledge hadn't thought in terms of home and hearth, except for his family place at the ranch. But even that he had changed to fit his new life, making it a part of the school and his work.

At the ranch he was safely cloistered from the world and emotional entanglements, except for those with his boys. After his experience with Blaine Kidwell, he was beginning to realize that wasn't an accident.

It was obvious enough by now that their relationship wasn't just a casual encounter, an incident. And yet she was so unlikely a woman to become involved with. He wondered if there was significance in that fact. In a way she was safe, but Rutledge knew his choices weren't motivated by fear. Did he love her?

To Blaine it seemed Cal's lightheartedness had turned vaguely brooding. He smiled and quipped after they left the house she had leased, but it wasn't a ready smile, and his humor seemed a little forced. He was distracted, and she decided that he, too, had come down to earth.

But she was thankful the tension between them hadn't resumed. As things stood, her furniture and household goods would be shipped down from Washington a week from Monday, giving her several days at the ranch to work with Rosemary and Jason. There was no way to get all of the things she had with her into Cal's plane, so they agreed that she would drive back in her car.

On their way to the Twin Palms, Blaine felt the need to address the reservation in him that she sensed. "Are you sure it's a good idea that I go back to the ranch, Cal? I can spend the week here just as easily."

"It's not only a good idea, it's imperative."

"Why?"

"Because I want you to."

"That doesn't exactly make it imperative."

"Depends upon your point of view." He reached over and took her hand. "Besides, how can we separate, fresh out of the honeymoon suite? People might get the wrong idea."

"You're worried? I've heard of performance anxiety, but this is crazy."

He smiled and pulled her hand to his lips, kissing her fingers. "As long as you're satisfied—the world be damned."

When they arrived at the apartment complex, Cal parked next to Blaine's car and they both got out. Without hesitating he took her into his arms.

"Drive safely," he said, pressing his cheek against her head.

Her arms were around his waist. "Thanks for the wonderful honeymoon."

"It ain't over yet."

She didn't dispute the assertion, but she knew better. Still neither of them seemed willing to let go, they just stood there with their arms around each other.

"If we aren't careful, people will begin mistaking us for part of the statuary around here."

"No," he replied. "We aren't rusty enough."

"You silly goose." She slipped from his arms and went to her car door. "I don't know when I'll be getting in."

"I'll make sure the place is cleaned up and stocked with food this time."

"Don't go to any trouble, really." Blaine got in the car and rolled down the window. "Have a good flight."

He hadn't moved, so she knew it was up to her to go. She started the engine. It wasn't until she was pulling out of the parking lot that she saw him finally turn to his car.

IT WAS ALREADY DARK and the moon was just rising when Blaine drove up the road leading to the main compound of the Rutledge

Ranch. Though she couldn't see much, just knowing where she was gave her a sense of being safely home. During the long drive from Las Vegas she had thought a great deal about the little house she had rented, meticulously planning the decor and arranging the furniture in her mind.

Cal had told her Jason would likely be given leave over the Christmas holidays, and she had begun making plans to have the house decorated to the rafters. She wanted it to feel like home to him, to make things as they had always been.

There was a cutoff from the road to the foreman's house that Blaine took to avoid the main compound. She saw no reason to disturb anyone at this hour, deciding that the morning was soon enough to check in.

When she came to the point where the road dipped down into the draw, she remembered Cal carrying her across the mud and kissing her as he held her in his arms. It seemed so long ago, yet she knew it was only days.

Coming over the rise, Blaine saw the roofline of the foreman's house against the sky. Drawing nearer, she could see a vehicle parked out front—Cal's jeep.

As she pulled up next to it, he rose from a chair on the porch. He walked to the car as she got out.

"You're late," he said with concern. "Did you stop for dinner?"

Blaine closed the door. "Yeah, in Beatty."

Without hesitating, he embraced her. He had showered, changed and put on fresh cologne since she had left him in Las Vegas. He smelled delicious, and Blaine snuggled against him.

"I didn't expect to find you here."

"I hadn't planned on it, but when I came by earlier to check the place out, I started thinking about you and couldn't drag myself away." He kissed her cheek.

"How long have you been here?"

"An hour or so."

"Cal, you've spent so much time with Jason's and my problems, I don't see how you manage to do everything else you have to do."

"I've been a little lax, I'll admit." He kissed the corner of her mouth.

"That's not good."

"The worst, I guess, is that I've accumulated about fifty laps for missing soccer practice."

She pulled back and looked at him in the moonlight. "That's terrible. The boys count on you."

"I'd do a thousand laps, if that's what last night would have cost me. Ten thousand."

She smiled and touched his full lower lip with her finger. "That's the most unusual compliment I've ever had...and the nicest."

He kissed her deeply on the mouth. When their lips parted she sighed, looking into his pale eyes that shone gray in the moonlight. "And I'll run ten thousand more to be with you tonight."

"But you can't. We're back at the ranch."

"It's okay. We have privacy here."

"That's what we thought last time."

Cal kissed her. "We'll be careful."

Blaine felt no more willpower than he was showing. "We shouldn't."

"I know. I can't help myself."

"I'm surprised you ever got as far as being ordained."

He kissed her again. "So am I."

She wiggled from his arms and went to the porch. "You're hopeless, Caleb Rutledge."

He came up behind her, slipping his arms around her waist as she fiddled with the door. "Hopeless, but hopeful," he whispered into her ear. He kissed her neck through the ebony tangles of her hair.

Blaine grew weak, her desire sapping her strength and killing any chance of resisting him. They went inside, not even bothering to unload the car.

THEY LAY NAKED on the bed, side by side. The moon was higher now, filling the small bedroom with pale, muted light. Cal trailed his index finger down one breast to her nipple, then down the other, his feathery touch sending shivers along her spine.

Blaine pressed his hand flat against her breast, stopping the titillation. "Don't get me excited again," she moaned. "I can't take it."

He kissed her temple. "It cost me ten thousand laps and that's all I get?"

"Lord, I've never made love so much in my life—or so long."

"Is that a complaint?"

Her teeth gleamed between her parted lips and she turned to him, running her fingers through his hair. "No. I'm just...overwhelmed."

"That's good," he said, and trailed his fingers lightly over her chest.

"Oh, Cal. What are we going to do?"

"About what?"

"Everything. Jason especially."

"There's nothing to do, is there?"

"I'm worried. Something tells me I should be. It's like a storm ready to break."

Cal rolled back onto the pillow with a sigh.

She looked at him. "What? Does that upset you?"

"I wasn't going to tell you, not until I found out what it was about, but..."

She sat up. "What, Cal? Is it Jason? Has something happened?"

"Not to him, no. It's the juvenile authorities in Washington."

"What about them?"

"We received a request for a status report on Jason. In effect, they're asking how he's doing."

"Why? Is that normal?"

"Periodic reports are not unusual, but this is a special request. Apparently one instigated through the courts in Benton County."

Blaine felt a clawing in her throat. "Agnes."

"Maybe."

"No, it's Agnes. I know it is."

"Well..."

"What does it mean?"

"They...perhaps she...want to know what's going on, I suppose."

"Then they'll find out about the fight?"

Cal was silent for a moment. "Yes. I'm afraid they will."

Blaine gave a plaintive moan.

"There's no need for us to be mentioned, or the fact that you'd been up to the lake with me. The report will just contain the essential facts about the incident and his injury. There's no way to avoid it."

"I don't care about myself. It's Jason I'm concerned with."

"That's what I'm getting at."

"What are you saying."

"The incident was a minor one, and we'll represent it as such. In itself, I don't think it'll be a problem."

"But if they knew I was here, and sleeping with you, my son's guardian, it might not be so good. Is that what you're saying?"

"Blaine, don't get excited. There's no need to upset yourself. It's just a bureaucratic maneuver that doesn't mean much. I'm satisfied that everything we've done, including having you here, has been in Jason's best interest. And if it comes down to that, I'll tell them so."

"You don't know Agnes. She'll turn it against us."

"There's no reason Agnes, or anybody else, will find out. After all, what you and I do in private is our business."

"But if she gets her hands on it, don't you think she'll use it?"

"You're getting yourself excited over nothing."

"I'm leaving tomorrow. I'm going back to Las Vegas." She started to get up from the bed.

Cal took her arm. "Blaine, calm down. Nothing serious has happened, and there's no reason why it will. This report business is a result of what I said to Agnes up in Prosser. She's upset, and fighting back the only way she can."

"But there's no reason to give her ammunition."

"We aren't."

"What do you call this, Father Rutledge?"

A silence fell over the room. He lay beside her, immobile, mute.

"I'm sorry, Cal. That was bitchy. I'm sorry."

"Look, Blaine, there are only two things that matter. One is Jason. The other is you and me. You're here because it's important that he develop a wholesome attitude and learn to cope with his problems. Rosemary and you together can do something about that.

"You're also here because of me. I want to be with you. The fact that you and I might benefit doesn't invalidate the good it might do Jason."

"Do you suppose Agnes will buy that?"

"Damn Agnes!"

Cal's tone was so sharp that Blaine felt stung by it. He immediately put his hand on her shoulder. "I'm sorry. Forgive me."

Blaine shook her head in amusement. "Look what that woman can do without really trying. This is probably all the result of a five-minute phone call to her lawyer."

"All the more reason not to let it upset us. We've got to live our life...and forget Agnes."

She looked at him, knowing he was right, but there was an abiding fear in her just the same. It was a fear she had known for years.

Cal kissed her shoulder and she lay down next to him, letting him gather her to him. She felt terribly weak just then, but for once it didn't matter. She knew that Cal, in his compassion, was strong.

CHAPTER FOURTEEN

ROSEMARY HODGES greeted Blaine and they sat in the armchairs, each taking the same one they had before. Though it had only been a few days, circumstances were very different than the last time they had met. Before, Blaine and Cal had only had an encounter. Now they had a relationship.

Although nominally these sessions were designed to deal with Jason's problems, Blaine knew that it equally meant exploring her life, too. Because of the incident at the lake, their conversation would necessarily touch on her relationship with Cal.

"How's it going?" Rosemary asked.

"To save time, maybe I should ask what you know."

"Cal told me that the two of you are...involved."

Blaine nodded.

"It was actually rather selfless of him to talk to me about it," the psychologist said. "Since we're associates, his personal life is not something we normally discuss. He didn't want to put you in the awkward position of having to talk around it."

"He's very thoughtful."

"Of course, you and Cal are only background to the primary concern—Jason."

"Yes, what do I do about Jason?" Blaine rubbed her hands nervously. "I've been living my own life, as you suggested. So what do I do now?"

"Well, I don't think you should announce what's going on but, on the other hand, you don't want to keep the fact that your relationship is evolving a secret, either."

"Which means?"

"Our objective is to help Jason learn to cope a little better than he has in the past, to learn to express his anger and frustration more constructively. Part of his maturation involves getting him to accept your separateness."

"How do I do that?"

"You don't, exactly. It's something he'll have to come to accept on his own. But the way the two of you relate will affect how successful he will be. In other words, the subtle messages he receives from you will affect his attitude.''

Blaine understood the principle, but felt a little bewildered.

''What we're talking about is communication, Blaine. I think part of the problem is that Jason has trouble telling you how he feels. He loves you and doesn't want to hurt you. He's loyal—a quality he learned from you—and he can't bring himself to say, 'Hey Mom, I don't like what you're doing.'

''You see, what you should be aiming for is not to get him to agree with you so much as it is to get him to express his own views, without acting them out in antisocial behavior. Children are not necessarily supposed to approve of what their parents do, but it is very important that they're able to talk about how they feel.''

''You're saying that Jason doesn't approve of me.''

''Let's just say that in our conversations he's told me some things he hadn't been able to tell you.''

''What?''

''He's admitted your work is a problem for him. On the one hand he's proud of you, but on the other he wishes you were more like other mothers. He identifies with you so closely that he personally carries the stigma of your uniqueness. Small-town prejudices often affect children more seriously than adults.''

''I know, I had my own to endure.'' Blaine sat staring. ''I guess poker has been my family's bane. Maybe I should have stayed at the bank.''

''No, that's not the conclusion to draw at all. In fact, to abandon your life for Jason would be counterproductive. You have an opportunity to help him learn to accept you as you are. Learning to deal with one's parents is the first step in learning to deal with the world at large. Life won't always accommodate him. You shouldn't, either.''

''He's never asked me to quit poker, and I never offered.''

''That much is okay, but we still need to open the channels of communication.''

''I'll talk to him about it.''

''That's good, Blaine. But I think there's a more pressing problem at the moment than your career.''

''Cal?''

Rosemary nodded. ''In Jason's mind your relationship with Cal is like the career issue—the same only different, if you get my meaning.''

"He's jealous?"

"Yes. And it's perfectly natural that he is. But don't forget we're talking about communication. Your objective shouldn't be to make him love Cal—it should be to encourage him to talk about his concerns and frustrations."

Blaine sat pondering the psychologist's words.

"And you might want to know that I've discouraged Cal from talking to Jason about it," Rosemary continued, "because I think it ought to start with you."

Blaine looked at her. "I'm sort of scared. He's my son and I love him, but I'm afraid I'll say the wrong thing."

"You won't go wrong if you speak from your heart. Don't try to apologize, justify, convince. Let him know it's okay to feel as he does. Encourage him to express himself and then listen to what he has to say. It may not come easily, he may even resist out of fear of hurting you. But in time it should come. Patience and love are the key, and in the short time I've known you, I can tell you have plenty of both."

Blaine felt her eyes fill with tears. She looked at Rosemary through the blur, and couldn't speak.

"Being a single parent is really tough," the psychologist said reassuringly.

"You know what?" Blaine said, sniffling. "I wish you were my mother." She took a tissue from the box Rosemary handed her and blew her nose. "Mine died when I was so young, I never really knew her."

"It's good that you can say that. Have you ever told anyone that before?"

Blaine shook her head. "I never had the courage. When I was little I used to think it about a teacher, or someone like that who I was fond of, but I could never bring myself to say anything."

"Well, that's good. It gives you an idea what Jason's going through. It's the same sort of thing."

Blaine blew her nose again and smiled at Rosemary. "Thanks, Mom."

The older woman smiled and reached out, taking Blaine's fingers. "I can easily empathize. I had a son, but never a daughter."

Almost as if it had been commanded, Blaine rose to her feet. Rosemary did, too, and they embraced. Blaine surrendered to the psychologist's comforting gesture, and then began to cry. They were deep heartrending sobs, long-felt emotion she had never expressed before.

Rutledge sat at Blaine's kitchen table and watched her at the stove. She reached into the boiling water with a wooden spoon and fished out a strand of spaghetti. Taking it between her fingers, she lifted it over her head and lowered it into her mouth.

He stared at the sensuous curve of her neck, marveling again at her delicate beauty. Rutledge smiled as his gaze traveled lower, his heart aching at the sight of her slender, feminine figure. She had been his, and the motivation he now felt was to possess, rather than conquer. He wanted her close to him, always.

Blaine peered into the adjoining pot on the stove and stirred its contents, leaning closer to savor the aroma. She glanced back at him. "Getting hungry?"

"Yeah."

She opened a drawer and took out some flatware, then walked over to the table and set their places. As she leaned close to him, he gave her bottom a little pat and stroked her thigh through the slim cotton skirt of her dress.

"Don't distract the cook."

"But I *want* to distract the cook." He reached for her waist, but she twisted, hopping away to make good her escape.

"There's a bottle of wine in the cupboard," she said, pointing. "Why don't you make yourself useful and open it?"

Rutledge got to his feet and ambled over, making a detour to where Blaine stood at the sink. He wrapped his arms around her, giving her a big hug. She didn't protest.

"What's happened?" he teased. "Recognized the inevitable?"

"I'm hoping you'll get satiated and go away."

"But think of all the years of celibacy I have to make up for."

Blaine gave a laugh. "You don't expect me to fall for that one, do you? Not with all your expertise with bridal suites."

"An avid student need not be a practitioner."

"Tell it to the judge." She stepped over to the cupboard and handed him the bottle of wine. "It's been in my car since Prosser, so I hope it's all right."

"Carrying it around in your car, huh?"

"Yeah. Just in case I got lucky." She lifted the pot of spaghetti from the stove and took it to the sink, where she began pouring it into a colander.

"Have you?"

"What?"

"Gotten lucky?"

She gave him a coquettish grin. "It's not been too bad so far."

Rutledge put the wine on the counter and grabbed her brusquely, playfully nibbling at her neck. She gave a little shriek and tried to escape again, but he held her fast. The friction of their bodies aroused him almost immediately and he held her more tightly. "How about an appetizer before dinner?" he breathed into her ear. "I've lost my desire for food."

"You'd better recover it. This is homemade spaghetti sauce."

Rutledge gave her a last nip, then let her go. "Okay. I'll satisfy your culinary pride before I satisfy you."

She ran water over the pasta. "Pretty confident, aren't you?"

"You're such wonderful inspiration." He took the wine bottle and corkscrew from the counter and retreated to the table.

Blaine quickly prepared their plates, heaping his especially full, and carried them over. He poured the wine. When he had finished, he picked up his glass, eyeing her, taking special pleasure in the sight. He held the wineglass aloft, waiting for Blaine to take hers. When she picked hers up, he clinked the glasses together.

"To *my* Queen of Hearts," he said solemnly. It sounded presumptuous and proprietary, he knew, but he didn't care. It was the way he felt.

BLAINE'S CHEEK WAS AGAINST his shoulder. The sheet covered their bodies, protecting them from the cool air wafting in the open window. Moonbeams angled into the room between the curtains, and she listened to the night sounds outside. A coyote howled somewhere off in the distance, its cry both threatening and lonely.

She felt the need to talk, but wasn't sure if Cal was still awake. She lifted her head and looked at his face in the dim light. "Cal?"

"Hmm?"

"You awake?"

"Sort of."

"Sorry."

He squeezed her against him affectionately. "That's okay, I was just drifting."

She didn't say anything.

"What's the matter, Blaine?"

"I sort of wanted to talk."

"What about?"

She took a deep breath and let it out slowly. "Jason." She knew he was aware that she had had a long talk with the boy that afternoon, and she hadn't planned on burdening him with it unnecessarily. But something about the night and the silence made her want to get it out.

"What happened this afternoon?"

"He was just as sweet as could be. He wouldn't say anything about you, about my poker, about his problems. He just kept telling me he loved me."

"He's having trouble saying what's on his mind, that's all. It'll happen eventually."

"I realize now what's wrong. In the past, when we talked, I was always looking for assurance."

"Have you expressed that to him?"

"I hinted around, giving him opportunities to say something. Rosemary suggested I start out slowly and not hit him over the head with it."

"It'll come. Don't worry."

"I'm afraid it's too late, that I've already messed it up."

"Of course not. It's never too late."

Blaine snuggled against him and he kissed her lovingly. "You're so good, Cal. You don't know what it means to me that you're so supportive."

"I've been part of the problem. I want to be part of the solution, too."

"It's not just Jason. I've worried about Agnes, too."

"I'll handle Agnes. Don't worry about her."

"Have you heard any more?"

He hesitated. "We've confirmed she's behind the inquiry."

"I knew it."

"It'll be all right. I don't expect it to go any further."

"How can you know?"

"I can't, for sure."

"She's capable of anything. Have you learned more?"

"Rosemary talked to the caseworker in Washington. He asked whether you've been seeing Jason."

"You see! I knew this would happen. What'd Rosemary say?"

"She told the truth. That we've concluded you're integral to the therapy program, and have encouraged your participation."

"Agnes won't accept that."

"She has no choice."

"I wish I had your confidence." She trembled.

Cal held her close and stroked her head. "Relax, Blaine. I won't let anything happen. Trust me."

FOR THE REST OF THE WEEK Blaine did her best to trust in Cal. She worked with Rosemary and Jason for an hour or two each day. Sometimes the three of them talked together; sometimes it was just she and her son alone.

Blaine could tell the boy was inching toward unburdening himself. Several times he seemed on the verge of venting his feelings, but pulled back at the last moment. During one session the psychologist prodded him a bit, but he held fast.

Following Rosemary's suggestion, Cal stayed clear of Jason, but he came each evening to the foreman's house to be with Blaine. Usually they ate together, and then he would stay the night.

Friday evening they had a late dinner and afterward sat in the living room talking. It was warm and Blaine was wearing shorts and a T-shirt. They sat on the couch listening to music on her radio. Cal held her hand on his lap, running his finger over her palm.

She stared at their hands, mesmerized by the sensation. "I wish Jason wasn't such a worry," she said after a while.

"Rosemary feels there's been improvement."

"There has. I can tell he's getting ready to say what's been eating him."

"Then you should feel relieved."

"I guess what's been bothering me is that everything's so up in the air. Something's about to happen. I can feel it."

"Well, you'll be leaving the ranch at the beginning of the week. That's been hanging over both our heads."

"I have no choice."

"You could stay here."

"I can't either, and you know it."

"Why not?"

"Cal, one of these days we've got to stop pretending and face facts. You and I both have been living for the moment, forgetting the realities." She looked at him, feeling so terribly fond of him. She stroked his cheek. "Maybe it's been good for us, I don't know. I've had a wonderful time. I've let go, but I'll have to pay for it. Tomorrow will come and there'll be the inevitable hangover."

"I feel like a bottle of cheap booze."

Blaine laughed. "Not cheap booze. A fine wine."

"A hangover is a hangover."

She kissed him lightly. "Better a good wine than a bad one."

"Why are you so philosophical, Blaine? I'm not ready to give up."

"I haven't given up. Besides, we still have two more days together."

"I'm not going to be any more ready to throw in the towel then."

"Cal, I couldn't have spent this week with you if I hadn't told myself it was a vacation, a party. I planned for it to end before it even began. That's the only way to survive something like this."

He grimaced. "That's far too cynical and coldhearted for me."

"Would it have been better if I had stayed in Las Vegas?"

"We've been together because we wanted to be together. It's been an experiment—a successful experiment—and I don't see why it should end."

"You've buried your head in the sand. It was risky for me to come. If it hadn't been for the sessions with Rosemary, I probably wouldn't have agreed."

"Thanks."

"That's no reflection on you. It simply would have been selfish to come without justification."

His look showed annoyance. "I can't help feeling a little demeaned. I wouldn't have done a thing differently if Jason didn't exist."

"I don't feel any less for you than you feel for me, Cal."

He got up and walked impatiently across the room, his anxiety apparent. "Why are you so convinced there's something wrong with us being together?"

"There's nothing wrong with what we've had...what we've shared. But there's no future. You know that as well as I do."

He glared at her. "Why is that so obvious?"

"Because I'm thinking of life as it is—me, you, Jason, your role, my role, who we are."

"What do you think I'm thinking about?" he shot back.

"You're thinking about sex and emotion, honeymoon suites and passion."

"And that's so horrible?"

"It doesn't last. It turns to disappointment and hurt."

"Why are you such a damned pessimist?"

Blaine's eyes flashed. "I'm a realist!"

"So, what are you saying? You're in this just for the fun? I'm just another card game you're milking for what you can get? Is that it?"

"No, Cal."

They stared at each other, Cal plainly angry. His words had stung, but she tried not to let them upset her. It was part of the price of being strong. Men always took rejection hard, even if it was sympathetic and well-intentioned. She had been disparaged before—accused of being cold. More than once she'd been called the Queen of Broken Hearts.

"Why can't you give us a chance?"

"A chance for what? Dragging it out until one or both of us is hurt? Until you're finally ready to face facts and cash in?"

"Life isn't a card game, Blaine."

"It's more a card game than a fantasy, which is what you think it is."

"Why are you so sure?"

"Because I know!" She was beginning to grow angry herself. Tears started to form, but they were tears of anger. She got to her feet.

"You don't know how I feel!"

"How *do* you feel?" she snapped.

"I've come to realize that I love you."

Blaine stared at him, trembling. She hadn't quite expected that and, though she didn't doubt his sincerity, she sensed his intent was to put her off. "What's love, Cal? I love you, too, but so what? I mean, the world out there—what we face—doesn't give a damn about the way we feel."

"How can you say that?"

"What does it mean, that you love me? Tell me what it means!"

His expression grew stony. "Okay, I'll tell you what it means. It means we owe it to each other to be together, to express our love."

"No, that's not love. That's desire. If you love someone, you sometimes have to deny them, and yourself."

He stood looking at her. Blaine thought she saw disillusionment on his face. Maybe he was beginning to see through his blindness. He didn't move. He just stared.

"Do you hate me?" she asked.

He shook his head.

"What are you thinking?"

He shook his head again.

"I've got to know."

He sighed impatiently. "All right. I was thinking about a discussion we once had in a theology class at the seminary."

Blaine saw the solemnity on his face.

"We were debating whether God was by nature vengeful or loving. It's a rather elemental question," he said, staring blankly. "I concluded that the answer was not in the nature of things, but in each man's heart." He paused. "After listening to you, Blaine, I think the same can be said of love."

She waited.

"Maybe you *are* right," he said evenly. "Maybe I am blind." He turned and went to the door. "But I'd rather love blindly than heartlessly." He looked at her sadly before walking out.

THE NIGHT was a long and painful one for Blaine. By morning the sting of Cal's words had not abated. He thought her heartless when she was only trying to protect herself—and him. But if that was the price she'd have to pay, she would, for both their sakes.

It was apparent that there was no point in staying around. She would have packed up and left first thing that morning but it was visitors' day, and she wanted to say goodbye to Jason. She decided to wait till the afternoon, when things were a little quieter, to go see him.

She spent the morning packing and cleaning the house. Cal was unhappy with her, perhaps even bitter, but she hoped he would not hold it against her and be vengeful. The tragedy would be compounded if Jason were hurt by it, too.

After lunch Blaine sat on the porch waiting for the end of the visitors' day to draw near. She knew that Cal was busy, and that he might have decided they'd had their last conversation anyway, but she hoped he might come to her and let her know it was all right, that he didn't hate her.

In light of the way things had ended, his admission that he loved her was almost more painful than heartening. It was also irrelevant to the realities of their lives. She was convinced it would be better if they didn't love each other. Still, despite everything, there was a longing inside her that she couldn't fight—a weakness that was more formidable than she.

When a vehicle appeared over the ridge, Blaine felt her heart leap. But after a moment she realized it wasn't Cal's jeep, or any of the other ranch vehicles. It was a car, a limousine. She watched with curiosity as it approached. When it finally stopped in front of the house, she rose to her feet. The darkened passenger window slowly slid down, and Blaine saw the sour, wizened face of Agnes Kidwell.

CHAPTER FIFTEEN

"I'VE BEEN TO SEE my grandson," the old woman announced.

Blaine slowly walked to the car. She looked in the open window at the loathsome face.

"Jason told me you were living here at the ranch. Needless to say I was shocked, and appalled."

Blaine waited, knowing the worst was yet to come.

"And I've been to see Rutledge. He as good as admitted what's been going on between the two of you."

"What did he say?"

"He didn't need to say much. Women like you leave the mark of guilt on a man's face."

"What's that supposed to mean?" Blaine snapped.

"That once you got your claws into him, you managed to drag him down into the sewer with you."

"You're the one in the sewer, Agnes. You're the one who's out to hurt every chance you get."

"Save the indignation. Our opinions of each other don't need to be restated. We both know how we feel."

"Then why have you come?"

"To give a warning."

Blaine smiled cynically. "Oh?"

"I want you to stay away from my grandson. That's why he was sent down here—to be free of you for a while."

"You'll never keep me from my son. Never!"

"Well, if you won't do it for him, maybe you'll do it for your lover—the wayward priest."

"What do you mean?"

"Caleb Rutledge has important responsibilities. The authorities have placed a great deal of trust in him, putting all these boys under his care. They would be as appalled as I if they were to find out he's keeping a harlot practically under these children's noses—the mother of one of them, and a poker player, to boot."

"You're despicable."

Agnes leaned toward the open window. "I'll be plain. I want you off this ranch, away from Jason, and away from Cal Rutledge, for that matter. I don't want you coming around or visiting. And if you don't heed my words, I'll see that the proper authorities learn what's been going on."

"That's blackmail!"

"Call it what you like. But Rutledge's future is in your hands. I'll take this to the board of directors, to the licensing authority, whoever is necessary. I'll see that he and his school are discredited, if that's what it takes."

"You'd try to ruin Cal, try to destroy everything he's built, just to get your revenge on me?"

"I'm not concerned with revenge. I'm concerned with my grandson." Her eyes flashed. "Apparently I'm the *only* one who truly is!"

In her rage, Blaine began shaking.

Agnes's tone turned uncharacteristically compassionate, "Why don't you find yourself a rich cowboy and ride off into the sunset with him? You'd be doing yourself a favor, as well as Rutledge...not to mention Jason."

Blaine glared at the evil face, her anger boiling over. She wanted to strike Agnes, throttle her, do whatever she could to annihilate her. But Agnes saw the blood in her eyes and pressed the button to raise the window.

Blaine watched helplessly as the opaque glass slid up between them. Then, as the limousine glided away, she did all that was left to do: she kicked at the fender futilely with her booted foot.

THE DEALER FLICKED the cards with a snap of his wrist, sending one skidding along the felt to each of the players seated around the oval table. He made the circuit twice, then repeated the process, this time turning the cards up for everyone to see. After watching the deal, Blaine lifted the corner of her hole cards, then scanned the up cards in front of each player again.

She stayed in the first round but folded on the second, when the odds turned against her. As the hand was played out she leaned back, mentally calculating the money in chips before her. She was more than a thousand to the good.

While she waited for the next hand to be dealt, one of the idle dealers came over to the table and handed her a note. Blaine opened it, then looked up to see Caleb Rutledge standing outside the poker parlor, leaning against the railing. Though the face was dear to her, it evoked an uncomfortable feeling, a spark of fear. Why had he come?

She leaned back to whisper in the man's ear. "Would you tell the gentleman I'll be tied up for quite a while? And ask if I can't just call him tomorrow."

As the cards were being dealt, she watched the dealer walk over to Cal, relay the message, then retreat. Blaine looked over the table and checked her hole cards, trying to get her mind back into the game.

The trey of clubs was showing and it was her bet. She checked, passing the opportunity to the next player. As the bet moved around the table she glanced up through the thin cloud of smoke. Cal was moving along the railing to where a pit boss stood at the entrance to the parlor.

The bet was hers again and she called without having paid close attention to the betting. As the second up card was dealt, Blaine looked at Cal. He was still in conversation with the pit boss. What could they be discussing?

The betting progressed with Blaine staying in, though her concentration wasn't on the game. She had been playing conservatively. Gathering her wits, she could see enough to tell that there were no strong hands. Only one player had folded. Her up cards showed a straight, though her hole cards didn't support it. The situation was ripe for a bluff.

Perhaps disconcerted by Cal's presence, she suddenly felt impetuous. She raised five hundred dollars.

One decent hand among her competitors and the ploy would fail. The player next to her folded immediately. The next hesitated—probably holding two pair or three of a kind—then folded, too. Blaine felt the momentum swinging her way. Only someone with a high straight or better would call.

The last two players threw in their cards. The bluff had worked, and Blaine had picked up the better part of another thousand. The man next to her announced he was cashing in and, as he got up to go, he glanced at Cal, who still stood at the entrance to the parlor. Why didn't he leave?

Blaine began nimbly stacking the chips that had been pushed in front of her. The dealer got out a new pack of cards, opening the cellophane and removing the deck from the carton. Blaine finished stacking her chips as the dealer shuffled. Looking up again, she was surprised to see that Cal was no longer there.

Feeling relief and disappointment at the same time, she tried to focus her concentration on her opponents, evaluating their psychological and financial conditions after the last hand. They all had to be pondering what cards she had held. The impulsiveness of her decision had probably helped—it was important to be unpredictable.

But why had Cal come to the casino? She hadn't seen him the previous day, after her confrontation with Agnes. In fact, she had loaded the car immediately after the limousine had disappeared over the rise, then had gone to Jason for a quick farewell before leaving the ranch.

Her son had told her about Agnes's visit, but he had seemed oblivious to the implications and Blaine had seen no point in enlightening him. It had been easier to leave quietly. Jason had undoubtedly felt more comfortable about her going, anyway.

As she reflected, the pit boss came up next to her and set a tray of chips at the vacant seat, obviously escorting a new player to the game. She looked up and was shocked to see Cal Rutledge slip into the chair.

"Cal..."

"If you can't lick 'em, join 'em," he said with an easy grin.

"This is foolish," she whispered under her breath.

The other players and the dealer were looking at them with curiosity. Cal took his chips and stacked them on the felt tabletop, then handed the empty tray to the pit boss.

"Thanks," Cal said, as the man withdrew. He looked around the table, nodding.

"You don't have to do this," Blaine said, leaning toward him.

"I'm a little rusty," he said to the table at large. "I haven't played since high school."

Several of the men chuckled, and the dealer repressed a smile.

"Tell me if I get out of line," Cal added.

Blaine rolled her eyes.

The dealer called for the ante and Cal pushed out his chip. The cards began flying across the felt. The ex-priest shifted in his chair.

"What are you doing after the game tonight?" he asked her out of the corner of his mouth.

"I'm busy," she whispered. She lifted the corners of her hole cards and looked over the table. Cal was staring at her.

The man next to him bet. Cal hadn't checked his hole cards and the dealer looked at him, waiting. When he pushed in some chips, Blaine winced. It was her turn and she saw his bet, matching it. The player on the other side of her folded.

The next up card was dealt and Cal showed a pair. All the players checked, including him. He still hadn't bothered to look at his hole cards. Blaine silently groaned.

She dropped out when one of the other players showed three fours. But Cal, still only showing his pair, stayed in. She wondered if he understood how to play Seven-card Stud.

When the final hole card was dealt, the player with three of a kind showing bet the limit. Cal finally picked up his cards, holding them as though he were playing bridge. Someone chuckled, and Blaine felt sick. *Fold, fold!* she silently screamed.

To her dismay, Cal called. She couldn't help a small groan. The other man announced a full house, fours over sevens.

"I've got a full house, too," Cal announced, nonplussed.

He turned over three sixes, and several people gasped.

"Sixes over tens wins," the dealer announced.

Cal grinned, and the loser got up from his chair abruptly. "Damned beginner's luck."

As the pot was pushed over to Cal, he looked at Blaine. "Can we go? I'll split my winnings with you."

She turned red and looked at the other players. "I'm cashing out. Sorry."

There was grumbling around the table as Blaine put her chips in a tray. Cal got up and moved behind his chair.

"Don't forget your chips, mister," the dealer said.

"Oh." Cal took a tray and hurriedly filled it. Then he followed Blaine, who had already headed for the cashier. He came up next to her at the counter.

"You could have lost a thousand dollars on that one hand," she said without looking at him. "What kind of a statement were you trying to make?"

"No statement."

"You bet without even looking at your hole cards."

"I looked at the end."

"Why did you wait?" she snapped, unsure why she was so angry.

"We played that way when I was a kid. It's more exciting."

Blaine looked bewildered and turned to the cashier, who was counting her chips. She silently watched. When she had been paid, she glanced at Cal. "Take my advice and quit while you're ahead."

"I would have won no matter what. The worst that could have happened is I'd have gotten your sympathy."

"Well, you got my attention. What is it you want?"

"To talk to you."

The cashier had stacked and counted Cal's chips and began paying him. Distractedly he took the pile of one-hundred-dollar bills and stuffed them into his pants pocket.

"I don't see the point in talking," she said, as they walked away from the counter.

"You left without saying goodbye."

"I was in a hurry."

"Agnes was at the ranch yesterday to see Jason. I thought you ought to know."

"I'm aware of that already."

They were walking through the casino.

"Don't you think we ought to discuss it, then?" he asked.

"What is there to discuss?"

"How we're going to deal with it."

Blaine glanced at him. She avoided looking squarely into his eyes. "I've already decided. I'm going to concentrate on the Nationals. They're only a week and a half away."

"What about Jason?"

"I'll see him later."

Cal took her arm and stopped her. She looked at him with annoyance. "Blaine, what's the matter with you?"

She pulled her arm free. "Nothing."

"I talked with Agnes, too," he said, as they resumed walking.

"Oh?"

"Yes. We had a rather pointed discussion."

"I'm sorry to hear that. I wouldn't wish her on anyone."

"One of the reasons I came here was to tell you about it."

Blaine had decided to avoid all discussion about Agnes and to stay clear of Cal, at least until she figured out what to do about Jason. She didn't want to do anything that would hurt Cal, or the school, and she would never abandon her son, though she hadn't concluded how to deal with Agnes's threat. Still, she knew that what the old woman had told Cal might make a difference.

"Okay, what happened? What did she say?"

"She told me she was shocked that I had permitted you to stay at the ranch."

"Is that all?"

"I politely told her to mind her own business, so she didn't say much more."

"You *didn't*."

"I did."

"Then what'd she do?"

Cal shrugged. "She just left."

"What do you make of it?"

"Sour grapes."

Blaine felt her insides tighten. "There's more to it than that. She'll destroy you if she has to, in order to get her way with Jason."

"I don't think so."

"I know so. She told me as much."

"Told *you*?"

"Yes, she came to see me after she talked to you."

Cal stopped. "Agnes talked to you, too?"

She nodded. They were in the lobby, and he pulled her over to a couple of chairs. They sat down.

"What did she say?"

Blaine related the gist of the conversation. Cal sat staring.

"That woman's got to be stopped," he mumbled.

"I feel terrible. It's bad enough what I've done to Jason, but I can't bear the thought of ruining you, too."

"Nobody's going to ruin me, or the school. You don't have to worry about that."

"She's capable of anything, and it's not like she doesn't have the ammunition. How would it look to anyone else—your board of directors, for example?"

"My private life is my business, nobody else's."

"I'm not just another woman." She pointed toward the casino. "I'm the Queen of Hearts."

"You're the woman I love."

Blaine closed her eyes, feeling the weight of responsibility his words implied. "It's not worth it."

"That's for me to judge."

"I won't let you do anything foolish. Besides, I've left the ranch. That's all Agnes cares about."

"What about Jason? You aren't going to abandon him?"

"No, but there's no need to throw it in Agnes's face. I'll figure out something."

"Well, you don't have to sneak around. If we have to have it out with her, we will."

"But there's more than just her to consider. She's already got the courts involved. What if they take Jason away from your school, send him somewhere else?"

Cal fell silent.

"And are you really willing to risk everything you've built for just one boy? Is that fair to the others? Believe me, Agnes will take this to your board of directors and the authorities. You can bet they won't give a damn if you love me or not.''

He rubbed his chin, brooding. "I can't let her get away with it.''

"Sometimes discretion *is* the better part of valor.''

"*You* never backed down in the face of her threats, Blaine.''

"Yeah. And look where I am—and where Jason is.''

"It was your right.''

"I put myself first." She took his hand. "Don't worry about me. It's only for a year, if we're lucky. And I'll see my son somehow...if you'll help me.''

"I don't like the idea of letting her bully us.''

"We don't really have a choice.''

Cal looked at her, and Blaine could see he wasn't the type to give up easily. Jason had been the same way, unwilling to let the teasing pass. In both instances she was ultimately responsible. They weren't to blame.

"I'll have to think about it," Cal said soberly.

"Just don't do anything foolish. Agnes can't hurt us if we don't let her.''

"I still don't like it.''

Blaine got up and pulled Cal to his feet, too. "Come on," she said, trying to cheer him. "I'll let you buy me dinner with your winnings before you go home.''

FOR THE NEXT FEW DAYS Rutledge worked hard trying to catch up with both his business affairs and his duties at the school. He participated in several intense practices with the soccer team, and thought incessantly about the woman in Las Vegas preparing for the National Poker Championships.

Circumstances, and Agnes Kidwell, had put Blaine beyond his reach. Her absence was painful, frustrating. And the fact that she was passively willing to accept her fate made him want to take matters into his hands all the more.

What was it about a woman's passivity that impelled a man to action? The more hopeless the situation seemed to Blaine, the more strongly he felt about doing something about it.

But dealing with Agnes Kidwell was only part of the problem. One way or the other, that challenge could be met. There was a bigger, more fundamental question that had begun haunting Rutledge: what to do about Blaine herself?

He had allowed things to drift, letting his emotions regarding her find their own level. He felt love, and he wasn't afraid to express it, but it was a safe admission. Circumstances prevented him from acting because of the wall between them.

Rutledge was wise enough to know that meaningful relationships, particularly long-term ones like marriage, required a certain identity of spirit, if not a breadth of shared experience. People with common backgrounds and similar values made better partners, and that was what marriage was—a partnership.

On the surface, he and Blaine Kidwell were as different as night and day. Despite her pride, she still saw herself as the girl from the wrong side of the tracks. Her chosen profession wasn't the most socially acceptable he could think of, but Rutledge had come to see it in less critical terms than he had at first.

He now understood why she had been so upset at the suggestion that she was a gambler. Though the setting of her work was... colorful...she was in truth a professional involved in a contest of skill and guile, not unlike the investors she liked to compare herself to.

But more important than any of that was the person he had come to know. Blaine was loving, good-hearted, courageous, intelligent, honest, caring and strong—not a bad list of qualities for any person, let alone someone he loved.

Yet in spite of all that, they seemed always to be looking at each other through a pane of glass. The image he saw was vivid and real, but she was beyond his reach.

Rutledge knew that Jason was part of the explanation. Though he and the boy's mother had become virtual allies in the child's cause, their roles separated them. There was probably nothing that couldn't be overcome but, for the time being, there would be that distance between them.

However, there was no doubt that the most immediate and pressing problem was Agnes Kidwell. Her threat had created a formidable barrier, even as it deepened Rutledge's personal determination to act.

The problem was, he wasn't the only one who stood to lose. And that made a bold response problematical. He couldn't lightly risk the well-being of his charges. The more Rutledge thought about the dilemma, the more he understood Blaine's reaction. Still their chosen course of submission, passivity and resignation, ate at him.

Rosemary Hodges found him sitting alone at a table in the cafeteria one afternoon. She walked over, a cup of coffee in her hand. "Mind if I join you?"

"No, Rosemary, I'd enjoy the company."

"I saw your thoughtful expression and didn't know whether to leave you in peace or rescue you from your loneliness."

"Frustration, not loneliness."

"Blaine and Jason?"

"Yep."

Rosemary sipped her coffee. "Jason seems to be in a consolidation phase, so I haven't pressed him, but I take it the problem had to do with his grandmother's visit and Blaine's leaving."

"In a nutshell, yes."

"Is your frustration personal or professional?"

"Both."

The psychologist waited.

"You see, Rosemary, the problem is my hands are tied because other people's interests are at stake, not just mine. If I had only myself to worry about, it'd be easy."

"And your interests and their interests don't necessarily coincide?"

Rutledge shrugged. "I don't know. Blaine and I don't agree on how to deal with the problem, and I can't risk screwing things up for her."

"I don't understand."

"Agnes Kidwell is threatening to make a federal case out of our relationship if Blaine doesn't back off. Blaine would rather comply than risk something happening to Jason, or to me and the school."

"That's consistent with her tendency to sacrifice."

"Yes, but inconsistent with my tendency to take a problem by the throat and fight it to the death."

Rosemary reflected. "I wonder how Jason feels about it?"

"Well, as you know, we haven't talked much since the incident at the lake."

"Yes, partly at my suggestion. But I wonder if maybe it isn't time for the boy to enter into some of the rather weighty decisions that are being made."

"You think I should talk to him?"

"It might be interesting to know how he feels. As I understand it, Blaine's concerns are not so much for herself as for him."

"That's true."

"Well, maybe there ought to be three votes instead of two." She smiled. "That way there'd at least be a clear majority."

"Rosemary, have I ever told you you're a genius?"

"May I remind you of that the next time we discuss my salary?"

Rutledge got up. "Sure, go ahead and remind me." He grinned, then reached across the table and patted her hand. "But you'd better hope this works," he said, as he headed for the door.

CHAPTER SIXTEEN

THERE WAS A KNOCK on Rutledge's door. He looked up from his desk. "Come in."

The door opened first a crack, then wider. The familiar, refined features of Jason Kidwell appeared.

"Hi, Jason, come on in."

The boy's gray eyes were full of suspicion and bore a touch of alarm, reminding Rutledge of the way Blaine had looked that time he had accosted her in the hallway at the Chaparral. Jason closed the door behind him and stood there. Rutledge got up.

"I want to discuss something with you, Jason, but not in my official capacity as head of the school. I want to talk to you personally—man to man."

"What about?"

"Why don't we go into the living room? Since this isn't business, there's no need to sit here in the office." Cal went around the desk and led the way into the front room. "How about some juice or something?"

"No thanks."

"I'm going to have some cookies and a glass of milk myself. Why don't you join me?"

The boy shrugged. "All right."

"I'll go and get the stuff. Make yourself at home."

When Rutledge returned the boy was sitting in an armchair, his bare arms stretched out on the heavy padded upholstery. He looked nervous and uncomfortable. Rutledge put the plate of cookies and a glass of milk on the table in front of him, then sat on the couch opposite. He leaned forward and took a cookie from the plate, gesturing toward it.

"Help yourself."

Jason chose a cookie, leaned back and took a small bite, his uncertain eyes still on Rutledge.

"Not bad for store-bought," Rutledge said, after taking a bite. "Of course, they're not like what my mother made when I was a kid."

Jason didn't say anything.

"Does your mom make cookies?"

"Sometimes."

"She's a good cook, I know. I've been lucky enough to taste her cooking."

The boy waited, his eyes unaccusing but tentative.

"You're practically a man, Jason, with rights and responsibilities, just like me. You've got yourself to worry about, but also your family—your mom." He looked at the boy, who stiffly held the cookie in his hand. "I care about you both, and since there are some important issues concerning the two of you and me, I thought we ought to talk about them. Do you feel comfortable with that?"

"Yeah. It's okay."

"I don't know how much your mom has told you in the past and recently, but your grandmother and she don't see eye to eye about what's good for you."

"I know. They hate each other. Gram's nice to me, but really mean to Mom."

"How do you feel about that?"

"I wish they didn't fight."

"What do you think the problem is?"

"Gram's jealous. Mom says it's been that way ever since she married my dad. It's the only thing I don't like about Gram."

"Well, there's more now. Apparently your grandmother intends to make an issue out of your mom's and my relationship. She intends to use it against us to have her way with you."

"What do you mean?"

"She's threatened to make trouble for me and the school if your mother doesn't stay away from the ranch."

"Why does she want Mom to stay away?"

"So that she won't see you."

Jason fell silent, his look brooding. He leaned forward and put the uneaten cookie on the table.

"To be blunt, Jason, I'd like to tell your grandmother to mind her own business, but your mom's afraid. She doesn't want your grandmother to send you somewhere else where she might not be able to see you. And, like I said, she doesn't want trouble for me and the school."

The boy bowed his head.

"I admire your mother for her self-sacrifice, but since this problem mostly affects you, I thought it would be a good idea to find out what you think we ought to do."

Jason looked at him questioningly.

Rutledge sipped his milk and took another bite of cookie. "I care for your mom very much, Jason. She's important to me, just like she's important to you. Your grandmother has created a problem between us, and I don't think that's right.

"I also think that your mother should be able to see you when she wants, without being afraid. She shouldn't have to sneak visits with you. In effect, your grandmother has gotten between you and your mother just like she's gotten between your mother and me. As I see it, we can either let it happen, or we can do something about it."

"What can I do, Father Rutledge?"

"I guess you can decide if it's worth taking a risk to set things right."

"You mean, take a chance they might send me somewhere else?"

"Yes. That's the danger."

"I don't know. I'm not afraid, but..."

"It's not an easy situation for any of us, Jason. I've thought a lot about it, and I've come to some conclusions. The problem boils down to who your mother is, and what she does."

"You mean her poker."

"Yes, her poker. Your grandmother has used that against her with you, and now she's doing it with me. The fact that your mom and I are friends—that we care for each other—has created some awkwardness for you, I know. Our relationship might raise some questions in other people's minds, too, like the board of directors of the school, or the government authorities who are responsible for us."

"Did Gram say she'd tell them?"

"She's threatened to, yes."

The boy's mouth hardened into a grimace.

"I may be guilty of bad judgment, Jason, and it's been especially unfortunate that you've suffered because of it. But I've come to realize the problem has to do with how your mother is perceived—what people think of her. That's where her poker comes in. If she did something else for a living, I don't think there'd be a problem."

Jason looked down sadly.

"But you know what? I don't think that's your mother's fault. I think it's Agnes's fault and my fault and your fault. None of us should be thinking about anything but the kind of person Blaine is, the kind of mother she is.

"Maybe your mother feels some guilt about her job, but she shouldn't. If other people want to look down on her, we can't do anything about that. But we can sure do something about how we feel.''

"I love Mom.''

"Sure you do. And I do, too, Jason. But we've both been guilty of apologizing for her—feeling shame, even—when there's no need to. You've fought for her in the past with your fists, and I'm wondering if it isn't time to fight for her again. This time, though, we'll use our minds and our hearts.''

"You mean, we ought to tell Gram off?''

"Yes. And maybe we ought to tell all the others how we feel. Maybe your grandmother's threats would lose their sting if we stand up on our hind legs and do what's right. If we love your mother and let people know we're proud of her because of the kind of person she is, maybe they'll judge her fairly, if it comes down to that.''

"I'll tell Gram, or the judge, or anybody else.''

"Are you willing to take the chance they'll send you away, maybe to a school where you won't be able to see your mother? Your grandmother might choose to make a fight of it.''

Jason nodded.

"All right. I won't wait for Agnes to start spreading stories. I'm going to go to the board and to the juvenile authorities in Washington and lay all the cards on the table.''

"What if Mom's mad?''

"I think in fairness I'll have to talk to her. Maybe we both should. What do you think?''

"I just want her to be happy.''

"Then let's start with a family conference.''

"Okay, Father Rutledge.''

Cal thought for a moment. "Tell you what. Whenever the other boys aren't around, you can call me Cal.''

Jason smiled. "All right.''

"Now, how about you and me doing some serious cookie eating before we get back to work.''

The boy reached for his half-eaten cookie and Rutledge, watching him, eased back on the couch. He felt relieved, his candor with Jason having cured the pain in his own soul every bit as much as it might have helped the boy.

BLAINE STARED at Cal's fireplace. It looked strangely dead and irrelevant in the middle of a summer day, but she remembered the crackling fire she had shared with him not many weeks before. That night had been the beginning. The uncommon ex-priest had not only given her back her son that evening, he had begun insinuating himself into her life, as well.

Now she had come full circle. Once more at a point of crisis, she was in danger of losing the son she had only recently reclaimed.

Cal had called the day before, summoning her to the ranch for a strategy meeting, but she couldn't help feeling all that was left for her was to sanction what had already been decided. She was afraid, and angry. Cal came back into the room.

"He's at a beginners' soccer clinic, Blaine. The dorm counselor said he'd send Jason over as soon as he gets back. It shouldn't be long." He sat down next to her on the couch and took her hand.

She studied his face, wishing her worry hadn't made her angry. "I wish you'd talked to me before you discussed this with Jason."

"I know you're upset, but I'm convinced that bringing him into this was the right thing to do."

"But it's such a heavy responsibility to shove on a boy."

"I wouldn't have acted if I hadn't thought he was up to it."

"Cal, I'm his mother."

"Yes, but that doesn't give you a monopoly on wisdom, even so far as he's concerned."

"I don't know that your record with Jason is all that much better!" Blaine snapped.

Cal took the blow in silence.

She sighed. "I'm sorry, that was unfair."

"The point is, nothing is settled for sure. I decided not to put the wheels in motion until Jason and I had spoken with you. If I'd talked to you first, you'd probably have objected, then I'd be put in the position of having to proceed against your will."

"What's to stop you from going ahead now, even if I'm opposed to your plan?"

"Nothing, except that I've already decided to respect your wishes on the matter. If the three of us can't agree, then we won't do it. But I felt very strongly that Jason ought to have a chance to give his input. He's a young adult, Blaine, and not your baby anymore."

She got up and paced. "Yes, that seems to be a recurrent theme."

"Every parent has to face that at one time or another. You're just doing it in a more dramatic fashion than most."

She looked at him impatiently. "What bothers me is that you've put me in the position of being a no-sayer."

"You can't protect him from the realities of life forever, even when they mean a possible disagreement with you. Maybe especially then."

"If you didn't have so much at stake in this, too, I'd feel resentful. I guess the worst I can think is that you're being foolish by wanting to bring this all out into the open."

"Right now I just want you to satisfy yourself that Jason wants this. The two of you can talk here alone—"

"No, we'll go out for a walk, if you don't mind. We used to do that at home when we wanted to talk."

"Whatever you prefer, Blaine."

They looked at each other, neither of them moving for a long time.

"You know," he finally volunteered, "the forgotten casualty in this whole nasty business is us."

Blaine turned and paced again. "No, you don't have to remind me about that. I've suffered over it these past days and nights as much as I've suffered over anything." She glanced at him. "That honeymoon of ours was a big mistake."

"Whatever the future holds, I'll never regard it as a mistake."

"Cal, you'll always be a romantic. A hopeless one."

"And you, the frustrating realist."

"That's why the honeymoon was cut short," she said sardonically. "We're incurably different."

"No we aren't. Our strengths and weaknesses haven't fully blended yet, that's all."

There was a knock at the door and Cal went to answer it. A moment later he returned with Jason in tow, still wearing his soccer clothes.

"Hi, Mom."

"Jason!" She went over to him and they embraced. "You're all wet," she said, stepping back and looking him over.

"I'm sweaty from soccer."

"And what's happened to your knee?"

The boy looked down at the skinned place where he was stained with grass, dirt and a trace of blood. "It's no big deal."

She glanced at Cal. Jason looked at the two of them.

Blaine put her hand on his shoulder. "Cal's told me about your talk, and I thought maybe you and I could chat about it before we make a final decision."

"Okay."

"Does your leg hurt too much to go out for a walk?"

"Naw."

"I'll be in my office," Cal said, "so come on back when you're done."

Blaine and the boy went out. They headed across the compound in silence. Kevin and another boy came in the other direction.

"Hi, Mrs. Kidwell," the boy said, waving.

"Hi. How are you, Kevin?"

"Okay." He grinned at them sheepishly and continued on with his companion.

"Have you two been getting along okay?" she asked Jason, when they'd walked a bit farther.

"Yeah. He's all right."

"The boys aren't teasing you about me any longer?"

"No, all everybody cares about now is the soccer season."

"Good to know our scandal can be so easily forgotten."

"Ah, Mom, you worry about things too much."

"That's what Cal says, too."

They had reached the head of the road leading to the foreman's house. The boy glanced at her. "Do you love him?"

"Cal?"

"Yeah."

"Well...yes, I care for him a great deal, but..."

"Don't worry, he already told me he loves you, so I know it wasn't just a roll in the hay."

"Jason!"

He shrugged. "I know about those things. You don't have to act shocked."

"I'm not acting shocked. I *am* shocked."

"I'm not a kid anymore, Mom."

"No, I'm beginning to appreciate that."

They were out on the road. The wind gusted, kicking up dust now and then. Blaine's hair blew across her face and she looked at her son, seeing a different, more mature young man than the image of him she carried in her mind.

"So, what do you think of Cal's idea of having it out with your grandmother?"

"It's not just Gram."

"No, you're right. I should have said having it out with everyone."

"I think it's okay."

"If it doesn't work, you know what it might mean. We might not be able to see each other, at least not like we have been here."

"Yeah, but Gram's been mean to you for too long. I don't think what she's doing is very fair."

"It isn't, but that's your grandmother's way."

"I knew she hated you, but I didn't know she was like that."

Blaine pulled the hair from her face. "Your grandmother's a desperate and misguided woman. The thing is, she probably means well. Despite the fact that I dislike her every bit as much as she dislikes me, I know she cares about you, Jason. She loves you."

"Then why does she have to make trouble?"

"She doesn't see it that way. She thinks she's looking out for your interests."

"Somebody ought to tell her."

"That's what Cal wants to do. But I know her better than just about anyone, and I'm sure she won't buy it."

"Maybe if I tell her I don't mind you playing poker she'll get off our backs."

Blaine put her arm around Jason's shoulders. "I think it's a little more complicated than that, honey."

"Well, it's the truth. I don't mind anymore. I'm glad you do."

She gave a little laugh at her earnestness. "Let's don't go overboard. It's enough if you accept me as I am."

"Cal said if I can fight for you with my fists, I can fight for you with my mind. That's what I want to do."

"He said that?"

"Yeah."

"Did Cal talk you into this, Jason?"

"No, he told me what he thought, and I think he's right. We both love you, so why not?"

She gave him a squeeze. "I'm flattered by all the men wanting suddenly to defend my honor. But I wonder if it isn't a case of misguided zeal."

"Of what?"

"Cowboys and Indians."

"I'm no kid, Mom."

She chuckled. "Let's hope Cal's not, either."

"He's not a bad guy."

Blaine smiled whimsically. "No, he's not, is he?"

They walked on in silence for a moment.

"Can we go back? I want to take a shower."

"Sure."

She spun around and they headed back, just as a tumbleweed came rolling down the road toward them. Jason took a couple of quick steps and gave the weed a soccer-type kick, knocking it into the ditch. Catching up with him, she put her arm through the boy's.

"Is it true that you don't mind my poker, or were you just saying that?"

"It's true. You're a good person and a good mother. That's what people have to find out. Including Gram."

BLAINE AND ROSEMARY HODGES sat in the back. Jason sat in the copilot's seat, intently watching everything Cal did. When they were airborne and headed north, Blaine looked at the ribbon of highway she had driven down from Washington. Though it was only weeks, it seemed like a lifetime ago. So much had happened, and yet the most critical event of all was in the offing. Jason's future depended on what would happen in Prosser the next morning.

Two days earlier Blaine had decided to go ahead with Cal's plan. She had moved back into the foreman's house so as to be available for the flight up to Washington as soon as Cal had worked out arrangements with the state juvenile authorities and Agnes's lawyer. An informal hearing was set to review the case.

Cal had also scheduled a special meeting of the school's board of directors in Las Vegas the following week, where he intended to disclose everything that had occurred. Blaine asked him what he planned to say, but he wouldn't tell her exactly, saying she had enough to worry about with Jason, and didn't need his problems to contend with, as well.

So much was at stake. Blaine had a sickly feeling of dread, but she felt a sense of relief, too, probably not unlike the way an accused person would feel when they finally got their day in court, though she knew Cal wouldn't approve of the analogy.

Rosemary worked with them to prepare for the hearing, and it was ultimately decided that she would make the trip as well, to bring a sense of objectivity to the proceedings. They all recognized the fact that Cal was hardly an impartial observer.

Out the window of the plane, Blaine watched the gradual change of hue in the intermontane topography. There was a brief glimpse of Lake Tahoe to the west, then Reno and, farther along, the vast wasteland of northeastern Nevada.

After several hours they crossed into eastern Oregon. Cal pointed out the Broken Lava Beds in the great open plain, and explained the geological formations to Jason, who was entranced with everything he saw.

The noise of the engines made it hard for Blaine to hear most of what Cal and Jason said during the trip, but the budding camaraderie between them was unmistakable. Blaine was surprised by it, but also fascinated. How could her son's jealousy turn so suddenly to friendship?

Whenever Blaine had seen Jason interacting with men, she wondered how deprived he had been growing up without a father. But the few men she had been involved with had never spent much time with the boy, so she hadn't really played the game of imagining him with a stepfather.

Caleb Rutledge was the first one she had cared about who had had a relationship with Jason, and it intrigued her to think of the three of them living together someday.

In light of their current mission, it was a particularly dangerous game she played. But Blaine found herself lapsing into such fantasies with increasing frequency anyway.

It was weakness. It subjected her to the possibility of needless hurt and disappointment. But it was impossible to resist. Cal loved her. That had to count for something. Or was it fool's gold?

As they neared the Columbia River, the irrigation circles began appearing on the rich, arid soil, looking from the air like the work of some colossus with a giant cookie cutter. Blaine stared at the distinctive landscape, the place that had been home to her all her life, remembering strange things, like the windstorms out of the south that carried so much dust people used to say the Oregon wheat fields were coming. It was a familiar place, but one full of poignant memories.

Cal soon grew busy with the landing formalities as they neared the Pasco Airport. Blaine watched Jason's keen excitement, and felt a sudden stab of sorrow when she thought of the tragedy that had befallen the boy. Why couldn't she just be wondering whether the man beside him might one day be a father to him and teach him to fly, rather than worrying that they all might be on the verge of being pulled apart from one another?

"Seat belts on back there?" Cal asked over his shoulder.

Rosemary, who had been reading, looked at Blaine, and they both said they were ready. Jason leaned forward and peered over the dash at the wide landing strip dead ahead, five miles or so away. Cal spoke to the tower and adjusted the throttles and flaps. Blaine looked out at the railroad and auto bridges spanning the Columbia to the west of their approach path, and knew it would be a fateful return.

CHAPTER SEVENTEEN

THE NEXT MORNING Cal and Rosemary were already in the coffee shop of the motor hotel when Blaine and Jason made their way down. Cal was reading the paper and Rosemary her book when they approached the table.

"Good morning," he said, smiling.

Blaine scooted into the rounded banquette next to Cal, and Jason followed her.

"You're looking bright and alert, Jason," Rosemary said.

Blaine patted his hand. "He slept like a log."

"The buttermilk pancakes are great," Cal said, "if you like 'em."

"Yeah. Sure do," the boy replied.

The waitress came with menus and, while Jason read, Cal leaned toward Blaine. "How's the mother holding up?"

"Didn't sleep more than an hour or two, of course. I'm more nervous than I was for my first big tournament."

"Don't worry. It'll be all right."

His knee pressed against her, and Blaine wished she could just let him hold her in his arms.

There was plenty of time before they had to be at the courthouse in Prosser, so they had a leisurely breakfast, the adults chatting and drinking coffee while Jason put away a double order of pancakes. When they were finished, Blaine and Rosemary went back to their rooms briefly while Jason went with Cal to pay the bill and bring the rental car to the main entrance.

Jason sat in front again, directing Cal through the Tri-Cities and to the highway leading to Prosser. The sights were familiar, yet vaguely depressing to Blaine, primarily because of the association with the hardships she and her son had been through.

The courthouse, which evoked the most painful memories of all, sat in a square surrounded by large shade trees. They went in a side entrance, climbing the steep marble stairs that were worn by the feet of generations of citizens. Blaine was aware of the tension and nervousness they all felt, and put her arm around Jason's shoulders while they waited for Cal to locate the meeting room.

They were about fifteen minutes early and sat for a while on the wooden benches in the hallway. Jason grew quiet and somber, sitting especially close to Blaine as they waited. She tried to maintain a calm demeanor, but agonized inside, doubting more strongly than ever that she should have agreed to the showdown.

After a while Cal and Rosemary went into the hearing room to discuss procedures, and Blaine and Jason were left alone. Blaine reached over and patted his knee.

"No matter what happens, honey, I want you to know I'm proud of you. You're doing this more for me than yourself, and I'll never forget it."

Jason was touched by her words but he didn't respond. As they sat quietly they heard the heavy clicking of heels coming down the hall. They turned to see Agnes Kidwell walking toward them.

She had on a dark wool suit, despite the heat. Her handbag was large and made of black leather. Following behind Agnes was her lawyer, John Bertrum, a heavyset bald man, who, as Blaine remembered, spoke eloquently and with vigor, though his voice always seemed to lack conviction.

Agnes paused briefly in front of them and looked down at the boy. "Good morning, Jason."

"Morning, Gram," he mumbled.

The old woman gave Blaine only a fleeting glance, then proceeded farther up the corridor. She sat on another bench and they heard the lawyer say he would go into the hearing room and call her when they were ready.

Blaine sat immobile, though she squeezed Jason's hand. She didn't look at Agnes, but felt her ominous presence just the same. She closed her eyes and asked herself if and how it could all have been avoided.

A few minutes later Cal stepped into the hallway and asked all three of them to come in. Agnes, who was nearest the door, got up and strode purposefully past Cal without acknowledging his presence. Blaine and Jason followed.

Inside the room was a large rectangular table with chairs all around. Rosemary sat at one end, and on the far side were a man and woman from the juvenile division of the state Correctional Department. The man, who was middle-aged and a little rumpled, introduced himself as William Dobbs. Then he introduced his associate, a younger plain-looking woman.

"Please be seated," he said.

Agnes went to the far end of the table, opposite Rosemary. Her lawyer sat next to her. Cal, Blaine and Jason sat across from the state officials.

"This is an informal hearing—a meeting really," Dobbs said, "initiated at your request, Mr. Rutledge. Accordingly, we will dispense with all formality. However, anything said here could provide the basis for a more formal hearing, which could lead to official action by the department, or the courts. I think you should all be aware of that before we proceed."

Blaine felt her stomach clench. She looked at Jason, who was somber, and beyond him at Cal, whose expression was intense. Rutledge was leaning slightly forward, obviously anxious to get on with the proceedings.

"Perhaps we should begin with you, Mr. Rutledge," Dobbs said, "since this meeting is being held at your request."

"Yes, thank you, Mr. Dobbs. As I indicated to you on the telephone, I thought it would be a good idea if we review the decision that was made to send Jason to the Rutledge Ranch and School for Boys. Quite frankly, my actions as head of the school have been questioned by Mrs. Agnes Kidwell, the boy's grandmother. Rather than leave things in doubt, I felt the matter should be brought into the open."

Blaine listened as Cal went on to recount the events beginning with Agnes's original visit to the ranch. She cringed inwardly as he began discussing his developing relationship with her.

His voice was measured, but earnest. He had the sound of a man speaking from the heart and, though she had good reason to be embarrassed, Cal's words moved her and she felt pride.

When he began describing their love affair, John Bertrum interrupted. "I'm wondering, Mr. Dobbs, whether it's appropriate to have the boy present for this."

The official looked questioningly at Rutledge.

"I would agree," Cal began, "that under normal circumstances it might be something to avoid. But, in a way, it's the essence of why we're here. My behavior and the boy's mother's behavior have been made the issue.

"The allegation is that our actions adversely affect Jason. The best way to determine if that's true is to bring things out in the open. The question is whether my effectiveness has been compromised, and hence the school's. Also, Blaine's fitness as a mother is an underlying issue—perhaps even the central issue."

"Why is that?" Dobbs asked.

"I'm convinced that were it not for Mrs. Agnes Kidwell's strong doubts on that score, none of this would be necessary. I don't think the problem is so much what Blaine has done, as it is who she is. Likewise, I don't think I'm being condemned for what I've done in private, but for the character of the woman I've chosen."

Agnes, who had been sitting in a stony silence, bristled. "That's true," she said. "Blaine *is* the issue."

"Just a minute, Mrs. Kidwell," Dobbs said. "You can say your piece later." He nodded to Cal. "Go ahead with your statement."

"I realize this isn't a trial in the formal sense," Cal continued, "but I think that Blaine has been put in a position of having to prove her innocence. I talked her into coming here because I think it's time the truth about her as a human being and a mother be known."

Cal looked up the table at Agnes. "I wish Mrs. Kidwell could be convinced of what I believe but, if she can't, I want as a minimum that others concerned know the truth. I want our actions and policies at the school to be judged on the basis of their appropriateness for Jason, not on Blaine's virtue or lack thereof."

"But that's absurd!" Agnes interjected. "This man has encouraged the involvement of the very woman who's responsible for the boy's problems. Mr. Rutledge's motives may be sound, but that woman's duped him. It's like inviting the fox into the chicken coop."

"Please, Mrs. Kidwell," Dobbs said. He looked at Cal. "Maybe you can elaborate on your program with regard to the boy—how the mother has been involved, and so forth."

"Certainly. I've brought along our school psychologist, Mrs. Hodges, for that very purpose."

Jason sat listening to Rosemary, feeling empty inside, knowing better than anybody what they were really fighting over. He looked down the table at his grandmother and wished she didn't hate his mother so.

Gram wasn't a horrible person, but she was so mean to his mother that he found it hard to love her. It was as if she was blind. Father Rutledge could talk all day, and that wouldn't change. If only *he* could do something.

Rosemary was describing his therapy program.

Jason liked Rosemary, and she made him feel good when he talked to her, but he knew without listening to her words that nothing she said would impress his grandmother. The psychologist couldn't be any more convincing than Father Rutledge. Gram just didn't understand.

He looked at the old woman again and caught her eye. She gave him a faint smile, but there was hurt on her face, and sadness, too. Jason knew there was a lot going on in her head, and much of it probably had to do with his father. He was the one who really made Gram sad.

Poor Gram. She was mean to Mom, but it wasn't really her fault. She didn't understand that he loved his mother more than anything, and probably that his dad had, too.

After a while Jason didn't hear anything. He just saw the worry on his mother's face. There was a different kind of pain on Gram's face. He felt like a soccer ball in between them.

The problem was, Gram was afraid—afraid she'd lose. Mom was worried what would happen, but he knew she didn't worry about his love. That was the difference.

After a while the man from the juvenile division started talking again and Jason realized they were going to take a break for lunch. The chairs around him started making noises as the people at the table began getting up.

Jason saw his grandmother's eyes fixed on him. They seemed to glisten, as though she was ready to cry. He had never seen his grandmother cry. He saw her try to smile, and then she turned away.

Gram's lawyer was conversing with Mr. Dobbs. Mom was talking to Cal and Rosemary, so Jason decided to go over to his grandmother. She looked surprised when he approached.

"Well, not afraid of your old grandmother, in spite of everything?"

"No, Gram. Why would I be afraid?"

She looked across the room at the others, who were still in conversation. "I would have guessed they had you hating me by now."

"I don't hate anybody."

She lifted her chin as she often did, studying him. "I'm sorry you have to go through this, Jason."

"I don't mind."

The woman smiled. "That's brave of you."

"You know, Gram, I wish you'd stop being mad at Mom."

Agnes looked up at Blaine, whose back was still to them. "Is that what she tells you?"

"It's kind of obvious."

She gave a half smile. "Yes, I suppose it is."

"I still wish you wouldn't."

"Jason, you're too young to understand these things."

"No, I'm not. I'm not a little kid anymore."

"I have nothing to say to you about your mother."

"Maybe that's what's wrong. Maybe we should talk about Mom. I know her a lot better than you do."

"You are growing up, but you're still a boy."

"I think you don't want to know the truth about Mom."

John Bertrum stepped to Agnes's side. "We'll be reconvening after lunch," he said. "If you don't mind, I'll run over to my office and you can join me there after you've eaten."

"That'll be fine, John."

The lawyer took his briefcase and headed for the door.

The others had ended their discussion and Cal came over to Agnes and Jason. He nodded toward Agnes, trying, it seemed, to look friendly.

"We're going to lunch now, Jason," he said.

The boy looked at his grandmother, who lifted her chin again. "What about you, Gram?"

"I'll be fine. I eat alone nearly every day."

Jason glanced back at his mom, who stood waiting with Rosemary, then at his grandmother. "Can I eat with you?"

She looked at Cal. "Well..."

"I'll ask Mom," he said, and went across the room. Agnes Kidwell and Caleb Rutledge looked at each other with equal surprise.

JASON TOOK A DRINK of milk and gave his grandmother a smile. She still seemed amazed that he was actually with her, having lunch.

"How come you have a funny look on your face, Gram?"

"To be honest, I still can't believe your mother let you come with me."

"She's not as bad as you think. That's what I was tryin' to explain."

"She's your mother. A child can't be objective about their parents."

"Kids aren't stupid, Gram."

"I wasn't implying you're stupid—"

"Don't you think I'd know if she was a rotten mother?"

"You have nothing to compare."

"What do you have?"

"I've lived a long time, Jason. I not only look at this personally, there are the standards of the community to consider, as well."

"I don't know about that, but I know that she's good. Father Rutledge and Rosemary say so, too."

"They want you to believe that."

"But they couldn't make me feel she was bad even if that's what they wanted me to think."

Agnes sighed. "There's no way I can explain it to you."

"What are you afraid of, Gram? Mom never hurt anybody."

"There are many ways to hurt. What happened to you may not seem like an attempt to hurt, but she's responsible, and it was inexcusable."

"What about my dad?"

"What about him?"

"Was it your fault he got killed, just because you were his mother?"

"That was different. He was a grown man."

"But he was your kid once. Didn't he ever get into trouble, or fights and things?"

"Your father was a good boy."

"So am I, Gram."

She bit her lip. "Yes, of course you are. I have no quarrel with you. It's your mother I don't see eye to eye with."

"Do you think she's horrible because she plays poker?"

"That's part of it."

"What's the other part?"

Agnes hesitated. "I don't think she's a very good influence."

"She doesn't tell me to do bad things. It was my idea to punch out Brian, not hers."

"No, of course she didn't tell you to do it."

"Then why are you mad at her?"

The old woman shook her head. "You're just too young to understand, Jason."

"Gram, I think you're the one who doesn't understand."

She stared at him.

"I love Mom, and she loves me. She'd do just about anything for me. She makes me wash and brush my teeth. She makes me study and save my money. She even told me that you love me."

Jason looked at his grandmother and could see the tears starting to well. She took a handkerchief from her purse and dabbed the corners of her eyes.

"Please, Gram. Let me stay at Father Rutledge's school and see Mom when I want to. That judge might think I'm a juvenile delinquent, but I'm a good kid, just like my dad."

Agnes bit her lip, but it was no use. The tears began spurting. She wiped her eyes furiously. Then, when she managed to gain control again, she reached into her purse and took out a twenty-dollar bill, putting it on the table. "Come on, Jason," she said in a hoarse whisper, "I've got to get you back."

BLAINE AND CAL slowly walked under the trees surrounding the courthouse. It was a blazing hot day, but in the shade it was tolerable. She wore a pale pink cotton dress with a string of ivory beads and white sandals. Cal put his hand on her shoulder, apparently sensing her need for reassurance.

"What do you suppose Jason had in mind, asking to go to lunch with her?" she asked.

"Maybe he felt sorry for her."

"Yes, Agnes is a pathetic creature when you think about it. I've had her at my throat for so long that I tend not to see anything but the evil. In his eyes she must seem more worthy of compassion."

"We're all worthy of compassion," Cal said solemnly. "It's getting over the walls that separate us that's hard."

"Well, maybe Jason's done that with his grandmother. I hope for both their sakes that he has."

They stopped at a bench and sat down.

"What do you think'll happen, Cal?"

"I don't know. My guess is these officials aren't particularly excited by anything they've heard one way or the other. I suspect they'll take their cue from Agnes. If she wants to make a big deal of it, they may feel obligated to press ahead, at least with a formal hearing. Your guess is as good as mine how that'll come out, but I can't believe they'd decide against you without proof that Jason's being hurt."

"Always the optimist."

"What's the realist's view?"

"I'm afraid to think."

Cal pulled Blaine against him and kissed her on the temple. "However it comes out, we'll deal with it together."

She caressed his cheek with her fingertips. "I want you to know that I was touched by what you said about us in there. Even if it meant nothing to everyone else present, it meant a great deal to me."

He kissed her fingers. "I hope with all my heart it helped."

Blaine let her head drop on his shoulder, thinking how much she loved him, and how ironic it was that they were sitting together in front of the courthouse in her hometown. Fifteen years ago—or two months ago, for that matter—who would have imagined that the girl from the wrong side of the tracks and a former Episcopal priest from

Massachusetts would be sitting together, holding hands, on that bench?

Cal looked at his watch. "We'd better go inside."

They walked together hand in hand up the steps of the courthouse. Blaine felt better about herself, and what had happened, than she had in a long, long time. Now, if she didn't lose her son, if things worked out with Jason, life would be just about perfect.

When they got back to the meeting room, Rosemary and the two officials were there, but the others hadn't returned. It was still early, so they sat quietly and waited. After a few moments the door opened and Jason walked in. He took his seat between Blaine and Cal.

"Where's your grandmother?" she asked.

"She went to Mr. Bertrum's office. She told me to walk on back."

Cal and Blaine looked at each other. Dobbs moved impatiently in his chair. Several minutes later the door opened again, and John Bertrum came in.

"Sorry. Sorry to be late. I was conferring with my client, Mr. Dobbs. She's declined to be present this afternoon, but asked that I make a brief statement on her behalf."

"All right. We're all here. Go ahead."

"Mrs. Kidwell has asked me to express her appreciation to you, Mr. Dobbs, for your concern over the welfare of her grandson. Although this proceeding was initiated by Mr. Rutledge, she is aware that it was instigated on the basis of her concerns. She asked me to inform you that she is personally satisfied that Jason's well-being is being met at the Rutledge Ranch and School for Boys. She joins with Mrs. Blaine Kidwell in asking that no change be made by the juvenile division in the placement of the child."

Blaine and Cal looked at each other, then she put her arms around Jason, who gave a whoop and clapped his hands.

Dobbs looked around the table, then at the lawyer again. "Is that all?"

"Yes, Mr. Dobbs."

"Well," the man said, shuffling the papers in front of him, "I suppose the exercise has been useful in informing us on the disposition of the case. Mr. Rutledge, so that there might be a permanent record in addition to our notes, could I ask that you submit a written report summarizing what you told us this morning?"

"Yes, certainly."

"Unless someone has something further to say, I see no reason why we can't adjourn."

"We have nothing further," Cal replied.

They all got up and Blaine embraced Cal, then Rosemary. John Bertrum walked over to them. He addressed Blaine.

"Mrs. Kidwell asked me to give you this note," he said, and handed her an envelope. Then he left.

Blaine tore it open and read.

Blaine,
After talking with my grandson, I realized he could not be the person he is if you were the woman I thought you to be. I'm sorry I never had the sense to recognize this before.

Agnes

CHAPTER EIGHTEEN

IT WAS DARK by the time they had gotten Jason back to the dorm and Rosemary on her way home. Blaine put her arm through Cal's as they walked across the compound. The night air was soft, fragrant. She pressed her body against him.

"I still can't believe it. It's like a dream," she said. "All these years and then a little note comes saying it's all over."

"Jason has opened other eyes besides Agnes's lately."

"I wonder what he said that made the difference? When I asked him what they'd discussed, he just talked in generalities. I don't think he knows himself what happened."

"I suspect it wasn't so much what he said, as the person Agnes saw. He's done a lot of growing in the past few months." Cal held her close. "We all have."

They went up the steps of the ranch house. He opened the door and they walked inside.

"I want you to stay here with me tonight."

Blaine looked at him coyly. "Agnes approves, so you think the whole world does?"

"I want us to think about us for a while."

She sat on the couch. Cal dropped down next to her.

"It is amazing we've had any sort of relationship at all," she said with a sigh. "These have not been the best of circumstances."

"The worst of it's over. We can begin to consider *our* future."

She looked into his eyes. They were soft, open. "You know, saying it like that scares me a little. In a way, I've been able to hide behind Jason and his problem. Now I've got to face you alone."

Cal's mouth bent at the corner. "Am I that scary?"

"You want to know the truth?"

He brushed her cheek with the back of his fingers. "Yes, the truth."

"I love you, Cal, but I *am* a little scared."

He frowned. "Not of me."

"Well...of what you represent."

His hand dropped from her face. "What do you mean? You're afraid of the relationship?"

"Maybe that's it—who you are, what effect you have on me."

He gave an ironic little laugh. "That pretty well covers it."

"Don't be upset with me."

"I'm not upset. I'm trying to understand you."

"It's not all that strange. I've been alone for a long time. You're...different, and my feelings for you are...unexpected."

"I don't know whether that makes me strange, or you."

Blaine's brow furrowed with concern. "I *have* upset you."

"No, I'm confused. I don't know, exactly, what you're saying."

"I love you, Cal, but I'm unsure...and I don't want to rush things."

He chuckled. "I take it, then, this is not the time to discuss the possibility of marriage."

She felt a lump in her throat and swallowed hard. Cal looked at her, waiting. She was looking down at her hands, thinking.

"Am I to take it there's a message in that overwhelming response?"

She turned to him, touching his cheek again. "No, Cal. It's just that I've been thinking about it, too. I love you, I've said that. I'm just unsure what conclusions to draw."

"Are you saying you don't think we should consider marrying?"

"I guess we are considering it. That in itself is a big step. I mean, at first I never would have thought we...the Queen of Hearts and an ex-priest."

"I think we're beyond that."

"Yes, but that was only the first hurdle. There's so much more that needs to be considered."

"And it will be," he replied. "We'll talk, but let's not let your famous realism get in the way."

"But we *do* have to be realistic."

"Blaine, I've never felt for anyone the way I do for you."

"Never? What about Laura?"

"I was a different person then. Younger, at a different place in my life. That doesn't mean I didn't love her. I did. But it's possible to love more than once, and to love differently."

"Maybe that's what concerns me."

"What?"

"Whether it's really you, the real Caleb Rutledge, who loves me."

He sighed with exasperation. "Don't you think I ought to be the judge of that?"

"Not necessarily, no."

"All right," he said, his voice rising, "what test do I have to pass? What proof do you need?"

Blaine's eyes misted. "I've got to feel it in my heart. I've got to know."

"What will it take?"

"Just time, I think."

"I guess I've got plenty of that."

"Don't hate me."

He shook his head. "I could never hate you." Then he smiled. "Want to turn you over my knee, maybe, but never hate you."

She took his hand in hers, rubbing the back of it as though it were a small animal. Cal looked at her sadly.

"I suppose you want me to take you to the foreman's house for tonight."

"No, I'll stay here with you."

"You will?"

"Of course. I love you, I want to be with you."

"So long as I don't mention marriage." He sighed with resignation. "I think we've got our roles reversed. The man's the one who's supposed to be afraid of the big 'M,' not the woman."

She pulled his hand against her cheek.

"Or are you just interested in my body?"

She nodded playfully. "Yes, that's it. I'm just interested in your body."

THEY LAY NAKED in the middle of Cal's large bed, the blankets over them, warding off the nighttime chill. Still Blaine was cold and snuggled close to him. He lay motionless, breathing evenly, but she knew he was awake. He had made love to her tenderly, but with a touch of reserve. Although he said nothing more, Blaine could tell he was hurt.

"How long have you thought in terms of marriage, Cal?"

He didn't reply for a moment. Then he cleared his throat. "I suppose from the moment I saw you, subliminally. Even the most elemental attraction raises questions in a man's mind."

"How long have you thought about it seriously?"

"It's been a growing thing. Coming back in the plane today I developed a strong urge to take action, to do something about it."

"Maybe it's just a reaction to what happened with Agnes."

"I have more faith in my feelings and judgment than that."

"I wasn't being critical."

Cal was silent.

"What did you have in mind for us? What kind of a life? There are so many things that would have to be settled. Where would we live, for example?"

"You like the ranch, don't you? I thought we could live here. You seem to like the outdoors as much as I do."

"Yes, I do. But what do you see me doing?"

"I guess that would be up to you, Blaine. But there'd be no need to play poker anymore."

"Why not?"

"You wouldn't need the money. I mean, why bother?"

"Cal, I don't play poker just for money. It's my career. I happen to like what I do."

He didn't reply.

"Is that a problem?"

"I just assumed...."

"Why would you assume that? I didn't assume you'd give up the school to come live with me in Las Vegas."

"Blaine, you said yourself you took up poker because you could make more in one day than you could working for a year at the bank."

"Yes, that's true. And I suppose I could have taken up bank robbery, too, but I didn't. I chose something legal, something I happen to love."

"But if you don't need to, why do it?"

"Cal, I think you're saying something different than what you really mean."

"What?"

"You can forgive my past, but you don't want a wife who's a poker champion. Isn't that what you're really saying?"

"I—"

"Admit it! It's the truth."

"I really didn't think about it. I assumed that you wouldn't want to play. Honestly."

Blaine lay thinking. Her heart was pounding. She felt the adrenaline flowing, but she also was beginning to understand.

"It's certainly something we can discuss," Cal said. "I hope you don't hold it against me...because I misread your feelings about it."

"I don't hold it against you, but I do understand my own hesitation a lot better."

"What do you mean?"

"You don't truly accept me for who I am. You don't want to marry

Blaine Kidwell, the Queen of Hearts. You want to marry someone you're going to remake, reform.''

"Blaine!"

"It's true, Cal, you just don't see it."

"Just because I misunderstood your intentions about poker, my motives are suddenly suspect?"

"No, there's a whole attitude behind it. I think I've sensed it all along. That's why I've felt uncertain, hesitant about us."

"You're jumping to conclusions. You can't condemn me that easily. I think you're looking for an excuse. You're afraid, and this gives you a reason to back off."

"Don't you think I want you to accept me, to love me for who I am?"

"I do."

"You don't. I *am* the Queen of Hearts, and that's the woman you'd be seen in public with, the woman you'd go to cocktail parties with, the woman you'd introduce to your relatives and friends, the woman who'd cook your Thanksgiving turkey, the woman—'' her voice filled with emotion ''—sitting next to you in...church.''

Blaine lay silent and still, trying to control the emotion threatening to erupt inside. When she'd finally calmed down, she got up from the bed. Cal, who had been as silent as she, reached for her arm, but she was already on her feet.

"Blaine, where are you going?"

"To the guest room." She gathered her gown and robe from the chair by the bed.

"Don't leave. Stay with me."

"I can't. Not now."

RUTLEDGE LOOKED AT HER over his coffee cup. Blaine was obviously uncomfortable and distant. She hadn't engaged his eyes, though he had been watching her.

She wore slightly more makeup than usual, but it didn't cover the red rims around her eyes. She fiddled with her English muffin.

"So, what's going to happen?" he asked. "Has my slip damned me to purgatory forever?"

There was a touch of annoyance on her face. "No, Cal. Of course not."

"When do I get to see you?"

"The Nationals are at the end of the week. I've got to concentrate on that—get my mind back on my work."

"First things first?"

"Please don't be bitter. I was being honest with you. If we can't be honest with each other, then we've got nothing."

He felt chastened by her words. She was right. He was bitter. "I take that to mean there's still hope?"

"I don't feel any differently toward you, Cal. I just think we both have a lot to consider. After what we've been through, we need time to be apart, to get some perspective."

"That's fine. I have no problem with that. I just feel that you've made up your mind and you won't forgive me."

Blaine looked at him squarely. "It's not a question of forgiveness. It's a matter of who we really are and what we really want. You just don't leave things like that to chance."

Rutledge was impelled to argue, but he could see there was no point in it. Blaine had made up her mind, at least for the time being.

After several uncomfortable minutes of silence, she took a final bite of muffin and dropped the rest of the piece on her plate. "I'd better go. You must have a ton of things to do, and I'm sure I'm as rusty as an old gate." She got up and looked at Cal, who hadn't moved. "What we both need more than anything is to get back to work."

Rutledge followed her to the front door and carried the bags she had waiting in the hall to her car. He put them in the back seat. They stood facing each other, and he could see she wanted it over with quickly.

"I'll call you after the tournament," she said a little sadly. "Maybe we can meet for dinner."

Rutledge nodded.

She shook her head, repressing her emotion. "Cal," she whispered, "I do love you." Quickly she bussed him on the cheek and jumped into the car.

RUTLEDGE WATCHED Blaine's Grand Prix disappear down the road. He turned away and came inside, feeling frustration and anger, though he wasn't sure who he was angry with. He was innocent, though. He'd had no ulterior motives, no scheme or plan. It was a simple misunderstanding of her intentions.

Maybe his own feelings *had* been projected a bit. Maybe he'd assumed she'd want to quit poker because to him it was something a woman would only do out of necessity. But that was a far cry from wanting to change her. The problem was with her, not him.

And yet, he had to admit her stinging reference to the Queen of

Hearts had left him feeling uneasy. She did have a point. In truth, he did see himself married to an *ex*-poker player.

He'd been accused of having a rescuer mentality in the past. Maybe Blaine Kidwell was just the latest example. Maybe she did have cause for complaint.

Rutledge looked around his house and felt antsy. He needed to get out, and away. He went to the small office outside his own where his secretary worked and found the room empty. It was still early, she wouldn't be in for another forty-five minutes. Taking a pencil, he scratched a note on a pad, then went to his room to change his clothes.

GRABBING THE SADDLE HORN, Rutledge swung his leg up over the chestnut's broad back, slipped his pointed boot into the stirrup, then turned his mount up the trail. Saluting the wrangler standing in front of the shack, Rutledge gave the horse a little kick with his heels and leaned forward, bringing the animal instantly into a loping gallop.

He rode for half a mile or so to the point where the trail entered the mouth of the canyon, and reined in his mount, letting him walk over the rocky ground. Rutledge and the horse were both breathing deeply and he felt the moisture of his own perspiration at his temples and on his neck.

Galloping in the hot sunshine and feeling the sting of the dry, sage-tinged air was an elixir, a cure for ailments of the spirit. When he'd first come home after Laura's death, he had ridden for days in the desert, climbed mountains, pushed every horse he rode to its limits. He hadn't been able to get enough of nature, enough pure air to cleanse himself of the pain, the sadness, the self-pity.

And here he was again, fleeing into the wilds, into the constancy and indifference of nature. Once more it was a woman, and a loss, that drove him to solitude and escape. It wasn't until he had pushed himself and his horse to a point of exhaustion, until his bones and muscles ached with fatigue, that he dismounted and sat by a raging stream to reflect.

The longer he sat, the more he was consumed by his surroundings. Nature enveloped him and he became a part of it, losing a little of himself to the vastness and majesty of creation. It was a religious experience, but it was also communion with life—the living world of which he was a part.

Once he had merged with it, he could step back and see himself more clearly and humbly. He thought of Blaine, too, because she was a part of his world, and a part of him. She gave his life greater meaning; she fulfilled him as a man because of what they had shared physically and spiritually.

In the great harmony Rutledge beheld, only Blaine was missing. He wanted her in order to be whole. But was the image of her in his mind Blaine as she was, or as he wanted her to be? That was critical, because that was the concern, the doubt, that she had expressed.

Separated from her and alone, but at peace with his surroundings, Rutledge realized that what he wanted wasn't Blaine, but rather Blaine as he would have her be. The commitment he had made in his heart was conditional.

Instinctively Blaine had realized it, though he had criticized her for it. The discovery filled him with shame and regret. She had been right.

Wearily Rutledge got on his horse and began riding back toward the station. He thought about Blaine as he rode, wondering what he owed her—an apology, it would seem, at the very least. He pictured himself admitting to her that she had been right. He imagined her gracious acceptance.

Strangely the silent dialogue with her gave him a sense of peace. It was not unlike the confession of sin. He felt unburdened. He also felt closer to her, because now he was able to see her more clearly, the woman she really was.

Blaine Kidwell was the Queen of Hearts, not an imaginary creature temporarily in the role. He could not make her different, because she could be no one but herself, just as he could not become someone different than the man he was.

Who do I love? he asked himself. *The woman I created in my head, or the real Blaine?* Rutledge had a tremendous urge to see her and find out, because he didn't know. Only now that he had figured out who she was could he hope to discover the truth.

The sun was dropping behind the mountains to the west as he traversed the last half mile to the station. He didn't know any more about what the future held than when he had left that morning. The difference, though, was that he had gained the wisdom to be accepting of the result. He would think and meditate for a day or two, and then he would go find Blaine.

JASON KIDWELL LOOKED DOWN at the pasty mashed potatoes on his plate and wrinkled his nose with disgust. He was hungry, but growing up with his mom's mashed potatoes and gravy made the cafeteria food punishment.

"You gonna play soccer this fall, Jason?"

He looked across the table at Terry Hardwick who was the only other novice in his dorm. "I don't know. I'd like to, but I don't know if I'll be good enough."

"They'd probably let you be reserve goalie, anyway. At least doin' that you get to use your hands."

Jason nodded and took a trial bite of the potatoes.

There was a loud shout from the end of the cafeteria and one of the older boys stood up and heaved a Frisbee down the long table, skimming it over the heads of the boys. Jason ducked as it passed overhead, then turned to see another kid at the far end snatch it from the air. There was a general roar of approval and the proctor, who'd been looking the other way, turned around with a suspicious look on his face.

"How long do you suppose this'll go on?" Terry asked.

"Probably until the proctor catches them, or it lands in somebody's mashed potatoes."

Benny West, sitting next to Terry, grunted his agreement, his mouth full.

There was another shout and the saucer went sailing back toward where it had started, except this time it rose in an arch beyond the reach of the intended receiver. The boy lunged for it and went skidding across the floor, just as a nearby door opened and Father Rutledge walked in. The Frisbee was about to hit him in the stomach, and he instinctively grabbed it as the boy stopped at his feet.

There was a general gasp, then laughter. Cal tapped the mischiefmaker on the head with the missile, then shouted at the proctor. "Hey Bob!"

The young man at the other end of the cafeteria turned around and the ex-priest snapped the Frisbee behind his back, sending it like a bullet the length of the room and into the proctor's hands. The assembly cheered and Cal helped the boy at his feet stand up before giving him a gentle push back toward the table. Then he raised his hand for silence. A hush came over the cafeteria.

"Three rules of etiquette, gentlemen. Never talk with your mouth full, keep your elbows off the table, and never throw a Frisbee in the cafeteria unless you're darn sure you can hit your target."

Jason laughed with everybody else. There was scattered applause. Cal made his way among the tables until he came to Jason. He leaned over and put his hand on the boy's shoulder.

"Hey, sport. After you finish, would you mind meeting me on the soccer field? I'd like to talk to you."

"Sure, Father Rutledge."

Jason and his companions watched the man walk back out, tousling a head here and there along the way.

"What's that about?" Terry asked.

"Probably sendin' you to the minors," Benny said with a laugh.

Jason shrugged. "Beats me."

CHAPTER NINETEEN

BLAINE KIDWELL SAT at the table opposite a jolly-faced woman with half-rimmed reading glasses who looked as though she ought to be running the bake sale at a church bazaar rather than the National Poker Championships. But Elinor Gebbling did run the tournament, and with great efficiency. She looked through the registration documents before her and peered over her glasses.

"Everything looks to be in order, Blaine. Your entry fee's paid, and everything I need is here." She picked up a plastic-covered clip-on badge and handed it across the table. "Might as well put this on, even though everybody knows you."

Blaine took the badge and looked at it. Her name was typed neatly in oversize, uppercase letters. There were no misspellings as there had been her first year. She clipped the badge on the pocket of her blouse.

"There're two other women in the tournament this year. Betty Starks from Texas, and Maryanne Byewalter from Ohio, I think."

"It's nice not to be alone."

"I think you've started something."

Blaine smiled and rose to her feet.

"Half an hour till the first round begins," Elinor said. "There's coffee and doughnuts in back, if you like."

Blaine nodded.

"And good luck."

"Thanks, Elinor."

Blaine made her way through the crowd of mostly men. Several greeted her, others just looked, some staring at her name tag. She saw Bedrock Butler in the midst of four or five admirers to one side of the casino, but walked on past.

"Mornin', Blaine," she heard him call over the general hum of the crowd. "How's the Queen of Hearts?"

"Hi, Al," she said, giving him a little smile. The year before it had been "Mr. Butler." She wondered if he'd remembered.

"Hope to see you in the last pair," he said, his voice slightly taunting.

"I'll be glad to make it that far." She moved on.

Lloyd Harris, the casino manager, saw her and came over. "Hi, Blaine. You're looking pretty as a picture." He put his arm around her shoulders.

"I'd rather look mean and intimidating."

Lloyd laughed. "Hope you make it to the finals, honey."

"Thanks."

"Listen, would you have a minute to do me a little favor?"

Blaine looked up at him. "Press?"

"Yeah, a little girl up from the *L.A. Times.* Doing a human interest piece. Mind?"

"Now?"

"You can sit down for a minute with her in back. She knows you'll be starting play soon."

"All right, Lloyd."

He kissed her temple. "Thanks, doll."

Harris led her over to a chipper young woman who looked fresh out of school. A camera was slung over one shoulder, a large bag over the other.

"Blaine, this is Tamara Moorehead of the *Times.* Tamara, Blaine Kidwell, the Queen of Hearts."

They shook hands, and Lloyd showed them to a small room off the poker parlor. The young woman dumped her gear on the floor next to a chair and sat down. Blaine sat next to her.

"I appreciate you talking to me, Blaine," she said, pulling a notepad from her purse. "I know you've got to get started in a minute."

"No problem."

Tamara gave her a disarming smile. "You married?"

Blaine was a little surprised at the question and the directness with which it was asked. "No, I'm a widow."

Tamara took a note. "Kids?"

"Yes, I have a son, Jason. He's fourteen."

More scribbling. "Where do you live?"

"I recently moved to Las Vegas."

"You involved with anybody? Is there a man in your life, I mean?"

Blaine looked at her disapprovingly. "What's that got to do with poker?"

"I'm doing a human interest piece. Poker's the backdrop, the hook. I write about people."

"I don't normally discuss my personal life."

"I wasn't prying, Blaine. The woman winning at a man's game is an obvious line for this story. It'll be in there, but it's a lot more interesting what a husband or boyfriend thinks. Women work nowadays either because they want to or because they have to. That's not news. But when a woman makes more than her husband, or has an unusual career, it's interesting to people how the couple deals with it."

"I see. Well, I'm not married."

"Do you think being the Queen of Hearts would be a positive or a negative in a relationship?"

"I suppose it would depend upon the man, wouldn't it?"

"Would you say generally your image and reputation make you more attractive to men, or less attractive?"

Blaine grimaced. "Don't you want to talk about poker? I came in second to Bedrock Butler at the Western Championships recently."

"I've got all that. Would you say you feel defensive about your work?"

"No, I love it."

"Would you give it up for a man?"

"No!" Blaine looked at her suspiciously. "What is this? Why are you baiting me?"

The reporter hesitated, then admitted, "There's a rumor that I picked up. I do my homework before I start. And I don't like to throw things in people's faces unless I have to."

"Your subtlety overwhelms me."

The woman smiled. "People care about these things, so, out of necessity, I do, too. The conflicts in a woman poker player's life are a lot more interesting than her cards."

"My conflicts are my own business."

"So your career is pretty important to you."

"Second only to my son."

"But I understand it's been a problem—even for him."

"You do do your homework."

"Blaine, I had an illegitimate kid when I was eighteen. I've worked my way through college in spite of it, and have busted my butt to be the best at what I do. *And* I'm a good mother—not the best from a time-devoted standpoint, but not a bad one, either. These are the things modern women share. My job is to make the sharing possible."

Blaine contemplated her.

"You don't have to talk to me if you don't want to. But you can't ignore the fact that you're interesting because you're an achiever, a role model. Everybody cares about you.''

"Where do you draw the line between caring and prurient interest?''

"Let me try it this way. What message do you have for the millions of women who are out there struggling like you in their own small way?''

Blaine thought, feeling halfway moved to cooperate. "Nothing terribly profound.''

"If you feel it, it's profound.''

"I'd say be true to yourself. Give to others, but be true to yourself first.''

Tamara wrote on her pad.

Blaine continued. "Every relationship needs compromise on both sides to work, but you can't compromise on who you are, and people shouldn't ask you to be someone you aren't.''

"Love can't conquer all? Even for the Queen of Hearts?''

"Maybe especially for the Queen of Hearts. Men love to fantasize about queens of one kind or another, but they don't marry fantasies.'' Blaine tried to smile. "It can be a lonely life.''

"Why do you do it?''

"Because I'm true to myself.''

"What kind of a man would it take?''

"One who could love me unconditionally.''

"Beauty marks and all?''

"Warts and all.''

"Describe the ideal man for the Queen of Hearts.''

Blaine smiled vacantly. "A country preacher.''

"That's a surprise. Aren't you the opposite of what a clergyman would want?''

"Not for one who believes what's in his Bible.''

The reporter scribbled some more. "Know any?''

"Yes and no.'' She stood up. "Sorry, Tamara, I've got to go play poker.''

Blaine stepped quickly from the room before the girl could see the tears filling her eyes.

SHE FOUND A QUIET CORNER and sipped a cup of coffee before the players were called to the tables. The aroma of the drink reminded her of her first morning at the ranch when Cal had fixed her breakfast. She remembered how he had looked at her from the stove, and it hurt terribly inside.

Hundreds of times she had seen herself kneeling on the floor of the cabin, her hair dripping into the soup kettle, her breasts bare, when she looked up to find him beside her. Her insides wrenched when she thought of him taking her, shivering and afraid, into his arms.

"A misunderstanding" he had called it, when his true feelings had wrenched them apart. And she knew he believed that's all it was.

Cal wasn't a bad person. He simply had his beliefs, as she had hers. He had permitted his love to conquer a great deal. But sometimes the gap was too wide, even for love. That was what she should have told the reporter. But it was too painful. It was enough that she was able to admit it to herself.

The players began moving to the tables and Blaine found her place. Lloyd Harris always made sure she sat in a prominent spot, where the crowds could see her. She was his pet, his showpiece. She was good for business.

Blaine didn't want to let him down. She didn't want to let herself down, either. Caleb Rutledge had the power to weaken her resolve, rob her dignity, turn her into a submissive, hungry creature, but not even her love for him could destroy her.

She would never be able to look at Cal's face without wanting him, but she never would surrender, either. She was the Queen of Hearts, and whether she continued playing poker her whole life or moved on to something else, she'd always be a poker queen.

Blaine had studied the assignments and knew most of the players at her table. As she took her seat, she looked around at the faces of the men. Several quipped with one another, but she recognized it as nervous patter. There was an air of camaraderie, but there was no doubt about the fact that it was to be a struggle to the death. Only one of them would survive the round.

Blaine looked at the chips neatly stacked in front of her, verifying the count. Other players were doing the same. The man on her left was rubbing the tips of his fingers on the felt to soften his touch. The dealer looked placid as he lightly thumped the sealed deck of cards lying before him.

"Ready gentlemen, ma'am?"

There were nods and grunts, and the dealer broke the seal. Though her mind was beginning to focus on the fifty-two cards being removed from the carton, and on the competition seated around her, Blaine's eyes rose absently to the mass of faces on the other side of the railing.

One at the back—a face nearly lost in the obscurity—came into focus. Blaine recognized the pale eyes and sandy-blond hair of Caleb Rutledge.

She stared at him for a moment. He was looking at her, his eyes fixed. He gave no sign of recognition, though their locked gaze was apparent enough. Blaine felt suddenly weak.

The cards purred softly as they were shuffled and she looked down at them, their red and white pattern clear against the green of the felt tabletop. The playing surface with its markings, the hands of the players, the chips, were all vivid under the bright light, yet the face in the obscurity of the crowd was more real than any of it.

Blaine suddenly felt unsettled; her concentration was lost. She looked up at Cal anxiously and he was still there, his face calm, his gaze clearly focused on her.

The dealer called for the ante and Blaine mechanically moved her chip to the spot before her. Then the cards began flying across the surface of the table, stopping with incredible accuracy beneath the waiting fingers of the contestants. She looked at her hole cards and calculated automatically as the up cards came out in a more deliberate fashion.

Among her first three cards she already had a pair, but the significance paled beside her awareness of the man in the crowd. She looked at Cal again, and for the first time he forced a smile—a thin, weak one, but it said positive, conciliatory things. It was Father Rutledge and Cal both out there, and she was glad. Blaine didn't feel alone.

THE FIRST ROUND at Blaine's table lasted longer than usual. Among the players only she and one other, a man named M.C. Kirk, were of national stature. They were the last pair and started the showdown with the table stakes divided about equally between them.

As the last player eliminated left the table, Blaine looked up at Cal again, as she had been all morning. He was with her constantly, a silent ally. She wasn't sure why he was there, or why he looked at her as he did, but she drew comfort from it, nonetheless.

Kirk folded on two hands in a row and Blaine took the small pots. On the third hand of the showdown her opponent won a sizable pot with a flush over a straight. Kirk had finessed the betting nicely and Blaine saw an opportunity to project vulnerability, to sucker him into overconfidence.

She folded early on the next hand. On the one after that she called, and lost, feeling Kirk's confidence building.

Blaine still had enough of a stake for a decisive hand, but she wanted to pick her spot carefully. They traded a couple of small pots, Blaine declining to raise on a strong hand, and was sure the time was right for her gambit.

Feeling buoyed, but maintaining a sober demeanor, she looked up at Cal for reassurance. He was there, and she was happy, encouraged on two fronts. Her heart quickened its beat.

On the next hand Kirk's first two up cards were diamonds. He bet heavily and Blaine smelled a flush. She had a pair in the hole and felt the time might be right to press him. She raised Kirk's five-hundred-dollar bet a thousand. He blinked, but didn't hesitate to match her bet.

With the next card Blaine bet another thousand. Kirk raised a thousand and she sensed it would be the pivotal hand. His last up card was another diamond and Blaine saw the tension drain from his face. She figured he had to have a flush. She was dealt another eight, giving her three. All she needed was a fourth, or a pair out of the last hole card, to have a winning hand.

Blaine decided to bluff if she didn't get her card, knowing she'd have to bet her entire stake without hesitation to be convincing. The last card slid to a stop in front of her and, in spite of herself, her fingers trembled as she lifted the corner. It was a king to go with one she had showing, giving her a full house. She'd beat Kirk's flush without having to bluff! The trick now was to draw him in—make him bet everything and lose.

He opened with five thousand dollars. Blaine promptly bet everything, leaving him stunned. He sat thinking. A number of players from other games began gathering around. She saw Bedrock Butler peering over several shoulders.

Would she bluff, or had she beat his flush? That was Kirk's dilemma. She could see him vacillating. He knew the Queen of Hearts was tough, but what did that mean—bluff or not? Blaine sensed he would call, and she was glad now she had the cards to back it up.

In the deadly silence at the table she looked up at Cal. He didn't seem to be aware of what was going on—he couldn't be with other games in progress. Yet he seemed totally with her. She stared at him through the smoke, half forgetting the drama at the table.

"I'll call," she heard Kirk say. He pushed his chips forward. The dealer made a quick calculation, then looked up at Blaine. She flipped over her hole cards and announced a full house, eights over kings.

Kirk gave a faint groan and got shakily to his feet. He disappeared into the crowd, brushing past the observers, including Butler. Blaine felt her shoulders slump a bit. She'd won the first round.

While her winnings were being stacked and counted she got to her feet and looked out at the crowd. Cal was gone. He'd disappeared. She sighed heavily. The euphoria she'd felt a moment earlier evaporated as quickly as it had come.

DURING THE BREAK while Blaine waited for the second round to begin, she wandered around the casino, its restaurants and shops, looking for Cal. He was nowhere to be found. She wondered why he had come, to be with her, only to disappear.

Finally, she settled into a corner table in the coffee shop and ordered a chicken salad sandwich and a glass of ice tea. There were several other poker players from the tournament in the restaurant. A couple of them said hello, but fortunately no one bothered her. She sat there, worried and nervous, as though she had lost rather than won that morning.

Blaine knew the problem was Cal. He was there, with her, but out of reach—always out of reach. The frustration, the uncertainty, the anxiety were torment—a taste of hell. It seemed the most important thing in the world was to find him, to be with him, to talk to him. Yet she had to be true to herself and do her thing, be who she was.

When she made her way back to the poker parlor she sought out Elinor Gebbling to see if Cal might have left a message, but there was none.

"What does he look like?" the woman asked. "Maybe he's been wandering around."

Blaine described him, feeling more as if she was making out a missing persons report than talking about the man she loved.

"He doesn't sound like a country preacher," a voice said beside her.

Blaine turned to find Tamara Moorehead standing at her side. "He isn't."

"I've been thinking about what you said," the reporter remarked casually. "I felt I couldn't let it drop, not until I understood."

Blaine thanked Elinor and she and Tamara turned and walked slowly away. "I'm going through some difficult problems right now, and I don't feel like talking about them."

"I know what I do is prying from your standpoint, but it's all part of our common experience as human beings."

Blaine smiled at her, but didn't comment.

"You don't have to give me any specifics, but could you talk about feelings?"

"Off the record?"

"No," Tamara said, "on the record."

Blaine sighed with resignation. "The hardest part is when you have your whole life figured out—you're in control because you know that's the best way to survive. Then somebody comes along and makes you doubt your values, your decisions, yourself. You're tempted to give in, but you can't, because you know it's not you. You'd be giving him what he wants, not who you are."

"Why is it men don't have the same problem?"

"I think it's because they've always had two different lives—one out in the world, another at home. Traditionally we've had just the one, and our instincts take us there, no matter how self-sufficient we become."

"So, it's an insolvable problem?"

"No, but it takes more than love."

The reporter contemplated Blaine. "If you had to choose, how would you decide?"

"The way Shakespeare put it—'to thine own self be true.'"

"You have a strong sense of who you are, don't you?"

"I try not to be weak."

"Does it make you happy?"

Blaine looked at her for a long time. "I think the stronger I become, the more vulnerable I am."

"Why?"

"I have less to share."

A man approached them. Blaine looked up into the face of Bedrock Butler.

"Howdy," he said, grinning. "Saw what you did to Kirk this mornin', Blaine. Mighty nifty."

"Thanks. Understand you won."

"Yep, I eliminated one of your lady friends, along with a few of the boys. If I'm as lucky this afternoon, and you are, too, we'll be meetin' in the final round tomorrow."

Blaine nodded. "I suppose so."

He looked at Tamara and Blaine introduced them.

"Well," he said to the reporter, "writin' about the girl who beats the boys at their own game?"

She smiled. "Something like that."

"Let me tell you a little secret, then. I'll bet you five thousand dollars the Queen of Hearts would never have shoved all that money in the pot this morning without a pat hand."

Blaine watched Butler, her expression sardonic. "Let's hope we get the opportunity to find out, Al."

He winked, then walked away.

"What was that all about?" Tamara asked.

"It's guys like him who make a woman either weak or strong."

"He's what makes you play?"

"Partly, I guess."

"But it takes a preacher to make you cry?"

Blaine nodded. "It seems to have worked out that way. At least this once."

BLAINE PLAYED through the second round as though she was in a trance. She kept looking for Cal, but he wasn't there. It didn't seem to matter what happened at the table, and she hated that. She tried to focus her mind by thinking of Bedrock Butler, her conversation with Tamara Moorehead, her career, even Jason. But the fire just wasn't there.

Despite a lackluster performance, Blaine found herself holding her own against a fairly balanced table. No one seemed able to make significant headway against the others. It was a circumstance in which a player often became rash, and Blaine knew she'd have to guard against it.

One of the weaker players at the table succumbed to the temptation and overplayed a couple hands in a row, once bluffing without having prepared properly. Blaine took the hand and a fairly sizable pot. It was time to press the others a bit, but she lacked the concentration to do a credible job.

Another indecisive hour drifted by and she glanced up to see Cal suddenly among the onlookers in the crowd. Her heart stopped as he acknowledged her awareness with a subtle nod. He was back! Why? Where had he been?

The expression on his face seemed to say everything was okay, and Blaine took heart. She felt her powers returning, the adrenaline flowing. With an occasional look at him for reassurance, she plunged into the game.

The table was quickly reduced to three players, a young college type, who was clever but comparatively lacking in experience, and an old dog from the Las Vegas area, whom Blaine only knew as Toby.

She folded early on several hands in which her opponents savaged each other. Eventually, the college kid got the upper hand and forced Toby out.

Blaine immediately decided to let her young opponent's overconfidence work to her advantage. They had never played together before, and her performance thus far in the round gave him nothing to fear. Under Caleb Rutledge's watchful eye, Blaine set up the young man over the course of a dozen hands, then moved in for the kill, blindsiding him with four of a kind against a straight, then bluffing him out of a winning hand.

With his confidence suddenly shaken, the dollars seemed bigger to the youthful contender than they had before, and he broke under pressure. Happily looking up at her supporter in the audience, Blaine got up from the table, knowing she'd made it to the final round. When she had tended to her winnings, Cal was waiting for her at the entrance to the poker parlor.

"I didn't know whether you were a mirage or real," she said, slipping her arm around his waist without hesitation.

He kissed her on the temple. "Your guardian angel."

"But you abandoned me earlier. What happened to you?"

"I had a luncheon meeting with the school's board of directors. I had to go."

They began walking through the casino, away from the hubbub. "You met with the board today?"

"Yes, I'd scheduled the meeting before we went up to Washington."

"I'd forgotten. What happened?"

"I resigned."

"Resigned? What for?"

"I didn't feel I could continue handling the day-to-day operations. I felt it was time to step down and bring in a professional educator as headmaster."

Blaine squeezed his waist. "Did it have anything to do with Agnes's threat...with you and me?"

"Even though Agnes backed off, I felt I had to come clean with the board. I explained the entire episode. They were prepared to overlook my transgressions, but I knew that the time had come to move on."

They exited the casino, their arms still around each other.

"Where are we going?" she asked.

"I came in a cab, so I was hoping you might give me a ride."

Blaine pointed to where she was parked and they headed off that way. "Where do you want me to take you?"

"Someplace where we can talk."

"My house?"

Cal grinned. "Do you trust me?"

"No. But then, I don't care."

They got in the car and, despite the intense heat inside it, he immediately took her into his arms, kissing her deeply. "I missed you."

"I missed you, too." She started the engine, turning on the air conditioner. The gradually cooling air blew over them. Blaine pushed back the dark strands of hair from her face. Putting the car in gear, she guided it out of the parking lot. "So what's going to happen if you've quit the school? What are you going to do?"

"I plan to spend more time on my business interests. Of course, I'll stay involved in the school...I'll still be chairman of the board. And I plan to be at the ranch a lot. With the plane it's not difficult."

"You won't live there?"

"No, I've started house hunting here in Las Vegas."

"Why here?"

He reached over and caressed her cheek. "To be near you."

Blaine hardly said anything the rest of the way home. She wondered what it all meant, not knowing what to think, what to hope for. When they had parked the car in the garage and went into her house, Cal immediately took her into his arms, pressing his long, hard body against her, trapping her.

"I've been thinking about you a lot," he said, gently turning their melded bodies from side to side. "It took a while, but I finally figured out why you were upset...not comfortable with my love."

"Why?"

"Because I hadn't really accepted you as you are."

"There was no reason why you should. You had the same obligation to be honest that I did. Blaine Kidwell is not necessarily the right woman for every man."

"She's right for me. I figured that out quite a while ago."

"You were deceiving yourself."

"No. Blaine was not the problem. It was the Queen of Hearts who troubled me, just as you suspected."

"But I *am* the Queen of Hearts."

"Yes, I finally figured that one out, too. It wasn't hard to accept, once it dawned on me what I was doing. But believe it or not, it isn't as obvious as you might think."

"What are you saying, Cal?"

"I don't just love the side of you that fits into my preconceived notions. I love the woman I watched play poker at the casino today."

Blaine couldn't help feeling skeptical. "But how can you change...just like that?"

"I didn't change. I just gave my self permission. Love is the absence of fear, you know. And most of what we fear is in ourselves. That was true of my feelings for you."

She pressed her face against his neck. "I know you're sincere, but I'm afraid to believe what you say."

"You know what Shakespeare said in Hamlet—'This above all: to thine own self be true.'"

Blaine laughed. "I quoted that myself today, to a reporter."

"To a reporter?"

"Yes, I was explaining why I couldn't marry you."

"You said *that* to a reporter?"

"Not in so many words, but I think she got my message."

Cal looked hurt. "You mean I'm going to be publicly rejected?"

"No, a woman always has the right to change her mind."

"Then you *will* marry me?"

She nodded, her heart swelling.

"What changed your mind? What I've said?"

"It was that face I saw in the crowd today." She tried to blink back the tears of emotion. "The Queen of Hearts could see that you loved her, as much as you love me."

Cal squeezed her fiercely. "You know what? You're both right."

RUTLEDGE COULD FEEL the tension in the entire casino, somehow extending far beyond the poker parlor, reaching out and drawing people to the scene. He glanced over his shoulder and saw that the crowd was now twenty or thirty rows deep. All eyes were on the platform where the final pair were locked in a struggle to the death.

He could hear the whispering as people crowded closer. "Who's the woman?"

"Blaine Kidwell."

"She the one they call the Queen of Hearts?"

"Yeah, she's playin' Butler, Bedrock Butler."

In spite of Blaine's determination to remain calm, Rutledge could sense the tension just below the surface. It had been a Herculean struggle—the two players having gone back and forth, first one gaining the advantage then the other.

At one point early on it had looked as though she was going to put him away, but Butler came charging back with a series of winning hands. Blaine had been down for quite a while and was gradually drawing back to parity.

Rutledge had been standing for hours, but he hadn't noticed the fatigue; his mind was focused constantly on the woman he loved. He watched the cards being dealt as he surveyed the placid faces of the competitors. As the betting progressed he sensed it would be a pivotal hand. The bets and raises were larger than any of the previous ones. It looked as though well over fifty thousand dollars was in the pot before the last hole card was even dealt.

Rutledge felt every muscle in his body tense. The crush of the crowd made it hot in that packed corner of the casino. Between that and the tension, he began perspiring more heavily. He could see that Blaine's shoulders were rigid, and Butler was fidgeting nervously.

The final card was dealt. Butler studied it for a moment, then announced he was going all-in. There were gasps and whispers from the crowd. Rutledge swallowed hard. He was a wealthy man, but seeing what looked like a couple of hundred thousand dollars put into play—all or nothing—was a heart-stopping experience.

Blaine sat motionless, looking at the pile of chips on the table. He knew her mind was working, focusing on the calculations that were required, the systematic evaluation of every element of the equation. Was Butler bluffing? She had to read that, too. Was he capable of risking hundreds of thousands of dollars on a mind game?

Rutledge waited with the others. Silence settled over the gathering. The dealer was frozen, a mechanical statue. Only Butler moved, fidgeting. There was no money in front of him. His entire stake was bet on the superiority of his hand.

Blaine looked up at him. There was a hush as the Queen of Hearts spoke. "I won't sleep tonight unless I know, Al. I'm calling you. What have you got?"

Her money went in and on the dealer's signal Butler turned over his hole cards. "Three tens," he said, a slight quiver in his voice.

For an instant Blaine's expression froze, then a smile touched her lips. Rutledge knew. "Queens," she said. "Three ladies."

Butler sat staring down at her cards. In spite of himself, there was dismay on his face. He had lost more than many men make in a lifetime in just one hand. He didn't say anything. He just got up slowly, then walked away.

Blaine turned to the audience, who began talking in louder tones. Rutledge could see her searching for him. He lifted his hand. She stood up and moved toward the railing. There were shouts, and someone whistled. He pushed his way toward the railing to meet her.

An instant later they were together, embracing. Rutledge held her, pressing her soft body against him. Behind him, around him, he heard applause. There were more whistles. He was kissing her. He didn't care. She'd won. The Queen of Hearts had won. And he, Caleb Rutledge, had taken a chance and won her heart.

EPILOGUE

BLAINE DROVE up the twisting road, past the large sprawling homes with views of Las Vegas from the flank of the mountain. Near the top she turned into the driveway, past the flowering cacti and succulents at the entry. It was late spring, the air was fragrant and pleasantly warm.

Blaine pulled into the garage and got out of the car, easing her stomach past the steering wheel. She carried a pastry box into the kitchen. Jason was sitting at the table, drinking a glass of milk.

"Hi, Mom."

"Hi, honey."

"What's in the box?"

"None of your business."

"Must be a birthday cake."

Blaine gave him a look of mild annoyance and put the box in the refrigerator. "If you don't marry a girl with infinite devotion, the rest of your life will be one disappointment on the heels of another."

"What's that got to do with birthday cake?"

"I had the whip hand in a perfectly good game of Texas Hole 'em, and had to leave in order to pick up this cake before the bakery closed. How many wives have the devotion of a mother?"

"I don't know. Maybe I should ask Cal." Jason gave a comic laugh.

"Don't be smart, young man, birthday or not."

He grinned. "You're only sixteen once."

"Thank God. Speaking of your dear stepfather, where is he?"

"Somewhere."

"Thanks for the clue." Blaine walked through the house to the master suite. She found Cal changing into his sweats.

He smiled. "How was your game today?"

"I think I'm getting soft. Don't have the killer instinct I used to have."

Cal walked over and put his arms around her. Then he put his hand on the swell of her abdomen. "There's something about an expectant mother that just isn't fierce."

Blaine laughed. "I realize that well enough. I just haven't been able to figure out how to use it to my advantage."

He kissed her cheek. "Just don't go into labor after you've pushed your stake into the pot."

"Oh, I'd wait around to see the outcome."

Cal laughed, then hugged her. "I imagine you would."

"What child would want to know he cost his mother a bundle of money, coming at the wrong time?"

"Yeah, talk about fuel for an emotional complex."

Blaine tweaked his nose. "Anyway, there aren't any tournaments I want to play in around Halloween."

He sat on the corner of the bed and started to put on his athletic shoes. Blaine watched him.

"Going for a run?"

"I thought I'd go down to the park and kick a soccer ball around for a while. Want to come along?"

"Maybe, if you don't stay too long. I'm planning a pretty elaborate meal for Jason. You know, Sandy's coming over. She's the first girl he's brought home, and I want to make a good impression."

"I think it's supposed to be the other way around."

"Well, whatever."

"Maybe I'll ask Jason if he'd like to come, too," Cal said. "Of course, now that's he's switched to track, he may not want to fool around with an old soccer hack."

"Nonsense. You only flew up to the ranch twice a week last year and you told me none of the boys could keep up with you."

"Admittedly, that's what I said...."

"Get's harder to lie each year, is that it?"

Cal nodded. "Maybe it's time to take up golf. You want to ask Jason if he wants to come, or shall I?"

"I have a feeling he'll be shaving, showering and applying cologne for the next two hours. Why don't just you and I go?"

He got up and put his arms around her again. "All right, just the three of us." He smiled, then kissed her deeply on the mouth.

Blaine put her head on Cal's shoulder and rested her hand on her stomach. "If it's in the genes, he'll be a soccer player, too."

"She'll."

"Cal, I've told you, it's going to be a boy. I'm sure of it."

"Nope. A girl."

She gave him an emphatic look. "A mother knows these things. I'm absolutely sure!"

He took her by the shoulders and looked deeply into her eyes. "Want to bet?"

Blaine laughed. "Why, Caleb Rutledge, you know I never gamble."

HARLEQUIN®

A M E R I C A N ◆ **R O M A N C E**®

LOOK FOR OUR FOUR FABULOUS MEN!

Each month some of today's bestselling authors bring
four new fabulous men to Harlequin American Romance.
Whether they're rebel ranchers, millionaire power brokers
or sexy single dads, they're all gallant princes—and
they're all ready to sweep you into lighthearted fantasies
and contemporary fairy tales where anything is possible
and where all your dreams come true!

You don't even have to make a wish...
Harlequin American Romance will grant your every desire!

Look for Harlequin American Romance
wherever Harlequin books are sold!

Harlequin® Historical

From rugged lawmen and
valiant knights to defiant heiresses
and spirited frontierswomen,
Harlequin Historicals will
capture your imagination with
their dramatic scope, passion
and adventure.

Harlequin Historicals...
they're too good to miss!

HHGENR

Harlequin Romance®

Delightful

Affectionate

Romantic

Emotional

Tender

Original

Daring

Riveting

Enchanting

Adventurous

Moving

Harlequin Romance—the
series that has it all!

HROM-G

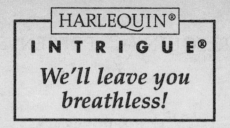

HARLEQUIN®

I N T R I G U E®

We'll leave you breathless!

If you've been looking for thrilling tales of
contemporary passion and sensuous love stories
with taut, edge-of-the-seat suspense—
then you'll *love* **Harlequin Intrigue!**

Every month, you'll meet four new heroes
who are guaranteed to make your spine tingle
and your pulse pound. With them you'll enter
into the exciting world of Harlequin Intrigue—
where your life is on the line
and so is your heart!

THAT'S INTRIGUE—DYNAMIC ROMANCE AT ITS BEST!

HARLEQUIN®

I N T R I G U E®

INT-GENR

HARLEQUIN PRESENTS®

HARLEQUIN PRESENTS
men you won't be able to resist
falling in love with...

HARLEQUIN PRESENTS
women who have feelings
just like your own...

HARLEQUIN PRESENTS
powerful passion in
exotic international settings...

HARLEQUIN PRESENTS
intense, dramatic stories that will keep you
turning to the very last page...

HARLEQUIN PRESENTS
The world's bestselling romance series!